Sanctuary

Sanctuary

Dale Allen

To Britt,
Best Wishes as a future
Athens business tycoon.

Dale
9/15/04

iUniverse, Inc.
New York Lincoln Shanghai

Sanctuary

All Rights Reserved © 2004 by Dale Allen

No part of this book may be reproduced or transmitted in any form or by any means, graphic, electronic, or mechanical, including photocopying, recording, taping, or by any information storage retrieval system, without the written permission of the publisher.

iUniverse, Inc.

For information address:
iUniverse, Inc.
2021 Pine Lake Road, Suite 100
Lincoln, NE 68512
www.iuniverse.com

ISBN: 0-595-30255-6

Printed in the United States of America

Athens, Georgia

This novel is dedicated to my wife Kim and my son Joshua. In these pages, you will find the best traits of many friends and family that I am proud to have. I hope I have done all of you justice. Thanks to everyone for the encouragement as the adventure begins...

Contents

Do Angels Weep? ix
Book One: Dominion 1
    Epilogue *12*
Book Two: In The Blink Of An Eye 13
    Interlude *19*
    A Christmas Miracle *22*
    City of Dreams *31*
    Interlude *33*
    Epilogue *39*
Book Three: Sanctum, Sanctorum 40
    Interlude *46*
    Interlude *54*
    Epilogue *106*
Book Four: Blessed Be The Children 107
    The War Years *109*
    Epilogue *169*
Book Five: Thy Secret Name 170
    The Story of Jarred *184*
    War in Heaven *189*
    The Final Seeker *191*
    The Journey Home *195*
    Epilogue *197*

Do Angels Weep?

With the glimmer of angel wings do I whisper Thy secret name.
The moon is but a pale reflection in the light of your soul.

Such is one, whose heart is a searing flash of darkness on a midnight plain.
A being who has known the fire of rage and the nothingness of desolation.

When the world ended in a rush of ebony stillness, your eyes were there to shine like a beacon to the lost.
Your heart beating softly brought solace to the Beast.

The fury of hell, I have known. Heaven is only an angel's breath away.

All the pain and suffering one has known is but a drop in the ocean when compared to the infinitesimal second of an angel's kiss igniting eternity.

Perhaps, we are only the dreams and nightmares of angels.

Your light is all that binds me to that gossamer strand of paradise.
Never let your light dim. For the sake of angel's who no longer weep for the Lost One.

Book One
Dominion

Pete Beck settled back into his first class seat, sipping on his Jack Daniels. Damn, it was good. The smoky liquid spread warmth in his tired body. Looking out the window of the sleek starliner, he watched the outer planets of the Sol system slip away. About another hour to the jump lanes and he would be to Epsilon 7 in another six hours.

He opened the file in front of him. Stamped across the top, in red, was "Top Secret-Department of Planetary Diplomacy-Eyes Only." How many of these had he done already? Ten? Pretty high flung shit for a street cop.

Beck had started as a beat cop in the Federal Police Force of America. There he had gone to the Bureau of Investigations. He had gone to night school, while working for the Bureau and had obtained his law degree. Not really wanting to practice, he stayed as a supervisor, and was assigned to New Washington as liaison to the Diplomatic Service. His wife, Maggie was the picture of patience as he struggled with what he really wanted to do with the rest of his life. His daughter Rachel, was getting ready to start junior high school and his three-year-old son, Joshua was just ready to start anything he could.

While working liaison, Beck had been fortunate enough to make friends with a young up and coming senator from the Southeastern States, named Samuel Robert Jackson. Sam, with his youthful manner and his blunt honesty roared into the presidential elections seven years ago and won by a landslide.

Six months after taking office, Sam called Beck into his office. "Pete, I want you to take a Presidential Liaison position with the Planetary Diplomatic Service." Beck laughed and said, "Mr. President, I—". "Call me Sam, damn it." Beck smiled. "Okay, Sam. I'm not a diplomat. I'm a glorified cop, for God's sake." Sam waved this off, saying, "Pete, not only are you a damn good investigator and negotiator, you are my best friend and I trust you. I need you for this. I have the Business Coalition, all four major political parties, including my own, and every other major interest group on my ass about our planetary relations. Now even the Catholic delegation is getting in on the act. I personally think everybody has watched too many Star Trek reruns, but I have to deal with it. I need you on the front line. I want to make sure my back is covered and I don't want to look over my shoulder while its getting covered." Beck sighed. "I don't know what to say, Sam." Sam whispered, "Say yes."

So, here sits Peter Beck. Of common beginnings, now the Senior Liaison Officer for the President. A cabinet level position. Beck laughed to himself, "Hell, at least the pay is better." Beck's position was the first of its kind. With the accidental discovery of altering two simple molecules, a young freshman college student at Fresno Nevada Coastal College had opened the gates of the solar system.

Creating a new form of energy, which responded to gravity, true space travel was born. After only ten years of extensive exploration in the "neighborhood," so to speak, the people of Earth found that life was abundant. The good thing was; a lot of Earth's little problems went away. All it took was people finding they were not alone and pulling together to solve those problems. The bad thing: Politics as usual.

After the initial shock, everyone wanted a say in our relations with the new worlds we had discovered. So far, the count was twenty-five worlds within travel distance and populated with beings that we could communicate with. Embassies had been set up on these worlds to develop a communication link between the populations. A constant crosscurrent of arts, science and philosophy. The benefits were enormous for both worlds. Most of the time, everything ran smooth. When it didn't, Beck went to work. His job: Make sure it works for everybody's sake. There is no room for error.

Beck closed the file. They were twenty minutes out from Epsilon 7. E-7, as it was commonly known, was our oldest ally. Actually, one of our closest galactic neighbors, we did not know they were there due to their orbital position in relation to their sun. A fast friendship evolved. The people of Epsilon were highly intelligent but also held very deep religious convictions. They were happy and all the ones Beck had met had a great sense of humor. They looked very human except for the vertical slitted eyes. Something to do with the development of their sun, Beck guessed. They were a beautiful people, though opinionated. He should know. Maggie was Epsilonian.

Beck was met by the Ambassador to Epsilon. Shuttled to the embassy, Beck went to business immediately. The senior staff officers broke it down for Beck. It pretty much matched the file.

Epsilon 7 was on the verge of civil war. Between two religious factions. The people of E-7 had all but eradicated violence, yet in the last six months; a reputed subversive had started a campaign to upset the theocratic parties of the planet. In doing so, this man threatened disaster.

Epsilonians were open-minded. They welcomed varied opinions about almost anything. Except religion. That was taboo. The Sydot was the major religious body of the planet, although other faiths were tolerated. The rebel faction was known only by a symbol. According to a Senior Intelligence Officer on staff, it looked very similar to an ancient Greek symbol roughly translated as "Dominion." As the staffer went on to say though, it was not very likely that the symbol would mean the same on this planet. The situation got very unstable for awhile. Riots, underground activity and midnight meetings by the radicals. Finally, the

Epsilonian Enforcement Division managed to capture the leader. Now the Sydot's are demanding a trial. The people are still arguing and word is that his underground is still active. The staffers closed their briefing.

Beck stood up and said "This is President Jackson's concern: Rumor has it, that the leader is not Epsilonian. My job is to find out who planted him here to start an insurrection and what ties he may have to Earth. Other than that, I stay; we stay, out of the local politics and judicial system. Understood?" There were murmurs of "yes sir" around the table. Except for the aged Ambassador, a veteran of countless assignments. The staff left. The Ambassador took Beck to his private office and spoke quietly, "Mr. Beck, there are two new developments that I don't think are included in your briefing folder." "And those are?" asked Beck. Sighing, the Ambassador eased down into his chair. He looked into Beck's eyes and said, "First, the Vatican has sent representatives to monitor the situation and offer advice to the Elders of the Sydot."

"Shit," said Beck quietly. He was sure Sam did not know of this. "And the second?" Beck asked. The old Ambassador sat still for a full ten seconds and in a whisper said, "The being that is imprisoned, says that he is the Saviour of this world." At that moment, Beck wished he were a lowly street cop again.

"Twenty-four hours? Is that all that's it been since he had set foot on Epsilon?" Beck stretched his aching muscles. Seems like days, he thought. Beck, sitting in his embassy quarters, reviewing the past few hours.

He had placed a call into Sam about the Catholic situation. The President was not happy about it but it didn't surprise him either. He said he had known it would happen eventually. He was just hoping for later. A quick call to Maggie and the kids, then he was off to meet with the Elder Council of the Holy Sydot.

It had not gone well. Beck had never fully realized the scope of power the Sydot had. Epsilon 7's civilization, over the course of thousands of years, had developed a theocratic system and a civil system of government. They seemed to operate pretty much in unison, but clearly, the Sydot had the final say. This was why they didn't have much of a crime problem. The Sydot handled their members "mistakes" in house, so to speak. Since this covered about eighty-five percent of the planet's population, the civil judicial process only had to take care of the non-aligned and the smaller, independent religious sects. The Elders welcomed Beck cordially, but were very quick to point out that they blamed ungodly radicals from Earth for promoting this blasphemy. However, they assured Beck, the matter was under control and would be handled by Sydot justice.

Beck then went to the Enforcement Division and said hello to the Chief, who was a very good friend and just so happened to be his father-in-law. Chief Johab gave Beck a bone crushing bear hug and showed him to his office. There he briefed Beck on what he knew of the situation.

"Well, Peter, it has been a strange six months," said the old man. "Our intelligence section first heard of this man down by the coastal city of Nerada. Reports of a cult sprang up down there and people started whispering about supposed miracles that had happened. We pressed our sources for a name. All that came back was a symbol, which you have already seen. We were never sure if the symbol meant the man or the group." "Surely though", Beck replied, "Your people have always shown great tolerance for other beliefs, right? I mean look at you. You are not Sydot, yet you are the chief enforcement official of this planet." Johab smiled and said "True, to a certain extent. The Sydot cares nothing for the civil branch. The problem with these radicals, is that almost from day one, they branded the Sydot as evil."

Johab went on to explain that the Sydot's own intelligence section picked up on these actions quickly. Rumor was that Inquisition Teams had been sent out. The civil authorities did not sanction this, but not much could be done. The teams had reportedly "interrogated" some members of the sect. Some were said to have died as a direct result of their "questioning". Beck was shocked. Johab told him not to be these were common methods used internally in the Sydot for generations. If you were inside their system of justice, you just didn't talk about it. If you were outside the system, you tried not to think about it.

"What kind of miracles did this man supposedly do?" asked Beck. Johab laughed. "Things like feeding a thousand with a single meal. Acts of healing and visions seen in the sky. Some even said he arrived in Nerada by walking across the ocean." Johab continued, "As his followers grew, he became so bold as to destroy a Sydot financial center. That was when the Elders declared all out war against this subversive."

Beck sat in his room, sipping the last of the whisky and finally settled into a deep sleep. He dreamed of a dark, stormy day. A hill. Three empty crosses.

The next day, Beck was allowed into the Epsilonian Maximum Security Prison, which presently had a total inmate population of one. A man known only by a symbol.

Beck looked into the sparse cell. It wasn't the most spacious or comfortable looking room in the world. Neither was it the dungeon that the Sydot claimed this monster deserved.

In the corner, a figure in shadow sat. Beck entered the cell. The figure looked up and stepped into the light. Beck held his breath. Seconds passed in time with the beat of Beck's heart. Beck couldn't help it. He burst out laughing. "My God man!" Beck sputtered, "People have built you up way out of proportion." The man just smiled.

Beck sat back and looked at the prisoner. Maybe six feet tall. Close to it. Well muscled, toned but graceful. Short cropped black hair with just a little premature grey. His dark eyes looked on the verge of laughing. Like he knew something that you didn't. The man was totally non-descript, except maybe for the scar running across his left cheekbone.

"So," Beck asked, "Who are you?" The man stared through Beck into his soul. Beck felt a shiver run up his spine. The man spoke in a mild voice; "I am Dominion."

Beck sat down across the table from the man. "What is Dominion?" he asked. "Dominion is. That is all." replied the man. "I do not expect you to understand, Mr. Peter Beck of Earth. Not yet anyway." Beck was surprised. Although he held a high level position, his work was normally done very low profile. He was not a well-known person.

"Why are you here?" asked Beck. The man smiled. "Why do you think I'm here, Mr. Beck?" Beck snapped, "This is not going anywhere. To answer questions with questions will do you no good. I'll be straight with you. The government of Earth believes you are a terrorist setting up a cell on the world of our closest friends. Evidently, the Epsilonians feel the same way. Now, I'm here to get your side of the story. If you don't want to tell it, I'm needed other places. You are, after all, just a common criminal, right?" Beck's words were designed to provoke a reaction. It was a method he had used countless times. He was sure of a response. He just didn't expect the one he got.

The man fell back on his bunk laughing. "Time. It is always time. Too little time. Too much time. It's time to do this. It's time to do that.," the man said in between chuckles. "Peter, I am a simple man. All you have to do is ask. The hard thing will be to listen to the answers. Listen closely, my very important man Peter, and I will give you all the answers you will ever need."

Beck had the guards bring a pitcher of water and an ashtray. He lit a cigarette (still not stylish on Earth, but nicotine free) and offered the man one. He declined with a shake of his head. Pouring both of them a glass of water, Beck looked at the man and said, "Okay, you promised me answers. I'm yours for as long as it takes." This seemed very funny to the man. He laughed again and said, "Peter, only the Father knows how true that is."

Beck sat and listened to the man, asking few questions. Guards would quietly come and go, bringing food, drink, and cigarettes for Beck. Hours went by. Guards rotated off shift. They spoke to their families of what they had seen. Family spoke to other family and friends. Word rippled through the city. Stories of two men sitting in a solitary cell that even when dark glowed with a soft blue light. As would later be said, when Beck entered that cell, he was sane. When he walked out twenty-four hours later, no one could say.

The man spoke in a soft voice and the walls of the cell expanded until they disappeared. "Peter," he said, "I am from your planet Earth. Not that it matters. It is just that way. I know of your Earth or at least I did. It has been many years since I walked the paths of your planet. I was once a soldier. I have been many things. I have seen billions of planets. I have walked the dust of worlds undreamed of. I have swam in oceans the color of which your mind cannot conceive. I have loved and I have hated. I have been born of woman and I have died." Beck stopped him. When were you on Earth?" The man's dark eyes looked into a distance only he could see. "Peter, I walked your Earth a little over two thousand years ago by your time reckoning. In a small country that your Middle Eastern Consortium now claims."

Beck sputtered. "Are you trying to tell me that you are Jesus Christ?" The man smiled. "No, but I knew the man you speak of."

"I was born Roman. I became a soldier and fought many battles. This scar is the legacy of one such skirmish. I was full of myself and soon found myself in a compromising position with a local politician's wife. For this, I was banished to a small town and placed on post guard. I knew the man you speak of. I knew his family. I watched as he taught the multitudes. I was there when he berated the priests of the temple. I saw him arrested. I witnessed the mock trial. I am a testament of his suffering and torture. I supervised the erection of the crosses. I watched him nailed to it. I heard the wails of his women and the cry of the thief. I witnessed the dark clouds of that day. The rain. Lightning, like I'd never seen before. I saw a bright light, like that of the sun except it was spinning in the sky. I heard the agony in his voice as he begged his Father not to forsake him. I smelled the sweat tinged with blood. I saw the whisper of life leave his ravaged body. I felt the earth tremble as the heavens roared their rage and I was sure the time of the end had come. All of this I know, Peter. As surely as I know I removed my spear from his side."

Sweat rolled down Beck's temple. Yet, his spine felt as if a cold finger had brushed it. What scared Beck, was that he could see it. Not only see it, but also smell and touch it as well. Everything the man said was as if Beck was there with him. He could smell the dust of the village. See the fear in the faces when the storm came. Hear the cries of agony.

Beck again focused on the man across from him. "I don't understand what you are trying to say," he said. The man replied, "I am only telling you my simple story. Nothing else."

"That terrible day, I threw my spear to the ground and never returned. My death was ordered because of the faith I followed. When it came, it was not kind. At the end, I was grateful that it was over. I knew I would go to a better place. I was wrong." Beck's eyes widened.

Beck was a self-proclaimed agnostic. He didn't really disbelieve in God; it was just that no one had shown him substantial proof. With what his planet had been through, almost destroying it, he just didn't believe that his tiny planet was deserving of divine intervention even if there was a God. Maggie was raised to believe in a higher power, but one that promoted self-destiny. Beck often wondered though, if he still had some optimist left in him. After all, his children were christened with biblical names. Now, to hear this man speak his worse theories were correct. In the end, it just didn't matter.

"I awoke from my death fully aware of who I was. Or at least who I had been. I expected to find my Father's home. The minor inconvenience of my torture and death had not even earned me a morsel of that place. Where I awoke is not important. There were many other souls there. It is a place of transition. A place of choices. Peter, have ever wondered what the Father's greatest gift to you was? Is it your perfectly balanced functioning body? Is it your higher intelligence than that of the simple animals that you were given dominion over? Is it the promise of a better life after your suffering? All of these are great gifts. He loves you so much. He could have given you all of these things without the pain. He could have set your destiny in the way of things. Think of it. No pain. No suffering or conflict. It would have been paradise, yes? Yet, would you be what you are? With no direction of your soul, would that have been love? The Father loved the people of your tiny speck of dust that you call home so much, that he gave you the greatest gift of all. The gift of free will. The gift of choice. As he did all his other creations. Billions upon billions upon billions. On to infinity. With the power to make slaves only to his will, He made you as he is. Do you deserve such love, Peter of Earth?"

"Do any of us deserve such love?" said the man. "In my new life, I was again given a choice. Settle for what I had earned and go there in peace. The Father does not measure us, we do. The other choice was to go on seeking Dominion. Peter, you have asked what Dominion is. It is not a thing or a name. It is what we aspire to become. Dominion is the highest level of love we can return to the Father. Dominion is to touch the face of God."

Outside the prison walls, the people clamored. The priests ranted about the evil within. An evil so great, it must be wiped from the face of the world.

The man sipped his water. His eyes were beginning to look tired; as if what he saw sucked his spirit away. He smiled softly at Beck and continued.

"Peter, you have heard the stories of heaven and hell. You have read your holy book, have you not? I say to you, all these things are true but not in your way of thinking. Man presumes to know the mind of God. Man made his choices, then tried to blame it on the Father. Let me ask you something. Why is it that you only use about ten percent of your brain? Do you think it was created that way? What if I told you man had one hundred percent of his brain capacity? Would that make him a super human? An angel? Perhaps God? Perhaps you should look at your "Garden of Eden" story in the light of what man lost, not that he was cast out. Heaven and Hell. Angels and Demons. All of them exist Peter, but not in your narrow scope of seeing. The battle for creation's souls is infinite. Imagine grains of sand on your largest oceans as being worlds. On every one of these worlds, its inhabitants have made their choices. Some good. Some bad. Some so bad, they do not exist anymore, except maybe as a version of your hell. Most, like your Earth made both good and bad choices. These are the battleground. Any father of these errant children would have dismissed them long ago and turned his back from them. Not my Father, Peter Beck. My Father and his children. One day, he will bring them home."

"I have been many things on many worlds. Each time, I serve the purpose of the Father to bring his children home. I have died thousands of times. You lose the fear of death, if you know what death is. You are an eternal butterfly constantly shedding its ugly shell. Countless of my brothers and sisters do the same. Every time we die a new death, we are given the choice again. Some choose to live where the choices have been made are good. Some, "retire" in your terms to the level they have obtained. They do not have to suffer anymore. They forget their agony and yours. Beauty and friends adorn their days. The Father welcomes them to rest in his peace. Others seek Dominion. There is spoken of a final Dominion, when the last seeker will pass. Then all of creation can be at peace. Before that, much blood will be spilled. It is the balance of creation. Sacrifice. You would think that not having the fear of death, would make this simple. It is not so. So very few seek Dominion. The Father in his way does not dictate Dominion. It is a choice. It is a final choice. To seek Dominion, you must know that in the end you are alone. The Father has forsaken you. You must face the final battle with all your own frailty and look into the abyss of desolation. Your soul will be lost. Your tears unseen and your cries unheard. In all the vastness of creation, you will stand alone if you seek Dominion."

The man wept.

Beck watched as the man wiped his tears away and stood up. "It will be soon," he said. "They will come for me soon." "Who?" Beck asked. "The priests."

"Why would the Father forsake you?" Beck asked the man.

"He cannot watch what we do on that day. Do you not think one that knows so much love does not know the equal in pain? Your holy book says that he loved the world so much, he gave his only son. This is the selfish nature of man. The Father loves so much; he gives untold numbers of his sons and daughters, so that others may live. How much pain. How much sorrow. In all of creation, why could He possibly love us so much to give the blood of his closest children to a world that does not yet believe?"

"When the final end comes, the seeker must lose the light of the Father. He dies a true death. A death of the soul. Creation shows you all of what you have only seen an infinitesimal portion of. You see all the joy and beauty of creation. All the ugliness and depravity. You know the sorrow of the Father. Countless worlds. Souls to infinity. Each thought, each fear becomes you. You know the light and the depths of darkness. Every life and death. Every molecule that ever existed. On every world, every dimension of creation. You touch the mind of the Father and know his happiness and his pain. If your soul survives this, you are Dominion. Your earthly body returns to the Father. With more love than could be imagined, he welcomes you to his side. With your brethren, you await the time of the final Seeker."

The Sydot Inquisition Team met with the Elders and made their preparations. The site and method of execution was chosen. It would not be quick or painless. These were the instructions.

Beck looked at the man as the light from the rising sun shone on his face. A deep sadness for what this man faced, even if it was his imagination. He knew this man was not evil and would do everything in his power to see that he got the medical attention he needed.

The man turned to Beck. "Peter, you still do not believe though you hear the answers to what you asked. You, Peter of Earth, will be my testament. My witness. Your fear and despair will turn to belief. You will become the rock of my Father's temple. From your high place among men, will you be cast. You will suffer and be betrayed. In the end, you will face your first death. In the midst of this, your soul will be full of anguish. But, because you are special, I will give you a priceless gift." At this, the man touched Peter's forehead and it burst with a million lights.

High above his Earth, Peter soared. He knew this was a future not yet written of. He saw war and desolation. Man against man. Beast against beast. This was the final battle. This was Armageddon. Despair sat along side of Misery. Hope was a long forgotten treasure. The hope of mankind buried in the ashes of self-gratification. The final battle for humanity. Or its oblivion. Peter's sadness was endless. For all their striving, mankind had come to this. All the achievements, the defining moments that made man special had burned to a crisp. No longer would man rise to the stars seeking knowledge of his heritage. No longer would a dream of peace exist. We had made our choices. All of us. The choice was extinction. Was there no hope? No stopping the destruction? Beck cried, "My God, is there no one to stand? One soul? One bringer of Life?" As tears streamed down his face, Beck saw a mass covering half of his world, shining with the light of blazing diamonds. Closer he flew to the mass, which moved with a determination. The light blazed with the aura of a thousand suns. As Beck entered the light, he surely must be consumed. Instead, a voice, soft as the gentle whisper of a summer breeze, intoned "Peter, my son. My rock of faith. For the sacrifice you will give, this gift I give to you." The mass, Peter saw, was mighty army. Emblazoned upon their chests was a simple symbol: Dominion. Leading the army was a man and a woman. Though older and carrying the age and scars of battle, he knew them. Peter's heart swelled with love. For nothing could keep him from knowing them. Rachel and Joshua. His children.

Beck staggered back as if from an electrical shock. He stared into the eyes of the man. Sadness and love along with agony and ecstasy.

The Team entered the prison, neutralized the guards, and grabbed the man from the cell. Peter tried to intervene, but there were too many of them and they moved too fast. This could not be happening. Beck screamed, "Not this man. You people do not know what you are doing. Oh, God! Not this man. Anybody else. Not him."

The man looked at the dark, barren hill. A single metal pole stood. His captors had prepared the instruments for his "purification". Alone, so alone. The man walked up the hill. To suffer for this world's mistakes. To die for a people he did not know.

To seek Dominion.

Epilogue

In a future not yet lived, on a desolate hillside of a world unheard of, the man hangs his head. Pinioned to a cross bar by laser inserted spikes, his blood flows. Dripping like red tears. The beings gather around. Some in fear and loathing. Some in love. Three moons cast an eerie pallor to the scene. A wine colored ocean ripples. Red clouds rushing in, as green and blue lightning flashes. Lifting his head, the man cries to the heavens. "My Father, I know your pain. I am scared but I am not alone. For I know why you must turn your face." With his lifeblood soaking the dust of an alien world, he whispers, "And I forgive you."

There is silence in the heavens. Upon the multitude of worlds, a new day will dawn. No longer will the Father be saddened. Creation will know the bounty of his love.

All for the love, given by a single man. A single soul who spoke for all of humanity. The final seeker. A simple man who had died to end this journey of nightmare for a multitude of worlds. A man who would be best remembered simply as Peter.

Dominion.

Book Two
In The Blink Of An Eye

Sam Cochran was a dead man. The blood still flowed through veins. The heart muscle still pumped. The body still walked among men. However, what had made Cochran himself. His soul. His essence. It was gone. It left the exact moment, almost three years ago, that the bomb blew the car apart. The metal body of a vintage Mustang which contained the flesh and blood bodies of his wife and daughter. Lieutenant Samuel Cochran. Detective, Atlanta Police. He had died a while back. His body was just too stupid to lay down.

Hello, dear reader. Such a morbid introduction, yes? Well, my friends, it is the only way I know how to tell this story. Many of you will not believe it. Some will wonder at it. Some will at least…think. Most of what you will hear, I personally observed. The rest, I have pieced together over the past years from research and speaking with eyewitnesses. So come along. Be patient. I was not young when this happened and that was many years ago. Follow me. Learn of hope and terror. Damnation and redemption. Perhaps of miracles and heroes.

The streets of Atlanta, Georgia. Two short months prior to the Millennium. The city prepares for celebration. The dawn of a new age. Atlanta, the city reborn. Home to the Olympics, and world champions. We know how to throw a party. The time nears. A couple of blocks off of Peachtree Street, a small world of it's own exists.

The old wino lays propped against the box. The last of the grape wine dribbling down his chin. His eyes, dulled but awake watch as the unmarked police car pulls to the curb. Out steps Sam Cochran. Cochran walks into the alley and looks into the unseeing eyes of the businessman. The man whose torso has been shredded by hundreds of slashes from what appears to be a very sharp knife. Sam begins the examination by rote. His mind is somewhere else. It doesn't have to be here. He can do his job blindfolded.

Let me tell you about Sam Cochran. Born in Atlanta about 38 years ago. He lived a normal life, growing up in the "old" city. The one that existed with culture before crack cocaine ate it up in years to come. Sam joined the Army at the age of 18, enlisting as a Military Policeman. He soon became a detective and went into the Army Criminal Investigation Division as a Special Agent. He served stateside and overseas. He specialized in Anti-Terrorism for the Army and after ten years of serving God and country, he came back home to Atlanta. He applied for the Atlanta Police Department and was accepted. He paid his dues, earned his detective badge and loved his job.

He loved Jill, whom he met, fell madly in love with and married shortly after getting back to Georgia. But the true love of his entire life. A life filled with chasing bad guys who maimed and killed. The true love of Sam Cochran was

Rebecca. His "Becky". The child of his and Jill's love. The dark haired beauty who at the age of four, had her Daddy's world rotating around hers. With just that tiny smile.

Sam was a hero to his family, but he was also a real live, goodness gracious hero to the rest of us. He caught The Bomber. Yeah, not a bomber. The Bomber. The bastard that set the charge off during the Olympics. The symbol of peace in the City Reborn. The blast that killed two people. Well, it took awhile and there were a lot more heroes looking for the bomber. Maybe in the end, Sam was just lucky—or was it fate? Sam got a lot of publicity though he shunned it. He was a real hero and everybody wanted to thank him. During the excitement though, evidently everybody forgot that The Bomber didn't work alone.

One July night, as Sam pulled in the driveway of his house, his death began. Jill and Becky were in his old Mustang. Her car was just in the shop for an oil change. But, as they shouted to Sam, "We Want Ice Cream", he smiled. His eyes opened. He saw Jill's sweet smile and Becky's dark locks blowing softly in the wind. He smelled new cut grass from his neighbor's yard. His eyelid dropped ever so slowly, warm soft orange glows coming from the sky into his mind. The promises of a lifetime ahead flood through his brain. As his eyelid touched bottom and began it's ascent, he thought he could hear Jill turning the key. He thought, "It shouldn't be making that funny thumping noise", and as his eyes opened fully, Jill smiled…and died. The explosion engulfed the car hurling flame fifty feet away knocking Sam unconscious.

Maybe there is mercy after all. He didn't wake up for three days. That was seventy-two hours that he didn't have to suffer. He didn't have to worry about losing his sanity. For a blessed time, all of his being was not hungering to kill. But that would change soon. Sam's eyes would open. He would know that darkness had descended. He would welcome it. After he screamed until his throat bled. After he cursed everything on earth and in the heavens. After the tears, which should have flooded the city, and after the flame engulfed him over and over and over. He would welcome the darkness. Hell, he would savor it. Sam Cochran had died. What walked in his place was so hollow that it was fearsome.

Dear Reader, take a small break. Ponder on this man. Listen to what I'm trying to tell you about him. He was a good man. A fine man. But, he died. Then he went crazy. Then he lived again. Say a prayer, okay?

So, what would bring Cochran to "the block" as it was known? The block actually comprised about five city blocks off of Peachtree. The area was not touted in the tourist brochures. It was mostly old crumbling buildings that had not made the renovation list as of yet. The few brownstones mixed in along with a couple of local businesses, which were barely hanging on, gave shelter to the locals. A mixture of folks, who simply didn't want to move away from familiar territory and passively resisted the intrusion of crack, prostitutes and gangs into their home. Luckily for them, the block wasn't worth the attention of most self-respecting crooks. It was simply too poor. The area pulsed with its own life and rhythm. Sometimes it seemed as if a bubble had been placed in the middle of Atlanta and inside that bubble, a micro experiment in life and death was developing, oblivious to the rest of the city.

Let me introduce to some of the populace of this small world. The wino. What can I say? He was one of the most useless people in those five blocks. Hell, not "one of". He was the most useless. He had not always been that way.

He had once been a productive son of his parents. Served his country in war. Lived the American Dream. He had married a young woman named Rosealee at the end of the war. "Rose" and he had worked hard, both working when they had to. He had risen to a mid-level management job with Georgia Power from which he retired from after twenty-five years. Together, they had raised two sons and a daughter. All three had gone to college, graduated with honors and became productive members of society. For every day of every year that went by the man and his Rose met the sun with each other and fell asleep in each other's arms at night. Then, one night, in the space of a second, it all changed. A young punk stoned on a mixture of speed and heroin decided to see how far his .357 magnum would shoot. It didn't shoot any farther than the car carrying the man and his Rose from the nearby Publix grocery store. It entered the window, shattering the back of Rose's head as she finished saying "I love you" to her man. There are many rumors and stories as to what happened next. Suffice it to say the man went crazy. He screamed for his Rose until only a bottle could still the anguish. The laughing Dark One that he first saw on the night Rose died faded in the bliss of whisky induced sleep. Only much, much later would he ever read the testimony of the kid who pulled the trigger. He would shiver when the kid described the dark jester who urged him to test the magnum.

Freddy Jackson was baaaad. Not really. Freddy wanted everybody to think he was bad. In reality, he was a coward. Always had been. He had been raised poor and black. Screwed both ways from the get go. He couldn't make it in the white man's world or his own. Instead he just kind of shuffled between the both. Freddy was a hustler. He wanted to be a big time gangster but had a couple of things going against him. One, he was chicken. Two…. Well, deep down Freddy was just too good hearted to really hurt anyone. He talked a lot of trash but in all of my research, I have never been able to corroborate any act of violence that

Freddy claimed to have committed. But, if you heard Freddy tell it, he was the biggest, meanest loan shark swimming the ocean of the block.

Tito Marin was bad. No doubt about it. Arrested twice for murder prior to turning eighteen. He had never been convicted. The word on the street was that he had actually killed seven people. He was the leader of the emerging gang whose goal was to control downtown Atlanta. Anything that moved or crawled on the streets would be subject to Tito's control. If you wanted to do business, you had to pay homage to Tito Marin. His soldiers were everywhere. Armed and ready to do the bidding. Later, one would wonder, exactly who's bidding?

There was an angel on the block. Her name was Mary Margaret. "Just call me Maggie" was what she always said. No one ever knew her last name. It was simply Mary "Just call me Maggie" Margaret. The angel of 5th Street. She just showed up one day. Soft blonde hair, the bluest eyes and very pregnant. This isn't that all unusual in the city. A lot of the girls continue hooking up to the time they have an abortion or either have the baby. Nobody really knew what Maggie did. A lot of assumptions were made. After all, she was beautiful, even with that big round belly of hers. Nobody knew for sure. She would appear and always seem to have a little extra food or a blanket. Many times, she covered the wino so that he wouldn't freeze. She would roll him over, so he wouldn't choke on his own bile. She always had a smile and a kind word for Freddy. Freddy, normally talking a hundred miles a minute would become speechless in her presence. When she walked, electricity filled the air. I don't know how to describe it except that even the air flowed differently around her.

I swear one time; I saw a brick give way under the foot of a construction worker as Maggie passed beneath. The brick moved before it could hit her. I mean moved from its downward path, as if it had been pushed or deflected. I'm not crazy. I know what I saw. Then there was the "Roger" incident. Roger was a lowlife. No one liked him on the block. He had served time for rape and child molestation. But, he bullied his way around the block. He wouldn't mess with any of Tito Marin's people but everybody else was fair game. Well, he spotted Maggie soon after she arrived. One day, half-drunk, he followed her home. I think you can well guess what he had in mind. Roger was found dead the next day. The coroner's report, I would learn later, said that they could not determine the exact cause of his death. His heart had just stopped. They noted the anomaly that both his eyes were burned out of his head. They were never found.

Never far from Maggie's side was "The Dog". Nobody knew the Dog's real name. He just appeared one day like Maggie. He'd nuzzle the scraps that were behind the restaurants, drink water from the drains and try and stay dry in the abandoned buildings. We all got use to him. There were plenty of strays around, but he was different. He was well…noble. That's the only word I can think of. He was a full-blooded German Shepherd, black and tan with just a touch of silver. He weighed every bit of ninety-five pounds. The gleam of intelligence in his eyes was eerie. Once the animal sighted Maggie, he never left her side that we knew of. At least not until that night. Christmas Eve, 1999. But, that is for later.

Perhaps only Maggie knew that the dog's name use to be "Shep" and that he had a family in a nice house in the suburbs of Atlanta. A mother, father and two children that loved him with all their hearts and that he protected with all his. Until one night. One single night, when his family had left him overnight at the vet for his annual physical and shots. The one night that a gang of home invaders broke into the family's house and massacred his loving family without remorse. The killers screaming in delight at the Dark One's blessing and freedom from their earthly ties. Within a week, the invaders would all be dead. They would experience the true freedom from earthly ties and know the horror of what waited beyond. Shep dreamed of darkness and blood that night. After escaping from the kennels, he searched for his family and only found the old smells of the ones he loved mixed with that of death. So, Shep wandered into the wastelands to become another known only as the Dog. He searched for his new One. And in Maggie, he found that One. A voice whispered in the noble animal's head: "Protect".

Interlude

And I dreamt. Perhaps a vision. I saw a thousand worlds, which bled the color of deep red. I saw a thousand winged beings that wept tears of blue. Upon a world, I did not know, I saw a man cry to the heavens. I heard the man forgive his father for forsaking him. I felt a brush of the pain of the Father and I wept. I wept until I could weep no more.

I saw One. I saw a child. A child of light. I saw a bringer of darkness. A sage of death. It was dark and it laughed as it offered the child to its father with bloody hands.

I saw one thousand years of hell on Earth. Man against man and beast against beast. The darkness pulsed and grew. It laughed as the kingdom burned in flames. The prelude to extinction had begun.

I saw on thousand years of peace. I saw the adult who was the child. The reign of promise. The prelude to eternity.

I dreamt. I saw. Please…which one will be the truth?

Now, death had once again come to the block. To understand this death, we must go back two days ago. Forty-eight hours that would change the destiny of man. Forever.

The businessman had landed at Hartsfield International Airport, arriving from Switzerland. The man was met by three others and taken to a local hotel for a briefing. Unknown to him, two days later he would be dead. For now, his three partners were rushing to Nashville, Tennessee. They could not be late. Everything depended on it. The time of crisis was rushing towards them. Their partner would have to do the best he could in Atlanta with the help of the old man and the chosen. They prayed it would be enough.

On the same day the man flew into Atlanta, Sam Cochran sat on the third pew of a church downtown. It was a Catholic Church but that did not really matter. He sat there staring into nothingness. The screen of his mind played the bombing over and over. The bastard had died. Cochran and his team tracked him without mercy. In the end, he said he'd rather die than surrender. Cochran was glad to oblige him. It was sweet…for perhaps a second. The act consummated his hate, but it didn't bring back Jill or Becky. God, how he missed them. Jill's soft touch and Becky's hugs. The smell of his daughter which was full of innocence and freshness. Everything this world was not anymore. He wept. His hand went to the forty-five-caliber automatic in the shoulder holster under his left arm.

He caressed it like a lover. He pulled it out and slowly eased the hammer back. Cochran placed the barrel square between his eyes. One twitch and the pain would be gone. One moment of bravery and he would weep no more. Just one tiny squeeze. How long he sat there he didn't know but darkness had fallen. His finger tightened on the trigger. One last look around. His eyes slowly opened and a tear ran down his cheek. There in the darkness, the gun glowed with a blue light. His heart stopped. Ancient memory echoed in his brain. The memory of his Grandfather and the story of the Christmas miracle. Shaking, he lowered the weapon. And sat in the silence of the great chapel while he thought of long ago stories of miracles.

Two blocks away, Tito Marin was giving orders to his lieutenant, Chakro. Chakro was a thief, not a killer but Marin liked him. He helped keep his army organized. Chakro, half Mexican and half Cherokee, was Marin's right hand man. He could be trusted. The word was sent to gather the enforcers. Marin had made a deal with some very important people. Soon, if everything went well, Marin would control the firepower and funds to own Atlanta. Marin considered himself fortunate. The price of all of this was only one person. No problem.

The tall stranger, dressed in black to include his overcoat, stepped from the limousine. He hated flying. It had always bothered him. The rain had begun as he looked up Peachtree Street. He must have been tired from his long trip a passerby thought. His eyes are rimmed in red.

At the airport terminal, another stranger also dressed in black strode from the baggage claim area. The old man pulled his coat close around him to block the cold rain. The top of the coat just did cover the white collar. He went into the rain, which swallowed him up.

Mary spoke to the other one. Really, for the most part she listened. Sometimes, her pretty head would shake no. The Dog lay there and listened. Attuned to her feelings, every now and then he would let out a soft huff or growl. Mary bowed her head and held her belly as if she could protect her child from the words she heard. If only it was that simple.

On the block, Freddy hustled. The wino slept. The city pulsed as the block gathered its breath. Something was coming. Death had arrived in the big city. And it was hungry. Hungry for the One. Hungry enough for the many.

A Christmas Miracle

In the 13th year of Sam Cochran's life, his Grandfather had told the story to the family one Christmas Eve as they sat in the family room beside the roaring fire.

"It was so cold, your breath froze as soon as it left your mouth. I was in Germany in the war. It was a bitterly cold Christmas Eve and in a little known forest, my unit fought for our lives. Shells burst all around. Death flowed like a separate entity. It stalked American and German alike, touching them with its ice-cold touch and laughing when they drew their last breath. One dying Sergeant swore that he saw a dark jester laughing with glee at the carnage."

Granddad's unit had suffered about ninety percent casualties. My Grandfather himself had been wounded twice, but still he fought. As the shells pounded, he found a foxhole and slid into it. At the same time, another soldier slid in the other side. Grandfather heard the whimper of fear. As he turned, he recognized the soldier's German uniform. He was out of ammo for his rifle but he still had the forty-five pistol. He drew the weapon and pointed it at the chest of the German. It was then he noticed the German's submachine gun pointed at his own chest. Time slowed. He squeezed the trigger of the pistol. His supernatural vision saw the German do the same.

Suddenly, a blue light glowed around both weapons, pulsing with the beat of their hearts. In amazement, both lowered their weapons without firing. Maybe it was shock or exhaustion. They both placed their backs at the opposite ends of the foxhole and softly slid into a sitting position. And stared at each other. Midnight came and there was silence. It was Christmas. Omens and portents were spoken of later; of lights in the sky and winged creatures. Sightings of white horses with majestic knights and a glowing symbol of promise and hope.

All Grandfather knew was that he and another lonely, tired human being shared their pitiful shelter from the cold and their meager rations as a Christmas meal. Somehow, the food seemed to fill his belly, though he had been hungry for days. With warmth and fullness, he became drowsy and fell asleep. When he awoke with a start, expecting to have his throat cut, he found he was alone. Except for a small piece of chocolate, carefully wrapped in tissue paper along with the photograph of a smiling little blonde haired German girl. A little girl who obviously loved her Daddy very much.

Until the day Sam's Grandfather died peacefully in his sleep, he spoke with reverence of the Christmas Miracle of that day. He kept the blessed forty-five and passed it to his son who gave it to Sam on his graduation from the police academy.

The more Sam thought about it, the more he was sure the forty-five that he carried would guide his destiny. It was getting close to Christmas. There was a smell in the air. Was it salvation or damnation?

Cochran nodded as the coroner told him that the autopsy would be done within twelve hours. The doors slammed on the ambulance and it began its slow run to the hospital. No hurry for the dead. The man's name, according to his identification, was Francis Xavier Walsh of Bristol, England. Cochran shook his head. A normal visiting businessman, very common in the city of Atlanta. Common, except for the strange tattoo and the nine-millimeter Browning High Power resting in a suede shoulder holster. Could he be British Intelligence or perhaps some type of counter-terrorist operative? Cochran would have to put out some feelers to his contacts. For now, it was back to basics. Talk to the people on the street.

Cochran spoke to the wino that related what little he knew in a trembling voice. "I didn't really see anything. I'd had a little to knock off the chill, you know? I heard something though. I thought I was dreaming. I heard a voice saying something about it being a pitiful effort and was this all the Almighty Hated One had to offer. The voice was ugly. It came out of the alley but it was like everywhere. It irritated me, like...well, scratching nails across a blackboard. That's the way it sounded but not exactly. Do you know what I mean? I remember a soft voice. It sounded foreign. It said something about the son of liars losing. Then he said something about dominoes or domini. It sounded Latin. Then there was screeching and a scream. It sounded inhuman. I remember red eyes. I'm sorry. I was so scared. I'm so sorry." Cochran patted the man on the cheek. Perhaps one damned soul recognized its brethren. He walked on.

Freddy was shaking. He stood in front of the brownstone, which housed him along with his mother and sisters. He read the letter over again. It was not a long letter and Freddy read well. His mother had seen to that. The words just would not soak in. His brain kept rejecting them. Cochran walked up and asked him about the dead man in the alley. Freddy shook his head absently. No, he didn't know about some white dude getting sliced and diced. Right now, he didn't care either. Cochran slipped a card into Freddy's hand and asked him to call him if he thought of anything. As soon as Cochran walked off, the card slipped out of Freddy's numb fingers and he half sat, half fell to the steps.

The letter floated to the dirty sidewalk. Flashes went through the brain of Freddy. Flashes of his wild child years. His experimentation with crack, speed and shooting heroin. It didn't last long. Drugs were just not his game. Hell, he had only shot up a few times. Shared with a couple of other users maybe what, three times? Freddy's soul grew dark and cold. It only takes once. He turned and walked away from the warmth of his apartment. On the ground the letter lay. The testament of Freddy. The final laugh of the worst luck. The worse fear for anyone. Now, the new gift to the coward of the block had arrived just in time for Christmas. Part of the letter opened with the breeze. "We regret to inform you that the tests have been verified. You are positive for the HIV virus. We have counselors on duty and there are many new...."

Cochran was walking back to his car when he saw Maggie and the Dog. He was drawn to her. He would say later that he was just questioning a potential witness. But he would have gone to Maggie if he hadn't been canvassing the neighborhood. He was the moth and she was the flame. It was destiny. The dog looked deep into Sam's eyes. "Protect", the voice whispered.

The old man had checked into the Marriott, near downtown. A phone call to Nashville. Then he checked his baggage including the one, which had entered via diplomatic channels courtesy of the Vatican. It was about the size of a large trumpet case. The man sighed and removed his collar. He opened the case and tenderly removed the weapon from it. He did not have much time. He had to find the girl. God help him. He had no choice.

And the light shone upon me. Warmth filled me and I was not afraid. A being of greatness stood before me. The voice reverberated like thunder yet was soft like a thousand chimes blowing lightly in the wind. "Child," it said, "you are old in body but young in spirit. You will be the witness of this time to come. A time of sorrow. A time of great joy. It will be a moment in the way of man. A single moment which will determine his destiny. The choice will be vested in a few but will decide for the whole. You must remember and testify. You think you are weak and cannot do this, but you have rivers of strength that you have never dreamed of. A great darkness moves into your sphere in the guise of innocence. Events that were set in motion thousands of years before will culminate shortly. If you can see through the lies and deceit, you will prophet wisely. If not, beware the easy path. It leads to damnation." The being touched my forehead and I knew it had marked me somehow. My dreams ended with visions of liquid blue, which shone like fire.

The street was quiet except for the low wind moaning through the buildings. The wino snuffled and rolled over. Eyes watched him with hunger.

Maggie had taken Cochran's offer of a hot cup of coffee at the local diner. She told him she had not seen or heard anything of the murder. Her blue eyes showed sorrow for what had happened. "So sad", she said, "I have seen this before. Man is his own worse enemy." Cochran asked what she was doing on the street. Her soft smile made him blush. She said it was something she had to do and that she would be fine. Her baby was due very soon. Sam became a little bolder and asked her about the father. "Oh, he would be here if he could. It is just not possible at this time. But, I'll be okay Sam. I know this." Sam shrugged. He knew he couldn't change the world. He didn't really want to. He just didn't care about it anymore. "That's not true." said Maggie. Cochran jumped. Was she a mind reader? She smiled and said that he was mumbling to himself. She looked at Sam's soul. The charred, broken one. Sam would later believe that she had hypnotized him. She whispered things to him. Things that thrilled him and made his blood run cold. When she left him, he sat and stared while tears coursed down his face. Later, he would not remember. He did not see Maggie again until Christmas Eve.

In Nashville, the young FBI agent had worked undercover on this drug sting for three months. He was tired but he had gotten close to one of the biggest drug movers on the East Coast. The man trusted him. The agent had worked hard without rest to prove himself to his newfound home with the Bureau. Soon, it would be over. On Christmas Eve, he would coordinate the biggest raid in the city's history. He would be a hero. Then, he could rest.

In a motel on the east side of Nashville, the drug kingpin spoke with the stranger. He did not believe what he heard. His instincts had always served him well. But, the stranger showed him pictures, identification documents and case files. "Son of a Bitch", the kingpin screamed. "He will die a thousand times for betraying me. I will cut his head off personally. The world will be one less FBI agent." He then thanked the stranger and, as his soldiers showed him out, told him to get some rest. He was really getting red around the eyes. A dark laugh floated over the southern winter night.

Soon, so very soon. The Hated One would blink. Then it would be over. One or the Other. It did not really matter. The laughter was like airborne madness floating on the winds of the night.

The old man hung the phone up. Walsh had been a good man and a good operative. This would not help the agenda. He rubbed at his wrist over the faded tattoo there. He was getting too old for the field.

Chakro told Marin that the enforcers had been notified of the time and place of the meeting. Chakro asked Marin what was up with all of the secrecy. Marin snapped and said that it was none of his business. He would be told at the meeting. Meanwhile, Marin had to go meet a very important "client". The one that would make his dreams come true.

The morning was cold and crisp. The Christmas shopping had begun. Of course, they didn't have to worry about that on the block. No one bought their presents on that set of streets.

Freddy had a hangover. A bad one. He had gotten so drunk that he had blacked out. Whatever he had done, he had blown through all of his money. Shit, what did it matter? Nothing mattered anymore. He began to shake. It wasn't death. He had seen plenty of that on the street. He was just…so afraid of getting there. He was scared and there was no one he could tell.

The wino sat up looking around bleary eyed. The hot dark liquid burnt his throat. The coffee dribbled down his chin.

The tall stranger walked among the children at the school around the corner giving them treats. He walked the block, stopping to give the wino a sandwich. He spoke to Freddy in a low voice, telling him to keep his hopes up…medical miracles were in abundance. He spied Maggie up the block. As he walked past her, she stopped dead in her tracks. The Dog stepped between her and the man. A low growl sounded. The man smiled and stepped back saying, "Bless You Child" and in a lower voice, which could have been dismissed as the wind, "Of the whore who begets the whore."

The next day, a ten-year-old shoots his classmate. The maggots consume the uneaten sandwich next to the wino and Freddy's body is seized with spasms as his immune system breaks down totally in twenty-four hours. The bells ring as Christmas approaches.

Cochran reads the autopsy report. Nothing surprising is in it. Death was from massive blood loss due to hundreds of lacerations. No metal filings could be obtained to indicate what type of blade was used. The tattoo was of unknown origin. Some type of symbol but no known gang or occult affiliation. No anomalies, except for a "glitch" in the DNA. The coroner added a personal note saying that it was probably some type of latent mutation. Nothing important.

The old man looked at the symbol on his left wrist. He would make one last phone call before beginning. There would be no other communication until it was over. One way or the other. He spoke to the woman on the other end of the line in Geneva. He told her simply, "Begin the next selection." She acknowledged and with that, another cycle of The Order of Dominion was initiated.

Two days prior to Christmas, the snow came. It fell in a soft white blanket, covering the city. The old man made contact with me. I knew not why. He said that I was not a stranger to him and that I had been predetermined, whatever that meant. Over many cups of coffee and plentiful food, the old man told me of wonders. I did not believe, but the food and drink were good. I figured it was a good trade off to listen to a deranged old man. Ah, the innocence of ignorance.

He told me that I would be the Oracle of events soon to come. My job would be to chronicle what happened for posterity. If there were to be a posterity.

The old man said his name was Hans and that he was here at this moment in time to save a life. I laughed and told him the Red Cross was just around the corner. The slap from his right hand rocked my head back. My eyes watered. I looked at his collar. I sputtered that I had never known of a Catholic priest who would strike someone. His look would have burned through the back of my head, I thought. His eyes narrowed. His voice, barely audible, stated emphatically that he was not Catholic nor any of the other "diluted" faiths. Those were his words. Then Hans told his story. Believe. Or not. We will all see the truth shortly. Whatever it is.

Hans told me that he was with an order much older than anyone would think, whose job it was to protect certain pivotal beings from danger. This time, I kept my laughter to myself. It sounded like James Bond meets the clergy.

Then, Hans reached out and touched my forehead as if he could see the mark. His touch brought fire and a million lights exploded inside my skull.

I fell towards a planet. My Earth. Much older, perhaps at the dawn of creation. The birth of man was at hand.

I saw the experiment that was man. Crafted with such love, man made his first choice. The punishment was sorrowful but sure. Anyone that has ever read the first few pages of the Bible knows the basics. But, there was much more. Hans' story unfolded like a theatrical trailer. There were great battles over man who had been made in the image of the Father. His other children, great beings unto themselves were torn asunder. Beings which we call angels. A Great War was fought with man at the center. Divisions were made. The mold was set. During this time of wonder, children of angels and man were born into the world. Some became servants of the wicked. Others swore to protect man at all cost. From the time man was banished into the wilderness, these beings swore an oath to protect humanity. Thus, was the first initiation of The Order of Dominion. Wondrous beings with their father's liquid blue eyes, these sons and daughters over the ages waged constant battle with the sons and daughters of the Liar. The Order was very closed and secrecy prevailed. Most would not even survive the initiation phase of the Order. Of those that did enter, few lived to see old age. Down through the ages, the angelic blood diluted but the oath did not. Man never knew the majority of those that gave their lives in the service of Dominion. Some became famous although their true purpose was never known.

I saw battles with clubs and stones from the earliest of times. I saw both earthly enemies and those not of this world. As years passed, the battle continued for the very survival of humanity. Dagger, sword and gun. Technology brought new weapons to the war. The purpose remained the same. I saw the bravery of Dominion as well as the tears. I recognized people from our history. They shone in a different light within the truth of things.

At any one time, there would only be five protectors initiated. They would serve until their death. In addition, two Oracles would serve to document the service of Dominion.

With the advent of technology, the Order utilized a support staff, which gathered intelligence and conducted surveillance of potential targets. The Order had such an extensive library of information dating back to their formation, that even the Vatican asked them for help on occasion. Therefore, when certain favors were needed by the Order, the Throne of Peter was only glad to assist.

Now, according to Hans, time approached a critical junction. Events of staggering importance would be resolved soon. In two small cities on this tiny planet, the future of mankind…perhaps all of creation, would be decided. In the blink of an eye.

Cochran was back on the street. The alley where the murder had taken place yielded no clues. A background check on Walsh only deepened the mystery. The dead man did not exist at least as far as Sam could ascertain through any government records. The British government had been no help but was in a hurry to get the body of their citizen back. They were sending representatives to escort the body.

Cochran tapped into all of his sources. Rumor had it that an out of town enforcer imported just for the job had hit Walsh. When pressed for a name, the only thing that came up was a "Mr. Black", which was a description of how the man dressed, not his real name. "Why the hit?" asked Cochran. No one knew. Further rumors of something big about to go down. Very soon. Enforcers were moving into place. The people who lived by the pulse of the city were seeking a hole and staying there for the duration.

Maggie knew the time was near. She hurried to make sure her newly found charges were okay. The wino smiled at her as she spoke softly to him. Were his eyes clear today? She patted him on his stubble of his worn cheek and went to find Freddy. The Dog found Freddy first. Sitting on the steps, shivering as the light snowflakes showered him. Without a word, she went to him, held him and whispered softly in his ear. Slowly, the shivering stopped. He went into himself, almost in a trance. Seeking for the core of his being. There he would find the truth. Maggie felt the labor pains begin. It was almost time. Tomorrow. Would it herald birth or death?

Mr. Black met with Tito Marin. A simple plan was prepared. People were creatures of habit. There would be a time tomorrow when the hated One would follow its habit despite the pain. "That is when we strike, Mr. Marin", said the man in black. "The timing will be critical. At that moment, we will throw everything at once." The stranger shrieked with laughter that set Chakro's teeth on edge. "And He cannot win!" the dark one cried. "For at that precise moment the Other will set his plan into motion. At that moment in time, God will blink." A stolen car was prepared. Shotguns were cleaned and loaded. Knives were sharpened. While this took place, Tito stood on the roof of a building in downtown Atlanta, looking at the kingdom that was promised by the Dark One who stood beside him and laughed. Marin smiled nervously as the man's red rimmed eyes almost seemed luminous in the twilight. Nearby, carolers sang in front of a manger scene. One lady swore later that she saw the baby Jesus weep tears of blood. If we had only known, we would have all wept.

Hans Gunter Thielemann said his final prayer. He cleaned his gun for the last time. The blessed gun that had been with him for almost half a century. The one that he had nestled close to him in the service of Dominion since a cold December night he spent in a foxhole in a blood drenched German forest. He looked at the pictures of his beloved wife, long passed now. And the beautiful woman who had only been a bashful smiling child when he went off to war. A woman who stills loved her father with all her heart. And he with his. "Father, make me strong. I will miss her so much." The last tears that Hans would ever weep rolled softly down his cheeks.

Late that night in Nashville, the FBI agent and his team checked their weapons and equipment. The vans were ready. The surveillance gear was in place. The raid would take place at high noon on Christmas Eve. The agent kind of liked the symbolism. If all went well, by 12:15, the Bureau would be in possession of the largest cocaine shipment ever seized on the East Coast.

Across town, the men made their preparations also. Automatic weapons and grenades were laid out on the table. A knife, the size of a machete, was presented to the "Boss" who would have the honor of removing the head from the bastard traitor. By 12:02 tomorrow, his blood would be drying on the blade.

Two blocks away, three men checked their H&K MP5 submachine guns with laser sights. Laid out in the small hotel room was three black raid suits and night vision goggles. None spoke. They had worked together many times before. As the night closed in, they knelt in communion. By 12:01 on December 24, 1999, the world would know of salvation or destruction. The heartbeat of the world now sounded like the ticking of a clock. Tick…Tock.

City of Dreams

The Dog whimpered in his sleep. Dreams in black and white. Once, home was a loving family with the warmth and safety of the pack. Then, blood and death. Cold and hunger. Endless night with strangers all around. Then he had found the One. Blazing light and color flooded his brain. The voice whispers "Protect." The Dog dreamt of a child. The One he would give his life for. The blood of the child dripped on the city streets and became a river that washed over the world.

Freddy slept. He had wandered the city until exhaustion set in. He dreamed of his father. The one he had loved so much. The smiles and laughter of a happy childhood. A family together when he was so young. Death arrived. Not with a bang but with a slow sleepy killer called cancer. He watched as the light of his father's life slowly dimmed. The little boy was so afraid. Whispers of impending doom surrounded him. In order to protect him, they kept him in the dark. And the dark was a very scary place for one so young. He held no power over it or the black entity that ate his father day after day. The day they buried him, Freddy was to be afraid for the rest of his life.

The wino dreamed of a world awash in blood. He saw a man; a simple man hung on a cross. His blood would wash all of creation. A great battle was coming. The time of choices approached. As he shivered in his sleep, he looked downward and saw a world on fire. The crucified man's tears fell upon the flames and they dimmed. A great army moved across the face of the earth. A single symbol glowed with the hope for all of humanity.

Hans sank deep into darkness. The dreams of a warrior-priest who had known many battles. He dreamt of a cold foxhole and a Christmas miracle. The long walk away from that war the next morning and his enlistment in a different, more vital war that was thousands of years old. How he had been found and the discovery of the gene that ran in his blood, reflecting the remnants of his heritage from the beginning of man. The symbol that glowed in the night skies that cold Christmas night that led him to his destiny. A symbol that would be attributed to the Greeks but actually was as old as man. The symbol of what man would call archangels. In that one concept represented by an ancient letter, the hope of creation rested. Dominion.

Sam Cochran cried in his sleep. He dreamt of Becky as she grew, graduated school and left for college. She would go on to become a medical researcher who would be instrumental in finding a cure for...No, she was only four. He turned and reached for his wife. No, she was gone. But, he saw what was supposed to be. Before the death of his soul. Before he was touched by a power and chosen for his journey of sorrow. Becky, the four-year-old, sat by him and wiped the tears from his eyes. "Daddy, you are so brave. Soon, you must be the bravest you have ever been. I know you are so tired but we love you and soon you can rest. For now, you have to go back to the place. You know the one I mean. It's very important to all of us. When you get there, you will have to make your choice. Remember that I love you. Forever." With that, she hugged him tight. Sam's tears flooded the pillow he held in his arms. Like a child.

Interlude

He cried for his children. So much promise and hope. He felt their agony and desperation of the fallen. Everything had been in their grasp and had slipped through their fingers. Now, the world was in chaos. Man had sunk to his lowest level. The wars and hate. The self-obliteration. Was there anything worth saving? Yes. At the same moment humanity was at its cruellest, it rose to its finest moment. For every atrocity, there were acts of heroism. For every act of selfishness, there were those that gave everything of themselves. Their duality was perhaps their salvation. He could only hope and to keep loving them.

The liquid blue eyes watched as events unfolded. They prepared for what must come. This was the moment when it would be known, if their dreams would hold true or their worst nightmares would come to pass. Man. Blood of their blood. With their hope went humanity's also.

The darkness moved upon the face of the world. The Liar waited for his children to fulfill his dream. Crimson eyes laughed with delight as the sun turned black and the world beneath his feet burned. Every man, woman and child. Rubble under his feet to be desecrated before the Hated One. Eternal revenge for the loss of his heritage. The ranting of a rebellious child and the universe as his playground.

The Earth breathes. Time ripples and dimensions deconstruct. Eternity implodes. Perhaps we are only the dreams and nightmares of angels.

Chakro was pissed. For some reason, Tito had decided to brief the enforcers himself. Not that he really minded that part at all. There were some things that just didn't set with Chakro well and the use of force bothered him quite a bit. He thought it was better to live by your wits. But, it really bothered him that Tito didn't seem to fully trust him on this matter. He spat with disgust. Probably that red eyed son of a bitch who was always whispering in Tito's ear.

In Nashville, the three men slipped on the black skin-tight suits. Solid black, except for the small white symbol over the left breast. They pulled the gloves and hoods on. It was almost time. Less than three blocks away, the "Boss" finished telling his men how he wanted the FBI raid team wiped out to the last man. He would set an example for anyone in the future who thought they could go against him.

The young agent smiling had just finished breakfast with the rest of his team. He felt much better now. He hadn't slept well. Dreams of other worlds and strange symbols. Must be the excitement, he thought.

Sam Cochran walked out of the office and down into the streets. The shoppers were everywhere. Christmas Eve had arrived in the city. He checked the forty-five in his shoulder holster and headed towards the block. He didn't think, he just followed his instincts. Flashes of bodies and flames along with the face of a murdered man burned in his thoughts. What led him, he did not question. The answers would soon come.

Freddy was pumped. He felt stronger than he had in days. He just couldn't sit in the apartment. He'd go crazy. He pulled on his jacket and went out into the cold. Maybe he would shop, who knows? He headed toward the center of the block.

Hans' taxi dropped him close by. He wanted to walk to clear his head. In his right hand he carried the trumpet case which cradled a deadly lullaby.

Maggie wept. She knew it had been foretold. Still, it broke her heart. So much sorrow in the past and much more to come in the future. Because of her and the child she hugged in her round belly. The pain was constant now and she could hardly walk. She reached down and patted the Dog. It was almost time.

In the center of the block, the wino watched. Thoughts of younger days coursed through his mind. He flexed his hands and struggled to stand straight on two feet. Waves of nausea washed over him and his eyes blurred. Then, they cleared and the world stood still.

The men waited in ambush in the warehouse on the south side of Nashville. They grinned to each other and themselves. Nothing was better than wasting a friggin pig. Nothing. They felt like gods. One looked over his shoulder as if a dark thing just on the edge of his vision echoed his laughter.

The ghostly team entered through the roof. Laser sights turned on. Was it imagination or did the symbols on their uniforms appear to glow?

The young FBI agent rested is back against the rough-hewn wall. He gave the go signal to his well-trained team. On the count of three and they would enter. One. Two. Three…

Maggie walked down the cold Atlanta street. Freddy saw her across the block. He smiled and walked towards her and the ever present Dog. Cochran stepped out of the alley where he had returned to the crime scene hoping for inspiration. The wino grimaced as he propped himself against the wall next to the street. The sun was hazy, hinting at more snow later this day. A car engine roared to life just around the corner. Two of Tito's enforcers wearing long coats stepped from the alley. The other two were in the car. Tito and Chakro turned the corner just as Mr. Black stepped into reality from nowhere. Maggie stepped off the curb, her eyes wide…

And God blinked.

Maggie's eye slowly, ever so slowly descended. The car turned the corner screeching, almost on two wheels. Two thousand pounds of yellow Monte Carlo hurled towards the slow moving pregnant girl. This would be too easy. Out of the windows of the car appeared two shotguns. The barrels looked like twin railroad tunnels. The two thugs coming up from the side reached under their long jackets and pulled out short, stubby submachine guns. Stolen, they would never be traced. Their fingers tightened on the triggers. Tito grinned. "All of this world before me and more." What had been promised was about to be. Chakro looked into the blue eyes of Maggie and realized the price of Tito's world. Chakro, for the first time in his short life knew of damnation. Mr. Black laughed with glee. He had won, no matter what happened. He unsheathed an ancient dagger. His eyes were the color of molten steel now. The eyes of his true father.

Her eyes almost closed. Time flowed different in this place. The air was a thickness unto itself. Freddy's eyes went wide as he saw the two machine guns. From nowhere, appeared an old man holding an even older gun. A bead of sweat seemed to drip for eternity down his temple. Cochran saw the dagger and reached for his forty-five. The wino thought of the days when he had played fullback for his high school football team as he lowered his head and his legs slowly began to pump, pushing him forward. The Dog moved forward with the words in his brain, "Protect the Child."

As the car careened forward towards the girl, with legs of youthful power, the wino made it between the onrushing vehicle and her. His shoulder nudged her out of the way, throwing her to the sidewalk. The car slammed into his right leg crushing it along with his hip. For a moment the pain did not exist. Then, with the blood and shattered bones tearing open his skin, the agony overwhelmed him and he lay down to die. His vision grew dim. His eyes opened and he saw everything.

Because of the wino, the car had struck a fire hydrant instead of Maggie. Cursing, the two punks pointed the shotguns at her swollen belly. They could not miss at this range. The two with the machine guns pointed at Maggie's back squeezed the triggers. Freddy knew in that moment what must be done. He never hesitated. There was no delay or second thoughts. It was the bravest act I ever saw in a human being. He threw himself right up to the two men, covering both barrels with his body. His body, with its broken down immune system, was not immune to bullets either. They tore him to shreds with a muffled chuffing sound. His eyes open, he fell to the ground. But, he smiled. I swear he smiled. He had bought precious time.

The warrior-priest leveled his old gun, which glowed with a bright blue light. He pulled the trigger and I could see the bullets come out of the barrel and seek the two that had killed Freddy. It was like those lifeless pieces of lead hunted them. When they found their mark, their bodies exploded with their eyes aflame. As Hans turned, the Dark One screaming his fury, slashed his throat with the dagger. As his blood poured onto the streets of a strange city, Hans thought of the story that would be told of this day. He wondered as he sank to the ground if it would be distorted like the ones of old? Like the one that told of three wise men at the birth of a Holy Child two thousand years ago. They may have been wise. They had brought gifts; that was true. They had also brought sacred daggers and vanquished the dark assassins of that blessed night. Protectors all, through the ages. Now, he went to join his brethren. With the faith that another would take his place.

In Nashville, at the same moment, the laser sights appeared on the drug dealers out of nowhere. Silent death whispered in the warehouse. In the space of sixty seconds, fourteen souls were sent to their judgment. The three melted into nothingness.

The warehouse doors were kicked in and the FBI Swat team entered throwing flash bang grenades and spreading side to side. Silence greeted them. Then a body. And another. When all was said and done, the count was fourteen including the head of the gang who for some reason was missing his head. A ton of cocaine sat unattended as well as thousands of dollars that were undisturbed. The young agent would be a hero for sure. But, this would go down in the annals of the FBI as one of the strangest raids in history. As Special Agent Peter Beck sat in the corner, rubbing his eyes, he thought maybe he did believe in guardian angels after all.

Maggie's eyes touched bottom and began their ascent. Cochran whirled as he saw the shotguns. Too late, they fired. The Dog leaping upward took both blasts in his ninety-five pound body. Cochran fired, killing one of the men. The next round took Cochran's shoulder out in a bright spray of blood. Tito Marin, screaming in rage, pulled a nine-millimeter pistol and shot Cochran in the back. Cochran went down. As he lay there, fighting the pain he aimed and took the second shotgun shooter out with a shot right between the eyes. Tito drew a bead on Maggie.

Her eyes opened. She stared into the soul of a boy named Chakro. A thief by all means and a young man who had made his choices, living with the consequences. As the hammer dropped on Marin's pistol, Chakro twisted his arm sending the bullet into nowhere. They began to wrestle over the still smoking gun. Two more shots rang out and both fell with crimson coloring their chests. Chakro cried out to the skies, "Don't forget me". I swear I heard a voice on the wind saying, "This day you will be with me". What Tito Marin saw at the moment of his death, I do not want to know. I saw his eyes and it was a look of horror I shall never forget.

Cochran lay in a pool of blood. I never knew the human body had so much blood in it. I thought he was dead. But, the Dark One approached. What had walked in the guise of a man, I saw clearly now. Perhaps, it was because I was so close to death myself. It was death incarnate. The beast of Revelation lacked in description when compared to this beast. A dozen heads, all born of some hell I dare not imagine. Hundreds of razor sharp claws. Somewhere in my fogged brain, I realized what had killed the man in the alley. It was the eyes that were the most terrible. A liquid red which bespoke of carnage and chaos with no hope or salvation in them. Only hopelessness and misery. And fury. The fury came towards the girl.

Time stopped and the air rippled. As I saw the true nature of the Beast, I saw the power of Samuel Cochran. A symbol glowed on his chest bespeaking of his heritage as a son of angel and man. As he looked the Dark One in the face, he recognized it for what it was and he knew it. For at the time of the death of his family, he had seen this creature sitting on the hood of the car laughing right before the explosion. Sam had thought he'd just gone crazy. Now he knew the one that had stripped him of his family, life and sanity was right before him. All because the Beast knew what he was and it was afraid of Sam Cochran.

Sam smiled a bloody smile. It should be. As Sam struggled to his feet and raised his pistol, I saw a phalanx of angels surrounding him. The pistol became a mighty sword glowing with a blue flame. As one possessed, I saw Sam's eyes turn liquid blue and mighty warrior wings adorn his back. The world as we know it may have seen Cochran pull the trigger. I saw him swing the sword of the archangels and destroy the creature known as Death. With the screams of a billion souls, it went back to its father's domain.

As Sam Cochran lay dying in the street, Maggie wept. She looked at the carnage that surrounded her and she sank to her knees. The labor pains were coming rapidly now. An ambulance whined in the distance. Was all of this just because of her? No…she knew this, but…Freddy lay dead. The old man with the look of a priest lay crumpled on the sidewalk. The wino moaned with his shattered leg. The noble animal lay at her side; blood matted fur and his once intelligent eyes dim. She cried unto her Father and she lay there listening to the approach of the ambulance. Her hand reached out and touched the Dog. He stood for what all of them had meant. Protectors all. Her tears fell upon his lifeless body.

I received a gift as I lay there. I got to see Sam Cochran die. Don't judge me yet. It was a wonderful thing. I saw a multitude of warrior angels. Not the cherubs of tales but mighty, proud beings with the same symbol glowing upon their chests. They formed an honor guard for the fallen man. A blue light embraced him. A part of him rose from what was left of his shattered body. He looked a little confused, as I guess he should have been. Then on the edge of the light, I saw…then he saw, the little dark haired girl holding out her hand. Tears fell down his face as he ran towards her wide-open arms and tears ran down my face as I heard her say…"Welcome home, Daddy".

As tears mingled with blood, I saw the Dog's chest raise with a breath.

Epilogue

Well, my dear reader. It has been many years since that bloody night. I have finished my research and now add my final thoughts to this manuscript.

Precious Maggie made it to the hospital that day. A few hours later, she gave birth to a child of light whom she named Christina. Oh, there were rumors and miracles that night in the hospital on the cusp of a new age. But, that is perhaps for another story. Maggie was very special, as was her child. Her child will someday herald in the new age and reign in peace as has been foretold. Until that time arrives, we have been blessed. Mary…er…Maggie is very special. Just as special and beautiful as the other child that she had over two thousand years ago. Don't ask me how I know it is her, I just do. Right now, Maggie and Christina have been taken to the "Sanctum, Sanctorum" or sanctuary where they await as the time approaches.

The time is near. A time of great choices. There will be a terrible battle. But, there is hope. All because of the choices of a handful of pitiful, frail human beings that long ago Christmas Eve. Even now we reach out to the stars and other worlds. On one such world, a man named Peter Beck stands upon the threshold of revelation and the path to his destiny.

As for me, I'm getting older. I have to move slowly because of my leg and hip. But, I have almost finished my task as the Oracle. And because of the gift I saw when Sam went to his reward, I look forward to seeing my Rose when it is time.

Until then, I have my writings and my books…and my companion. A noble animal. I decided to call him Saint. I figured it was much more fitting than his old name. Yes, he is a wonder. I grow old. He hasn't aged a day since Maggie's tears. He is my constant friend and protector. I think he awaits the return of Christina. His eyes look as if he will always remember the edict to "Protect the Child". Who knows how long he will be with us? He, like us, could go at anytime. In a year. In a thousand. Perhaps, in the blink of an eye.

Book Three
Sanctum, Sanctorum

I stood on the rim of the world and watched as the sun turned black and the moon became the color of blood. I saw the cities in flames that the tears of the saints could not put out. Death stalked the Earth. I heard the cry from humanity. Where is my salvation? Where is my sanctuary? The winds blew and the storms raged. A small glow in the abyss of destruction shone like a gem in the midst of the blackness. The voice of a child whispered, "I am".

Samantha Duncan walked towards Piccadilly Circus. She had been in London for three months now, preparing for the time. It was December 22nd. The year of our Lord 1999. Tomorrow, she would go to her home in Glasgow. To await the birth of her child. A small smile played at the corners of her full lips. Hers and Michael's child. The memories flooded her mind.

Samantha had been a warrior. Born in the highlands of Scotland, she had been raised of sturdy stock to be sure. And beautiful, with raven hair, which lay about her shoulders. Her intense dark brown eyes with flecks of gold had intimidated many a man. She was recruited for the war because of the extra component of her DNA strand deep within her body. She survived the selection process and was trained for a war, which was fought all over the world and beyond, always in the shadows of reality. She had met Michael during a particularly horrible campaign and her child of love had been conceived. She had been retired from active duty. This unusual in itself, but hers was a special situation.

Stories would be written of her exploits to be remembered by those that came after. Soon, however this chapter would end. An ending befitting a warrior but not a mother. An ending in blood.

Jason Walsh watched Samantha from the corner of his eye. He was her protector but he tried to give her some personal space. It was hard for him not to stare at her. Even with her big round belly, she was a fetching woman. His eyes kept going to her hair. So black, it almost seemed to have a life of its own. The two white streaks perfectly balanced on each side of her forehead, she wore with pride. He had heard from his father, that the streaks were the legacy from a pitched battle with one of the Liar's own. She had won.

Jason smiled to himself and only hoped he would have such mettle as this woman and his father, Xavier Walsh, who served the Order of Dominion with such valor. After his mother's death, Jason had been recruited by the Order while he was serving with the British Special Forces in the SAS. He was still classified as an initiate. He had not been formally accepted. Normally, he would not be in the field but a crisis had arisen elsewhere and his father and the other protectors had been needed. So, Jason had his chance. He would never know how proud his father was of him or that it was a good thing that his mother was not alive. To lose both a husband and a child would have driven her to madness.

Into the nighttime throng they walked. Past the pubs and shops intermingled with strip clubs and porno theaters. As they turned a corner, it was as if they had stepped out of the world. Only silence and darkness existed. Jason's heart beat faster as his adrenaline kicked in. His combat instincts had been finely honed by the military. He moved closer to Samantha. Her dark eyes widened as the creature, which masqueraded as a human stepped in front of her. As its grating voice began to speak, another voice softly whispered to her inner self, "It is time."

"Whore. Did you actually think you would escape our attention because of what is happening over there"? It looked at Walsh. "Is this the best the Hated One can field nowadays. He thinks he knows of blood and pain. He is a child. A lamb for the slaughter." Walsh looked at Samantha. It was as if she had entered a trance. She held her stomach, cradling her unborn child. A serene smile crossed her lips as she whispered, "I have seen it. Future and eternity. I see it all."

As she lowered her head, the thing unsheathed an ancient dagger. Walsh hesitated because of Samantha's actions. The first slash across her chest bubbled with crimson. She never uttered a sound. Not during one of the fifty slashes. Walsh was moving fast and met the creature head on. As he closed in battle, he saw the eyes of his adversary. The color of molten lava. Angels would sing his praise for the bravery with which he fought. In the end, he would die on the dark streets of London in the shadows of an unknown war. He would enter the warm light that awaited him.

After it was done, the creature hid the bodies. They would not be found for three days. The rain began to pour. The tears of heaven unleashed upon the earth. If you listened very closely, you could almost hear the words, "Protect the Child".

It was a young Bobby who found the bodies. His nightmares would last a long time. He had been chasing a young pickpocket who was working the Christmas crowd. He had followed the waif into an alley and lost him. The Bobby pried the boards from an entrance to an old theater and entered the lobby with his torch on. As he played the light around the lobby, he saw the bodies, but kept going. His mind had refused to process the image immediately. When it did, he froze. His hand shaking, he slowly brought the light back. Back to the two poles at the side of the lobby. Two poles, which had been, modified as inverted crosses. The bodies of a young man and pregnant woman hung lifeless. In their own blood, was written, "Whore of the Angels" on the floor. When the ambulance arrived, the young police officer was still screaming.

Dr. John Hanover was tired. He didn't know whom he had pissed off to pull Christmas duty, but he was going to give the Chief of Staff a piece of his mind after the holidays were over. The trauma room never slowed. He shook his head. The blood, piss and vomit just never stopped. Not even for the holidays. It seems that it just gets worse. People get pretty inventive when it comes to inflicting mortal injuries to one another. Hanover thought, if there is a God, he must be on extended vacation.

Another page and Hanover was off to Trauma Room #3. He arrived to find the dead bodies of a man and a pregnant woman surrounded by nurses and an intern. His weariness exploded. "What the hell are you doing calling me down here for dead bodies. We've got enough down the hall that are trying to die on us." The staff flinched at his raving. They knew. They were all tired. One nurse spoke softly, "Dr. Solomon here, was pronouncing the deaths. He decided to try out his new stethoscope. He swears he heard a heartbeat." Hanover just shook his head. Everybody was exhausted. He started to turn. The young intern shouted, "Please Doctor. I'm not crazy. I know what I heard. I think her baby is still alive." Hanover snorted. He paused and turned around. He listened with his own scope while he looked into the ravaged face of the woman and thought that she must have been beautiful, once. His eyes narrowed and a small frown crossed his lips. He shook his stethoscope and placed it on her belly again. It was impossible but there it was. As steady as the ticking of a clock. The whisper of life.

Hanover bellowed at his personal team. "Get the woman to an operating room, stat. We're going in boys and girls." As the team worked frantically, all thoughts of holiday meals and family gone, they had little time to think of the miracle that they were a part of. It was just the beginning. Hanover sliced into the woman's belly. She had been torn up pretty badly. The child may have been damaged. Hanover, intent on his mission, barely looked up. The others had, however and there would be stories later of a soft blue light in the room that cold Christmas day. As the boy child was lifted from his mother's stomach, there were tears in the eyes of the team. As Hanover raised the child, they all gasped. One nurse crossed herself. The child cried and Hanover looked into its eyes. His voice shaking, he told his nurse to get his surgical clippers. As he did what he knew he must do for this child, he wept.

Years of doubt and questions faded. He wept the tears of rebirth. When it was done, he swore his team to secrecy for all their sakes. He then sent word for his parish priest. Father Emerson of the Holy Church of Saints and the orphanage. Father Emerson would do the right thing. Yes, he would provide the sanctuary for this child.

A child reborn as the Phoenix of legend from the ashes of destruction. "Ashe", thought Hanover. How fitting. The child's unsettling eyes looked through Hanover's soul as if he liked the name. Ashe's wounds were tended and they waited for Father Emerson.

That night when he got home from work, John Hanover gathered his family unto him and reveled in their love. And his own for them. Perhaps another Christmas miracle. He had regained his soul.

On the cold night wind, a child's cry could be heard. A cry so plaintive, that it seemed to reach to heaven itself. The cry of Ashe Duncan.

London, England
18 years later

Ashe looked up from his books as if in deep thought. After a few moments, he began to read again. At an astonishing pace. Father Emerson shook his head fondly. Of all the children who were or had been in his care, Ashe was the most special. Such a handsome lad. Deep black hair, just like his mother but with bright blue eyes. Father Emerson laughed softly to himself. The intense blue eyes of Ashe initially had frightened many of his young wards. Some had said that they were almost luminous in the dark. Over the years, they all had come to love the soft-spoken young man and now, hardly a word was spoken about it. Ashe, always thoughtful of others, sometimes wore sunglasses to soften the effect. He was big for his age. Very tall and broad shouldered. Not only had Ashe excelled in academics but had done very well representing the orphanage in a wide range of sporting events. Ashe had already been offered a scholarship to Oxford. A slight frown crossed Father Emerson's face. He somehow doubted that the young man would ever make it to that hallowed institution. That was not to be. Not for Ashe. An errant tear began to drop from the Father's eye. He quickly wiped it before Ashe could see. Beyond everything that set him apart from the others, was Ashe's compassion. Especially for an old man of the cloth who had been like a father all these years. One who loved him like a son he never had.

One month after Ashe's birthday, the phone rang in Father Emerson's chambers. He spoke quietly for a few moments, then slowly placed the phone back on the cradle. He went to find Ashe. A visitor was coming. It was time.

Ashe waited in the study nervously. He had never had anyone come just to see him. Father Emerson had said that this was a very important man who was flying all the way in from Geneva just to see Ashe. Random thoughts fired through his brain. "Could I be in some kind of trouble?" "Or perhaps, he knows something about my family." Even though a thorough search had been made for any of Ashe's relatives, following his miracle birth, none had been found.

Father Emerson and the other spoke at length in his private office. At times, the voices became agitated. Then soft again. The servants strained to hear but to no avail. Finally, silence descended and the two men exited the office walking into the study to meet with the subject of their conversation.

Ashe looked up as they entered the study. He didn't like the look in Father Emerson's eyes. The other was unreadable. He was tall. Not quite as tall as Ashe, but close. He could have been anywhere from forty to sixty. It was impossible to tell. The man looked to be in perfect health with a full head of brown hair, graying at the temples. He moved with the grace of an athlete but dressed in the attire of a successful businessman. Ashe noticed he wore all black. Except for the lack of a clerical collar, he would have passed for a visiting bishop. His gray eyes looked as severe as that of a trained killer. Ashe stiffened. Something was dangerous about this man. Then he smiled and softly said, "Hello son. My name is Micah." Ashe went to him. He felt drawn to him. Drawn by the aura of home and of safety. Of sanctuary.

Micah spoke of a Great War and of heritage and duty. Of sacrifice and rebirth. Ashe listened, enthralled. Every core of his being knew this was the beginning of his destiny. As his heart raced and his breathing became short, his eyes blazed with the thrill of what he heard. Even Micah became silent for a moment at the intensity of Ashe's stare. Micah touched Ashe's shoulder and said softly, "Son, hear what I say now. This is your choice. No one else can make it for you. I cannot say any of this will be easy. On the contrary, you will see much sadness and be a testament to many horrors of man and the Enemy. Your life will be subject to forfeit. There is only one promise I can make to you. You will never be forgotten. Your deeds will be echoed through the coming ages. Ashe Duncan will be remembered."

The next day, after saying his tearful good-byes to Father Emerson and his many brothers and sisters, Ashe and Micah left.

To seek knowledge. To know duty and honor. To seek sanctuary.

It had begun.

Interlude

In the Darkest of Ages

As the cold wind howled like the wolves of the forest, the knight pushed on. His armor torn and bloody like that of the body within. How long? Forever, it seemed. The battle. Such horror and blasphemy. The Enemy had laid in wait. His entire force had been ambushed. A bloody smile crossed his lips. They had fought with valor to the last man. On the smoke filled plain, metal clashed with the unholy flesh. The earth itself fought with rumblings. The heavens cried and raged as lightning lit the savage battle. When the sun broke, he and the wounded Beast were all that were left. Fifty of the best knights had entered that field. Now, it was only their King and this thing from the abyss. Face to face. They fought with talon, sword and will. In the end, his blessed sword found the creatures black heart and its lifeblood soiled the earth of that far off battlefield. Nothing would grow on that spot for a thousand years to come. But, for now the relic was safe. He staggered on.

Whenever he thought he could not go another step, he would open the bundle he carried and gaze into the prize. That which he had given his life and soul for. His entire obsession that kingdoms had been built for and legends given birth to. He sat against an old twisted tree in the dark and cold, dreaming of his wife and missing her so very much.

He thought of his friends and comrades along with their dream of a better world. There would be that. Sometime, somewhere. Their quest had been just. It had been the right choice.

As the life ebbed from the knight, he knocked at the gate of the small fortress. So softly, he feared he could not be heard but they were expected. As the priest dressed as a warrior looked into his dying eyes, he heard himself speak, "I have come so far. I have given my all. My kingdom. My wife. My life. All for the Holy Grail." At this, he managed a last smile. "Or at least that's what the Enemy thought, until it was too late." With his last breath, he gave the small bundle to the priest. With the utmost gentleness, the priest looked into the warm blanket and smiled into the liquid blue eyes of the child. His tears flowed unashamedly. Brushing the locks back from the bloody forehead of the brave knight, he whispered, "Well done my Arthur. You have reached sanctuary." And as his tears washed away the blood of the fallen protector, he swore, "You will be remembered."

And the Dragon roared.

Near Geneva, Switzerland
3 years later

Ashe ducked the sword. The flash of silver so close, he could see his reflection in the blade. Sweat poured from his face. As he rolled, the clang of metal on rock produced sparks. Ashe reversed and his dagger drove upward. And stopped just a hair breath from the chest of the man above him. Micah smiled as he laid his sword down. "Well done, but you almost lost it a few minutes ago. I should have had you on the rocks there." Ashe grinned and said, "True enough, but I guess you're getting a little old." Micah laughed softly and swatted Ashe on the butt with the broad blade of the sword and sent him off to the showers. After Ashe left, Micah's look became more serious. The young man was improving everyday. He was in excellent physical shape. He had become proficient with dagger, as well as the trusty 9mm Browning Hi-power that was Micah's personal favorite. Ashe was the top of his class when it came to a sword. Of all the modern weapons at the Order's disposal, Ashe favored the sword of the ancients. Micah thought, "He should have been a knight of old." He worried of Ashe's heart though. Only time would tell.

As the hot water cascaded his body, Ashe stretched. The great scars on his back seemed to glow in the darkness. The two crescent shaped wounds marred his otherwise perfect body. However, even they had an eerie symmetry about them that seem to make Ashe complete. As his body relaxed from the workout, his mind wondered back. To the beginning of what is now.

A short time ago it seemed. When Ashe had first arrived with Micah, after flying in to the airport and being met by a car and driver. The short drive to the countryside was beautiful. Ashe was so excited, he had hardly noticed the scenery. The small fortress dating back hundreds of years, sat nestled in the foothills of a mountain range. The original building had been expanded several times to become the size of a castle. When you added the seven levels concealed underground, the complex was enormous. Driving through the gate, after passing security, Ashe noticed the small, engraved symbol on each side of the gate. Other than that, nothing denoted that this was the home of the Order of Dominion. Ashe's new home.

Ashe settled in easily with the other young men and women living at the complex. They were in training. Most had been selected for support functions in intelligence and security. A few, very few were to be new initiates into the Order. Micah never stated exactly what Ashe's purpose would be, but started him into a rigorous training program. Physical training, weapons, intelligence gathering and history. History of man. Most importantly, the history of the Order. "Not only is it your heritage," said Micah, "it is your very survival."

After the shower and joining the others for dinner, Ashe went to Meditation. There were several chapels on the complex. His favorite one was the small Chapel of the Martyrs outside the Hall of Valor. As he sat there in the silence of the ages, he felt at peace. Out of the darkness, a soft voice spoke, "What was will be again. So it is promised. The choice received as it is offered." Ashe smiled. He loved the softness and the cadence of the voice. "And how are you this day, Gabriel?"

Gabriel sat in the darkness in his special place. At his age, it was getting harder to move around and direct sunlight hurt his sensitive eyes. As Ashe came closer, Gabriel smiled and his vibrant eyes seemed to glow a little brighter. Of all the souls in this place, Ashe held a special place in Gabriel's heart. They spoke of how training was going and what new recruits had arrived at the complex. Gabriel listened closely to the excitement in Ashe's voice when he mentioned a girl by the name of Mara who arrived just today. Ashe had only met one of the new male recruits. A young American by the name of Levi. Ashe jokingly told them "welcome to hell" and got a pretty good start from the new folks. Gabriel softly laughed. "Ashe, I hope your sense of humor will never leave you, my son." Gabriel got up with a soft rustle and turned to leave, "I must go now. I tire easily. May the Father commune with you, young Ashe." As Ashe watched the figure leave, he turned his face to the stars, visible through the skylight in the dome of the small chapel. As a meteor flew across the face of heavens, he thought of his mother. And father. Wherever he is.

As Ashe turned the corner out of the chapel, he stopped. Uncertain whether to go get some much needed sleep or go to his favorite place. Gratification won out. He turned towards the Hall of Valor. As he stepped into the enormous chamber, his breath stopped short as it always did from the impact of the place. In all of this structure with all of its history, nowhere was more sacred. Ashe thought, "So many souls. So many battles." The story of the Order was held in these hallowed walls. Ashe entered the portal leading to the long hall, glancing up at the words engraved there in Latin. "Protect" "Remember". The two words bound together by a symbol.

Dominion.

Ashe walked quietly down the carpeted hall, surrounded by hundreds of small alcoves bathed in soft glow. In each alcove sat a small pedestal holding a book. Behind most of the books, a statue was present. None of the statutes were alike. They were of different ages, genders and appearance. The likeness was that of the protector from varying moments in their service to the Order. The books were their stories, carefully chronicled by the Oracles. Stories of heroism and of service. For all too many, it was the story of the ultimate sacrifice for their fellows.

Ashe stopped to look at the varying books. Names from ancient to modern times reflected back at his gaze. As he continued, the names floated before his eyes. *Urial. Samuel. Joan. Gordon*...and on. Every name, a testament. Every book, a chronicle of faith and sacrifice. Ashe always stood in awe of these writings. He had spent much of his three years here reading the various books. Some were inches think. Others, unfortunately, were only a few pages long. All of these had statues behind them. It had been explained to him, that the books were started upon an individual's acceptance to the Order. Your statue was not placed until the time of your death. Ashe said a small prayer. There were so many statues. So much death. Was the prize worth the price?

Micah spoke informally with the Council of Seven. They discussed possible future missions based on intelligence coming in. They held a moment of silence in remembrance of the protector who had been lost just last week. What had appeared to be a routine mission had turned deadly quickly. Names of certain initiates were mentioned as a possible replacement. This would be discussed at a formal meeting. Talk turned to Ashe. Micah reported on his progress. The council was impressed. For his age and short time at the Order, he showed remarkable initiative and skills. One council member verbalized the one question they had all wondered, "What of his heart?" Micah sipped his brandy and looked across the room at his brethren. The family of his for over twenty years. He spoke. "I, as well as anybody should know the question we face concerning Ashe. Remember how I came to you? Broken. With the last of my spirit shattered. After what had happened, I felt nothing. I think that was worse than the way Ashe is. He knows great compassion. You worry that this will be a weakness when the time comes. I say to you, it is his greatest gift. After all I lost, I found sanctuary. After being hollow, I was filled. I regained my soul, including my compassion. We should not worry. At least Ashe has not lost his. We can only hope, he never does." The others looked at each other and slowly nodded in agreement. "When", one asked, "can we start the final tests?" Micah thought for a moment. "I will speak to Gabriel in the morning and seek his advice." The council nodded and left Micah alone with his thoughts. Micah looked to the heavens as if to seek an answer or solace. "Father forgive me. He is only a boy. An innocent thrust into this world." No answer was forthcoming. Micah sat alone and wept. Would Ashe forgive him? Could he ever forgive himself? The time was near.

Across the world as twilight descended, the man walked to the hill. Looking down upon the city, he touched the ground and brought forth fruit for his enjoyment. As he spread his arms above the windswept plain, thunder rolled and danced across the heavens. He said, "I am thirsty" and the spring broke forth in front of him with pure, clean water. He smiled down on his people and let his good will flow forth. He would soon bring his followers miracles and wonders that his Father had promised. The entire world, soon to be one and whole. As the rain poured, he cried, "Children, come unto me." The wind brought words to the man's ears. Words from his Father. The time of his ascension was nearing.

Liquid blue eyes watched. And waited.

Ashe dreamt. He walked down the long hall filled with books of the dead. The books bled until they formed a river, which flowed, to the source. The source was a woman whose face he could not see. She held the world in her hands. Her eyes pierced Ashe and he felt the pain in his heart and back. Burning like a white-hot flame. He was afraid as he doubled over in pain. Her hand softly touched his forehead and marked him as her own. She whispered in his ear, "My heart breaks for you Ashe. You are chosen. I cannot intercede." A single tear fell upon his face, awaking him.

The scream echoed through the buildings. Death had come.

Ashe awoke with his heart pounding. He could almost see her face. The scream echoed again. Ashe ran down the hall and to the right. Feet pounding from others were running towards the ungodly wailing. Black garbed security personnel with machine-guns and daggers sheathed in scabbards parted the crowd. As he closed upon the sounds, Ashe realized where they were coming from Gabriel's quarters. As he and the security team arrived at the door, there was only silence. Micah appeared from nowhere with his old Browning in his hand. He nodded to the security chief and they entered. Silence except for a dripping sound. Total darkness with a whisper of smoke. No, not smoke but mist. "Gabriel", Micah called, crouched just inside the door. The rest of the team entered in practiced movements. Movements, which would have been the envy of the world's special operations, teams. A voice from the back of the chamber softly replied, "I am…unhurt. Watch your step. It is….messy." The dim lights of Gabriel's room were illuminated. Blood was everywhere. The soft drip of it from the walls thundered in the silence. The attacker had been torn to pieces. What could be identified of him sent a chill through Ashe and the rest that were gathered. All of them recognized the clothing. It was the training uniform of the Order. It was one of them.

As Gabriel drank the clear liquid from the glass, Micah waited. Only Ashe remained in the room with them at Gabriel's request. Gabriel continued with his story, "As I was saying, I had just retired for the night. A sound caught my attention. As I arose, I saw a laser light appear on my chest. I heard the whisper of the bullet. It was slow. So I moved. Then I saw him and stepped into the light. I recognized him. I had seen him on the training field just a few days ago. A young man by the name of Rashid, I believe. He was new and had not been to one of my teachings yet. When he saw me, he screamed. I don't think he was properly briefed for his assassination assignment. I warned him to remain still and wait for the security team. Then he pulled a dagger from his belt and ran towards me. I tried to stop him but he entered the Holy Circle of the Old Ones. I saw his eyes die with the horror of what awaited beyond in them. The rest you know." "Damn", said Micah. "Our security system is the best in the world. With the background checks and everything else, they still managed to slip a ringer in." Gabriel patted Micah on the shoulder, saying that no one was perfect. He then announced he was going back to bed. Another room had been prepared for him until his could be cleaned. Bidding his goodnights, he departed the room.

Ashe sat in wonderment. He only understood a fraction of what had happened. He had been through the teachings and knew of the final tests. This was made clear to every new person almost from the beginning. It was your choice. To go on in folly would mean death. He had read of the powers of the blessed relics but had never seen the results of a violation of them. His stomach felt queasy. This was his first brush with the brutality of the Enemy. Micah spoke of the time nearing that would be a crucial time for the Order and the Enemy. Perhaps they were getting desperate. Micah told Ashe that he had had enough excitement for one night. "Go rest, you will need it tomorrow."

Ashe tossed and turned, thinking of what would have happened if the assassin had succeeded. He could not imagine this place without Gabriel. Ashe berated himself. Perhaps he had been "playing the game" but had not fully realized that this was real life and death. He swore to double his efforts. This attack would not be tolerated. Not at Sanctuary. He would ask Micah to be on the excursion team. He thought of his teachings from many of the books of worship. "Vengeance is mine", saith the Lord. Then Ashe thought of the look in his mentor's eyes. He wondered if Micah had ever read that passage.

Even Ashe was nervous as he watched the cold fury in Micah's eyes. The group stood silent as Micah's low voice issued the instructions. The battle plan was laid out with precision. "We have information concerning a major Enemy operation in the Western United States", said Micah. "It is now time to strike. This will be my team. For some of you, it will be a final exercise before graduation into the service of the Order. Pick up your gear from the quartermaster, eat well and get some rest. You will need it." The young ones slowly filed out of the operations room filled with their own thoughts. Ashe watched them as they passed. Jack Dalton, Shannon Gzar and Jifad Habkaazer. All seasoned students who had completed their training. Two others filed out last. Mara and the American, Levi. Ashe wondered about Micah's selection of these two. They were new. Surely he must have a reason for this. Ashe could only shrug. He caught Mara's dark, slightly almond shaped eyes. She smiled as she walked past. Ashe hesitated a moment to see if Micah had need of him, but the leader seemed to want to be left alone with his thoughts. Ashe headed to dinner. Then on to the Hall of Valor.

Micah leaned his head back and sipped the aged whisky. The twelve-year-old liquid burned as it meandered down his throat. He held his head back with his eyes half closed. The visions came. The clock. Ticking. No way to stop it. Time goes on. The fear and frantic search. The taste of victory and the poisoned bitterness of mistake. His mistake. The fury no man should ever know. He thought of the torture given at his hands. The blood and urine. Except they were the color of rotting pus. The screams not of this world. The finality of it. When the clock stopped and he had failed. Millions of souls rested on his conscience. His only thoughts were of the two whom were a part of his. The visions faded in the mist of the last of the whisky as he thought of dark eyes and soft ebony hair. Micah's eyes slowly opened. If ever a picture of hell could have been mirrored, it would have been in that grayness. His right hand carefully placed the glass on the table. His left dripped with blood from the gouges of his fingernails. The blood of Micah falls as if summoned by the Earth itself. A down payment for the blood which rested on his head. A payment, which would never be enough, Micah thought as he walked deeper into the bowels of the fortress. Deeper into sanctuary.

The man climbed into the abandoned building and went to the third story window. He had an excellent view of the quiet residential street in the suburbs of New York. He pulled the rifle out of his Wilson gym bag. After screwing the barrel in and setting the scope, he waited. His target jogged by every morning at seven am. Two minutes from now. As he sighted the scope down the street, he thought of his family. They would not understand this. If he were successful, perhaps they would never know. If not…well they would think of him as a monster. He quietly breathed the words as he peered down the barrel of the high-powered sniper rifle. Then he saw the runner. As he came into sight, he stopped to rest a moment. The man sighted the crosshairs directly on the forehead of the man. His finger slowly squeezed the trigger. A loud rumble began which built to a screaming pitch in the fraction of a second and made the shooter look up. Just as the building caved in on him. After the dust settled, the man lay in the rubble, broken like a discarded doll. He took a ragged breath and looked. Looked as the rats, hundreds of them coming towards him. Red eyes and sharp teeth. They looked hungry. His chest being crushed, the man didn't know if he could even scream.

Elric Legion stretched from his short rest and smiled at his bodyguards. Then he began his morning run again. As he passed the old building, one could see just a smattering of dust floating out of the windows. If one had very good hearing, you could almost hear the screaming.

After showering and changing into his suit, Elric Legion, Ambassador of the United States to the United Nations entered his limousine for the ride to work. He looked thorough the tinted windows at the blue sky and smiled. What a glorious day!

Back at the building, the screaming had stopped. The rats were hungry no more.

Ashe stared down the softly lit hallway, troubled. "What of this bloodshed", he thought. "It goes on and on." Was this a sacred duty? Or just plain vengeance. He stopped in front of a majestic statue with a thick book in front of it. Perhaps the answers lay in the past. Where it had begun, millennia ago. He slowly opened the book with the name revealed in candlelight. The book of the First. *Urial.*

Interlude

In the Beginning...

The man and woman wept. What had they done to deserve being thrust into the cold world? Had they only sought knowledge, which was their birthright? The beautiful one that had whispered to them no longer spoke. His truths had been penetrated and they held hate in their hearts for the first time. Hate, for the one who had stolen what had been given to them. They would call him Liar. As the night fell, so came fear.

Strange beasts wandered the land and the man and woman no longer held communion with them. The First One did not speak directly to them anymore. His messengers spoke of a Great War. The Archangel Michael said to them, "You, my loved ones are the center. In the way of things, you can know greatness if only you do not destroy yourselves. The choice made by you will bestow their heritage on your sons and daughters. Many of my brethren believe in you, some do not. They were the only beloved, now there is you. My home has been torn apart with rebellion just as yours was. I cannot remain but do not tremble as night approaches. Journey to the west. You will know great sorrow but you will persevere. You have been given dominion over this world now. How you use this gift will determine the legacy that you leave to your children. Take heart. We have beseeched the Father on your behalf and in his love, you will find sanctuary and a covenant. We will never leave you. You, who are the dust made flesh in the image of the One we love so much, we will love also. I will send an emissary to protect you and your offspring. This is our promise. So watch and wait while you remain true to your spirit and the love of the Father."

With that, Michael made his mark on the man. The symbol of the Protector's clan. The symbol of the Archangels.

Throughout the wondrous years of miracles and the time of man and angels together, the man's family held the truth. On the cold night of a new season, a star shines brightly in the ebony sky. More brightly than any of the others. Unto the family of man was born a child. A child with liquid blue eyes and snow-white wings. Human...and yet not. Upon his forehead was a symbol. That of the Protector. His name would be Urial. The First.

The man had lived many years after that fateful choice. A man not born of woman, who had known much happiness and sorrow in his long lifetime. He, who had first felt fear and loneliness and with his wife, journeyed far from their paradise to seek Sanctuary. He felt that the birth of the child marked both a beginning and an end. His time had passed. He closed his eyes. Forever.

The Book of Urial

The wind raged as the storm grew. Rain poured down upon the people. They cowered in their pitiful shelters. Those who had scoffed laughed no more. The rains came. They didn't stop for a long time. A lifetime for most.

Aboard the great ship was gathered every beast according to the plan of the Father. The tiny remnant of the great experiment called man was all that was left. The Liar had sowed his seeds of discord and man had angered the one who gave him life. A great purging of this world had begun. Death was gluttony for the Enemy. Once and for all, this lowly form which thought itself so noble would be wiped from the face of creation. The few who floated in the flimsy wood vessel were of no concern. The Enemy had secreted his agent aboard. They would not live to see land.

The family gathered and spoke in fear and wonderment. The noise of the other living souls on board chittered, growled and murmured. The Old Man spoke to his family of the promise he had been given. The promise of a new beginning given to him from the Father. All of his life, he had been true, even in the face of laughter and persecution. He had honored his Creator as well as his ancestors. Now, within the safety of this vessel, the hope of humanity huddled. And waited.

In the lower level, the creatures stirred. In future generations, many would be known. Some would change over the years. A few would not exist in the new world of man. The suppleness of the great cats. The timidity of the lowly mice. From majestic to minute, they too waited, for the fulfillment of the promise.

The sleek animal lay against its mate, breathing softly as it slept in peace. The equine body, gray with an almost silver tint was beautiful to behold and was one of the Old Man's favorites among his keep. The gentleness of creature was evident in its soft brown eyes, which gleamed with an uncanny intelligence. Crowning its regal head, was a single ivory horn. A movement in the darkness. Eyes gleaming in the stillness, the beast moved closer to the sleeping pair.

The Old Man, along with two of his daughters, made his way around the vessel taking care of his charges. As he approached the lower level, a shiver ran down his spine. He slowed as he peered into the blackness. It was as if the world had swallowed itself. As his lamp lit the way, he knew fear. That which had been foretold had begun.

The female lay in the blood of her life mate. Tears dripped from the moist brown eyes. The magical property of a unicorn's tears would be extolled in future years. For all the magic that could have been, now lay in a lifeless heap which had been torn to shreds in a fit of childish rage. As the Old Man's tears mixed with the blood and tears of his blessed favorites, the Beast rose.

In a grating voice it said, "Foolish man. You have believed that you are worthy of living in this world and of believing in hasty promises. Today, you will know the price of your arrogance. You will know the true insignificance of your puny existence."

As the Beast towered over the man and his daughters, the Dragon roared. Its obscene body undulated towards the humans, with a hideous mouth opened to reveal the gates of the realm of the hopeless. Dimensions where no hope or love existed. The Dragon spoke of vengeance. Once, it had been loved along with the others. With the advent of man, its claim to the Kingdom had been usurped. His kind had been branded outcasts. For this man would pay the ultimate price. "Old Man!" it screamed, "I will have your daughters in every way you cannot even dream of. They will scream for the pleasure of my attention. They will bow down on their knees before me and beg for my favor. All of this you can watch until I decide to pluck your eyes as you grovel waiting for your Hated One to intercede. As I swallow your beating heart and succor the sweetness of your blood, your final thought will be of defeat. No power born of this Earth can stop me." The Beast moved forward. The Old Man bowed his head as his daughters wept. And spoke one quiet word...*Urial.*

The first Oracle wrote of the battle that day. The silence descended upon the Dragon as Urial floated from above. The warrior wings spread the breadth of two men. The liquid blue eyes glowed with the fury of lightning in the darkness. In his right hand, he held the blessed sword of Michael. The sword which would be known by many names down through the ages. A sword forged in the soul of creation, honed by the very life force of the Creator. Urial spoke to the Beast. "It is now that it begins Son of the Liar. The choice you make this moment will determine how much blood will flow thorough the ages. Know now, that man is under our guardianship and forever will be. If you choose to walk this path, you will fail. The Father of Lies and his kind will know subjugation. My Order will defeat you at every turn. Choose wisely." The Dragon stood silent as if in communion with its Father. A moment of eternity within the walls of a speck afloat upon a sea of heaven's tears. The heartbeat of the world slows, slows...stops. The Dragon charged with a great roar. Talon and sword met. Blood flowed like rivers rushing to the ocean. No human had seen a battle of such. The conflict raged for hours. Two creatures, neither totally of this world staggered from each other's merciless onslaught. Talon. Sword. Blood. The first would not be the last. In the end, both lay in death.

The Old Man wept as the skies cleared. He wept for happiness and for sorrow. His sons and daughters would live as promised. Live, to start this world anew. With the whole of creation in his hand, humanity would start again. He cried as a father for Urial. The special one who the Father had entrusted in his care and he in his. The Protector that the Father had promised when the days were dark. And protected he had. But the death of Urial broke his heart. Never had he known a more pure soul. Yes, Urial had human blood in him. But he was so very much more. Perhaps he was what man had been meant to be. As Urial lay wrapped in linen soaked with herbs, the Old Man communed with the Father. "What will become of us now. I trust in your vision, but I am so afraid. I'm sorry if I did not do enough, Father. I gave my life. I gave the strength of my word and I've kept it. I've given everything." He cried to the heavens, "I bind my kind to you forever…Please be merciful."

The Covenant of Urial

On the third day, the ship touched the pinnacle of the mount. The sunlight beamed down upon the gathering of life. All the souls off boarded save one. The Old Man sat quietly in the bowels of the ship next to the still figure wrapped in linen. Through a small window, a shaft of sunlight lit the small room with a soft yellow light. Yellow light, which turned into a soft blue, little by little. The voice spoke to the man. "My son, do not despair. You have remained true to my spirit. I have delivered you to a new beginning. With this beginning, I make a new covenant with you. You will give life to this land. You will speak of me and my love for your kind and hold true and stand against the Rebellious One. In this new land, I will place my mark for your sanctuary. This will be a holy place like no other. The chosen will serve as protectors for the son of man. They will be the best from my love that I can send to you. The life of my life for you, my children. Urial was the first one. There will be many others. Protectors, all. Remember them and never let their story fade." The Old Man nodded with understanding. As he slowly rose to join the others, the soft voice said, "With this gift, I seal my covenant with you."

The Old Man turned as Urial arose. With the Old Man's warm embrace and soft tears upon his mighty chest, Urial smiled. "Come Noah, let us go to the place. There we will build. Home. Sanctuary."

Nestled in the ancient foothills sat the small fortress. The legend of Urial would be recorded for over a thousand years. Warrior. Teacher. Keeper of the sacred relics. Urial saw many battles. He celebrated with man, their victory. He cried with them, their defeats. Above all, he loved them. Through all, he loved them so much. He heralded the coming of the One. To three Protectors, he told of a child who would be born of a virgin. A child who would bear the weight of the world on his very human shoulders. A great man. Perhaps the greatest. If he lived to be a man. Already the Enemy moved towards the city, slouching as that of a beast. The three cunning, some would say wise, men hurried with Urial leading the way. Towards that small town. To the child. To make sure the child grew into manhood. To fulfill his destiny. They would protect the child and provide him sanctuary. He would cleanse the Earth with his blood.

The shots rang out. A close group of holes penetrated the paper target. Five hollow point nine millimeter rounds, directly thorough the heart. Micah holstered the weapon and removed his shooting glasses. His eyes narrowed as he thought, "I will have blood. Fear me, you bastards. I'm coming."

Mara rested in her room. Her long legs propped up on the edge of her bunk; she read the history of the Order. Her mind wandered to the upcoming mission. She was surprised that Micah had insisted that she come along. Nevertheless, that suited her just fine. The sooner, the better. She had been pretty much of a loner since arriving at the fortress. Her selection had been rigorous, but not as bad as what she had been prepared for. Since her arrival, everyone had been friendly; however, by nature she was not a very social animal. For much of her life she had been alone. Ashe did interest her though. There was something about him; she couldn't quite put her finger on. Some quality she couldn't quite place. It was as if a part of him did not belong. She knew that feeling well. He would be interesting company. Her full lips softly smiled. Very interesting company.

Levi sat in the dark of his apartment with the soft red glow of candle lighting his face. It was the color of blood in the subdued light. A grating sound accompanied his rhythmic breathing. As he did his mantra, he sharpened the dagger. Over and over. Until the edge shown with the color of the candlelight. Blood red. "Soon", he thought. All the preparation he had undergone. The time approached. Vengeance would be his. There would be no sanctuary for what had been done.

Jack Dalton checked his battle harness with the two Detonic mini forty-fives pistols. The Remington short barreled shotgun sat ready. "Let's kick some demon ass", he muttered to himself. He smiled. Dalton was almost a legend at the school for the Order. He was what the instructors called a "cowboy". Not seeming to fear anything, he threw himself into the training like he had been born for it. He had been on two other "live" missions and proved himself in battle. Jack seemed to thrive on the conflict and he inspired instant confidence in his classmates. As the old saying went, they would follow him into the gates of hell. "Well", Jack thought, "It might just come to that."

The sun dropped down behind the mountains. Snow was coming. It had already reached the upper peaks. Not just a snow. A blizzard of record fury. The wind raged and you could almost hear the scream of the Dragon.

A half a world away, Elric Legion sat in the small room adjacent to the rotunda listening to the finishing remarks. He rolled a shiny silver quarter between his long slim fingers. The secretary refilled his coffee. He smiled and admired her long slender legs that went well with her honey blonde hair and deep green eyes. So young and beautiful. "Ah, if only I were a little younger", he thought. As the loudspeaker outside swelled with the orator's voice, *"Now, I introduce to you, my fellow citizens of the world, the new Secretary-General of the United Nations...Elric Legion!"* He squeezed the coin into the secretary's soft hand and entered the great chamber to the thundering applause.

As the secretary slowly opened her hand, she marveled at the piece of gold, which lay there. She would have to tell all of her friends about it at lunch tomorrow. A planned lunch of old friends who got together once a month come hell or high water. A lunch she would not make it to. Not tomorrow. Not ever. Her friends would gather at the funeral to say goodbye after being horrified at the news that her raped and tortured body had been found in an alley the next morning. Robbery had been ruled out as a motive. She still had the small gold piece clenched in her once soft hand.

As Micah made his final preparations, the phone in his quarters softly buzzed. The voice on the other end told of changed plans by order of the Council of Seven. Micah turned crimson and his voice raised in protest. Until the soft words on the other end silenced him with three small words: *"She has returned."*

The Book of Salia

The dust of the village blew as the south winds howled. The woman moved rapidly through the throng of people. She wrapped her covering closer around her face to keep the grit out. She worried that she would be too late. The silence of the Beast was here at last.

The little girl wandered alone. Blood matted her dark blonde hair. Unusual hair for this region of the world. As unusual as her light colored eyes. As she disappeared into the blowing dust, darkness descended.

In the night were eyes the color of deep crimson. As the girl ran, the eyes came closer. Beneath them, a smile parted the unholy lips. Soon, it would have the tender flesh of its prey to use as it pleased. The screams of the innocent would honor his Father.

In the absolute silence of the alley, no voices penetrated the inky blackness. The girl stopped, her breath coming in quick gasps. As the creature stepped from the shadows, its razor sharp talons were unsheathed. The essence of nightmare shuffled towards the child. A child who's parents it had slaughtered a short while ago. A child, who now bowed to her knees in the dust. A child bathed in a soft blue light.

As the talons raised and began their final descent, the dagger entered its lower right back. Screaming with pain and rage, the creature whirled facing its attacker. The woman plunged the dagger into the demon again and again. A war cry from her lips, the slender woman with the darkest of eyes moved forward into the embrace of the forsaken. Blood flowed and howls filled the night air. In the end, the dust of the tiny village slaked its thirst on the blood of the slain.

Years later, a beautiful young woman, with eyes the color of the sea, would seal the vows of her marriage to her young husband named Joseph. In the eyes of their God and in the presence of their friends and families, their road to destiny would begin. And close by her side through it all was her closest friend. The one who had stayed at her side since that night. The one whom history but not her comrades would forget. A warrior and a priestess. A woman of quiet dignity and ebony eyes. A protector who would stay by Mary's side until the birth of her child. *Salia.* A name that would be lost in the history of the world but hallowed in a far off place of Sanctuary. The name of a woman whose lifeblood would stain the dust of another small village soon after the birth of the child. A simple woman, who once heard a small voice, whisper "Protect the Child".

As the young man sat at his Last Supper with his friends and followers, his soft brown eyes looked at the empty plate, which sat at the table. A plate that had been placed at each meal of his family for years. For honor and in remembrance. "*You will be remembered*", *he thought,* "*This I promise.*"

She had wandered the world, sharing the lives of the rich as well as the poor. She had shared her knowledge and learned the wisdom of others. She had shared their laughter and cried their tears. In the midst of it all, she and her mother had quietly waited for the time. On a lonely hillside, in remembrance of the one who had gone before, she said goodbye to her mother.

Alone, she had faced the Liar in the wilderness. All was offered to her. Riches and power beyond her dreams along with the supplication of the people before her. To rule as a princess forever in this kingdom on Earth.

She was told that if she cared at all, she would spare these insignificant beings the horror of what would come if war were declared. She saw the world in flames and the atrocities that would rain upon the children of man. She saw blood flow as the world died like a child before a ravenous beast. All of this could end before it started, if she would only kneel before him.

With tears in her eyes, she stood at the gate where she had returned. Tears of weariness and sorrow for what must come to the children. The agony and fear that they could not escape. The time of blood approaches. She wiped her tears and stood tall. There would be hope. Hope vested in the few who would fight for the whole. In the midst of hopelessness would shine the light of man's salvation. Her legacy to this world would be that hope. As her small hands rested on the ancient symbols of the archangels etched in the stone of the fortress, Christina bowed her head and thought of a single name, *"Jarred"*.

The doors opened, welcoming her to Sanctuary.

The Forgotten One sat in his place and screamed in rage. Rage at himself for not understanding. Not understanding how these puny beings could exist. Other beings, he might be able to comprehend but not these lowly self-serving bastard children. Why had his brothers and sisters decided to protect these insects that called themselves man. The One screamed. The cry of a billion lost souls. A cry that would make beasts die in the very spot they stood and blight the earth of all growing life. A cry from which no sanctuary was found. A cry of loneliness in the midst of eternity.

Elric Legion sat in his new office. After a day of greeting dignitaries from the various nations, he relaxed with a cold drink. His suggestions for co-operative financial support and medical care had been well received. Soon, national boundaries would become blurred. The people would be as one. His people and his world. Legion smiled as he communed with his Father.

Set well back in the deep northern woods of New York State, the cabin was warm against the encroaching cold. The assassins sat in a close circle as they made their plans. The first had failed due to the lack of planning and teamwork. This time, they could not fail. If the unthinkable happened, then the fate of their mission rested with the other one. Hopefully, that would only be a last resort because there was too much personal involvement. As the assassins finalized their plans, one nervously removed the white collar from his throat. It didn't seem to belong in this world of deception and killing.

The Council of Seven listened as Christina spoke. "The time nears. His rise in power will be swift. His army multiplies every day. His closest advisors have sought refuge in a compound in Wyoming in the Western United States. They await his ascension. There is a growing movement to consolidate the day to day operations of the civilized world under the command of his organization. Even the Americans are voicing their willingness to join. There is a very vocal opponent in the American capital. I have no way of knowing the fate of his movement but I fear he will be killed or worse."

As the dawn broke over the park near the Capitol, the man jogged surrounded by his entourage. President Samuel Jackson followed his morning routine. He wasn't a great runner but he tried to stay in shape when he was home. It was hard for him to focus this morning. He was worried about his best friend. Ever since Peter had returned from the Epsilonian mission, he had not been the same. Peter had told him the story of the man that he had met. Sam wanted to believe, at least in Peter. He feared for his sanity. Now it seemed, everything Peter said was gloom and doom. The end of the world as we knew it. The current of dark conspiracies everywhere hid danger.

Sam was under pressure from everyone from Congress to the United Nations to have Peter step down from his position. Sam shook his head as he rounded the last turn of the block. He could not, no would not abandon his friend. He loved Peter like a brother. The naysayers would have to…The copper-jacketed bullet entered just behind Samuel Jackson's ear, blowing his brain matter right and forward onto the closest Secret Service man. As the screams began nearby, echoing in the morning rush, crimson tinted eyes smiled coldly as the blood of a good man was soaked into the fresh earth.

Book Three Sanctum, Sanctorum

The team moved quietly into the Swiss countryside. Explosives were placed. Weapons were readied. No longer would the war be fought in the shadows. It was time.

There would be no sanctuary for the hated ones. Even they could not hide from the power of the atom.

The young housewife wandered the park in the small town in northwest Maryland. She had just come from the mall where, unknown to her, she had been exposed to a microscopic amount of a chemical agent which had been in development before she was born.

Primarily based on what was known as the bubonic plague, this nasty little bug had been altered beyond anyone's worst nightmare. The final product had been thought destroyed in the Gulf War years ago. This was not so, evil does not die so easily.

As the pretty brunette strolled, she stopped and spoke with people she knew, old and young alike. Each brief moment of pleasantness spread the contagion of horrible and painful death. Each tiny breath that emanated from her full lips sealed the death warrant for the souls around her.

Legion smiled as the delegations voted for the Universal Financial and Health Onimbus Plan. It was welcomed as a breakthrough for humanity. A beginning of world citizenship was at hand. The Implementation Committee displayed the new identification disc to an excited and approving audience. Would miracles never cease?

In a small cubicle inside of the metal and glass building of Advance Technology Incorporated, situated near Richmond, blood soaked the desk of a man. A man who the world had known as Frederick Johnson. An honor student, who graduated with advanced degrees from Harvard and MIT. A good man by most standards who believed in treating his fellows fairly and quietly excelled in his field of microelectronics. A man who had developed a prototype for the benefit of mankind. A man who loved his mother even when she began her tirade against technology as the end of the world and quoted her beloved Bible as the source of her knowledge. A man who had smiled gently as he patted her softly on the cheek as she had shown him the signs of the end. A man, who had sat in awe and then horror as he looked at his prototype, now mass-produced in the millions for the future. A prototype magnified in detail under the bright halogen light. The same man who had marveled at the intricate detail of micro electronic circuitry which could hold the entire life of a human being inside it. A man who realized that not only the life but the soul of a man. His mind burned as he read the tiny model number imprinted in the disc. A man who stared for hours at the numbers until his right hand closed around the trigger of the pistol which ended his agony. Frederick Johnson lay in a pool of blood at his desk beside the object of his life's work. A small disc which could store the intimate information of billions. The bright magnification coil still shone lighting up the disc and the numbers it bore. ATI-Model #666.

The storms gathered as if the Earth itself seemed to know war was at hand. As voices raised calling for calmness, they were beat down. Violence spread like the unknown virus dubbed the Maryland Curse. Madness spread to the streets as the economies faltered. Inflation ran rampant and the people crouched in fear. The light of hope faded. In a world on the brink of insanity, their eyes turned toward the voice of reason and comfort. The voice of Legion.

In the quiet hall sat a troubled Ashe Duncan. He had spent the last few hours in the company of the beautiful Mara. He felt his heart churn. He was drawn to her, as he knew she was to him. He felt guilty for having those feelings for her in the midst of Micah's sadness and rage. Something important approached and he felt that they had come to a turning point. When he tried to question his teacher and friend, the only reply he got was that the clock is ticking. With those simple words, the eyes of Micah burned with a knowledge that Ashe had never witnessed before. A knowledge that bespoke a vision of hell.

Ashe walked down the softly lit aisle until he reached the book. A book, which out of respect, he had never read while at Sanctuary. He gently touched the cover of the manuscript. Was it proper for him to look? In the end, to save his friend, he knew he must.

The Book of Micah

In the bright desert sun, Colonel Micah Sarentstein stood, surveying the carnage wrought by his troops. The terrorists lay dead, thirty in all. How much blood had they shed? Never again would the bastards kill innocents. Micah's men had seen to that. He slowly walked back to the waiting chopper. As the machine rose in the air, sunlight glinted off the points of the Star of David.

Colonel Micah Sarentstein was the most decorated leader of the elite Israeli Counter-Terrorist Group in the history of the shadowy Mossad. He had devoted his adult life to the protection of his adopted country. Born in the city of San Francisco, he was happy to hear of the assignment that would take him back to his native home. His wife Sarah and his little girl Jerrie were happy for the chance to spend time in America. The chance of a lifetime, they had chorused.

Micah coordinated all anti-terrorism information in the United States for his country and was the main liaison to his host country's intelligence agencies. On a cool October day, the beginning of the death of his soul started with a single piece of paper. Information had been received that a group known as The Crimson Jihad, led by an unknown fanatic, had placed bombs in three American cities. No demands had been forthcoming. Micah mobilized his personal team of specialists and along with the American federal agencies began the hunt for the devices and the persons responsible. According to their information, the clock was ticking. Twenty-four hours before death.

Micah kissed Sarah softly on the forehead. Her devotion constantly marveled him. He knew the fear she must feel every time he walked out the door. But she never said a word; she just performed her own little ritual upon his departure. After Jerrie gave him hugs and kisses, Sarah would hold his face in her hands close to her. She would gently kiss both his eyes, lips and finish by his right ear where she whispered, "Come back home". He told them he loved them and left for his mission. The last one of many.

The first bomb was found in Southern California. Three SWAT members died in the raid. Micah was there as an "observer". The terrorist cell was killed to the last man and woman. Horror engulfed the team as they identified the primary bomb component as nuclear. Information gathered at the scene pointed to Atlanta, Georgia and a leader known only as Kasesh. He called himself the Destroyer.

The warehouse was located in a rundown industrial district near Folks Avenue. A three-mile area had been quietly evacuated while the entry team stood ready. Micah and his counterpart Jim Raines from the CIA were dressed in battle gear. This time, they would personally lead the attack. As the flash/bang grenades exploded the team entered under cover of gas. In the dark and smoke filled rooms, laser lights pointed to targets that died with the whisper of silenced weapons. Blood soaked the concrete floor as the team moved through the building. The bomb was located and disarmed. The man known as Kasesh lay wounded with terrible leg wounds. Micah approached the evil and pointed the Browning High Power at his head. The head of Kasesh hung as if defeated with greased filthy hair hanging in his face. Kasesh slowly raised his eyes into that of his judge. As their eyes met, Micah felt true fear. Before him, in a defiant face of pure evil, Kasesh's eyes glowed in the darkness. The color of bright embers.

Kasesh sat chained in the room. The only answers he had about the third device were an outpouring of laughter and obscene utterances. Micah sat and watched as the interrogation continued with no success. The clock ticked. Kasesh spoke, "You pitiful excuses for beings. You will never win. I have been sent by my Father to blight your attempts at greatness. You will only be known now for your futile efforts. You can't even protect your own people. Especially you", pointing at Micah, "I can smell your blood. You are one of Them." At the puzzled look in Micah's eyes, Kasesh cackled. "You don't even know it yet, do you? You do not even know your own destiny. Have you not figured it out yet? I wear the skin of a human as if it were clothing. I am beyond death. I am Death!" Micah's heart beat sounded like the slow grinding of a clock on its final countdown. He rose slowly. He believed this creature. Beyond its human appearance lay the dark thing that Micah recognized from the bloody battles of the past. A thing that perhaps you could glimpse just on the edge of your vision, if you turned quickly. Micah stared into the crimson eyes as he walked forward. He unsheathed his dagger. Micah would introduce Death to his kin. Pain. The screams began. That of the inhuman thing before them and that of the men who would have nightmares forever.

Before the thing died, Micah had the names of two cities, Washington DC and Las Vegas. He tried to make his mind work. The horror of what he had seen and done would have driven a normal man to insanity. Perhaps, it had him. The men with him could only scream and cry. Tears from men who had seen terrible things in their long careers. Tears from men who now believed that evil was no longer an abstract term. They had seen true evil and it would scar their souls until they passed from this world. The clock was almost finished. Micah had to decide. Washington made sense. Micah rushed there with his primary team. A second team was sent to Las Vegas. Doubtful though, why would anyone make a point of blowing up a bunch of gamblers in the middle of the desert?

There was a small device found in the Lincoln Memorial. It was disarmed just in time. The team from Vegas had reported negative results so far. The clock ticked its final minutes and there was silence. Micah was exhausted and glad that it was over. He sat on the steps, smoking a cigarette and thinking that he was too old to be running around like this. He sighed as he ground out the last of his five cigarettes a day that he allowed himself. He missed Sarah and Jerrie. He packed up his gear and got ready to head home.

Hank was on a lucky roll at the tables. If only his fat harping wife would leave him alone about going to see that damn lounge show. He didn't see what she saw in that aging singer but she sure had the hots for him. Besides, with the chips stacking up in front of him, that brunette with the big boobs was sliding closer to his chair. Now, that was better than any lounge show. He ran his hand through his slick thinning hair and rolled the dice again.

Out on the street, another brunette named Mary Ann was turning her third and final trick for the night. She had made enough money to make her and her pimp happy. Now, the once Brody High Nebraska cheerleader could go home and not worry about any more bruises than she already had.

It was business as usual in the City That Never Sleeps.

The sun rose from the desert floor engulfing the neon dot of civilization. The power of the atom returned to the home from where it was born. As the shock wave traveled out, it also ran down through the desert soil, deep into the earth. It broke open a small fracture that had never been officially identified as a fault. This fault happened to be connected to a much larger fault. One that had troubled its neighbors to the west for years with major earthquakes. As the old song goes, "You ain't seen nothing yet."

Six months later, a man whom everyone considered a hero sat in a mental ward of a very private and secluded hospital. A man who could have done no more than he had. A man who had saved millions of lives with his determination and dedication. A solitary man whose eyes had once been bright blue. Now, the haunted gray eyes stared into nothingness. Everything that made him what he was had been ripped away. The man who had cursed his country and the rest of mankind. A man who had cursed his God for the death of his soul. He spoke of demons and dreams of the blood of innocents that dripped from his hands. A man who had died when his wife and daughter slipped into the sea with the other souls on that fateful day. Colonel Micah Sarentstein no longer existed.

As time would pass, the earth would heal. The man would find his way to a small fortress where he would find his purpose again. He would find solace and restoration. As the years moved forward, the legend of Micah was born. Soldier and teacher. Keeper of the Faith. His new family, The Order, was all that mattered. From the exterior it would appear that Micah was intact. Deep down, however was a small fracture, which had never healed. A fracture of guilt and mistake. Nurtured by the nightmares of the blood and screams of the innocent. Cleaved by the visions of the ebony hair of the woman who had whispered in his ear and of the laughing dark eyes of his only daughter. Can Micah truly be sane? Only the Father knows.

The people in their anguish cried for help. The sickness had spread from the Eastern United States, westward and beyond. It travelled with fun filled families on vacation, business travellers, and vagrants alike. The plague was upon us and did not discriminate between race, gender, or faith. The rich and poor died with the same burning fever and running boils, screaming in pain until their last breath rattled in their chest. Other nations began to count their mounting death tolls. The disease knew no boundaries and neither distance nor water seemed to impede its progress as it cut a swath through humanity.

The streets were filled with scared, angry and desperate people. And the predators stalked the weaker prey. Always in time of crisis, the slime and evil would surface. Not only did they survive, but actually seemed to thrive on the chaos and misery around them. In our cities and town of the small world we call home, the hunt was on with the massacre to follow.

National and international support systems crumbled. Law enforcement and medical resources were strained beyond relief as millions were sickened and died. Countries teetered on the brink of collapse with riots in the streets; economies bottomed out overnight and the fear of their leaders who did not know what to do. The world stood on the edge of its self-induced destruction.

From the New City, housed in a mountain of glass and steel, came the voice of reason and comfort. Elric Legion stood before the assembled delegates. His whispered voice thundered in the desperate silence. "I hear your cries. I will bring solace and unity to this world. My friends, the time of miracles is upon us." With that, he brought forward a young woman in the last stages of the Maryland Curse. The audience gasped at the sight of the running sores and pain evident in the woman's face. A doctor and nurse came forward with a hypodermic syringe filled with a crimson liquid. The shot was given to the woman. One minute passed, as there was silence in the great hall of nations. The woman sobbed as the fever wracked her emaciated body. Two minutes passed. The woman fell silent, a puzzled look on her face. Then her body convulsed in spasms. The delegates wept at the sight of her suffering, having seen the same over and over again in their own people. Five minutes had ticked by. The silence was absolute. Before them stood a woman in perfect health.

What would later be known as the Legion Compact was signed by all of the delegates that very afternoon. In return for the medical and financial assistance to recover from the plague's devastation, everyone agreed to form a worldwide consortium for mutual support and defense. A world currency and identification program, using the Advanced Technology chips, would be implemented immediately. For all practical purposes, Elric Legion now commanded the world.

As he sat in the dark enjoying the three hundred-year-old brandy, he smiled. A terrible smile below crimson eyes.

Across the world, people lined up for the chip implant. Many were inducted into the world's defense forces in lieu of payment. The wealthy paid for theirs and the poor bartered whatever they could for the life saving serum that would only follow after they had received the implant. The government leaders wondered though. Not everyone came for the implant. As a matter of fact, a lot of people had refused. As the executives sat in their paneled offices, their souls already beginning to rot, they could not help but wonder why.

The shotgun roared. Twelve gauge pellets riddled the approaching man's chest, shredding it into bloody ribbons of flesh. As crimson spurted from the gaping holes, the one time terrorist turned soldier died without a sound.

Jack Dalton racked another shell. His team had come under fire just outside the walls of Sanctuary. Shannon rolled to the left bringing her Uzi up into firing position. Their five-person team faced at least three times that in the surrounding hills of the countryside. Mark Chambers crawled forward sighting his M-16 on yet another shooter. His aim was true as the enemy's head snapped back with bits of brain matter and bone flying. They fought their way to the knoll where the main firing had come from. With reinforcements from the Security Detachment, all the enemy had been killed save one. He had been terribly wounded but was still defiant. Jack had faced this before and knew that what he looked at was not totally human.

Jack removed the holy dagger from his scabbard as he approached the creature. The thing smiled a sickly smile at the young man. It's rasping voice, oozed with the vileness of its home. "Tell Micah I do this in remembrance of my brother who died at his hands". The creature howled with peals of laughter as he pressed a red button on top of a small console. The laughter continued until the quick slice of Jack's dagger silenced it as it separated the head from the shoulders of the blasphemy before him.

As Jack, Shannon and the others stood before the device, the crystal numbers continued their countdown. Jack turned to the Security Chief and said, "Tell Micah to come. Bring everyone. The end is here." The timer sat atop the nuclear device counting down in cold red digital numbers. The indicator read, 23:57:45. One day until the fires of destruction. One day left for Sanctuary.

Mara and Ashe lay close together in the tangled sheets. Ashe listened to her soft, even breath. He thought of the love they had made. Had it happened so fast? Or not soon enough? They had become so close in the past few weeks. He enjoyed her easy laugh and soft touches. She made him feel alive amidst all of the blood and death around them. Sometimes though, she seemed sad as if there were a part of her forever out of his reach. She rolled over and curled against his chest, her warm breath blowing softly across him. His mind languidly floated in the currents, which led to sleep, and he dreamt.

The woman stood before him again. He recognized her face now. It was Christina, but older and somehow different. Perhaps it was the grief and pain of a certain knowledge that hardened the usually kind face he was used to. She looked sad as she gazed upon him. In her hands, she held the world that dripped with the blood of the innocents. In the shadows, another woman waited. She was with child and she held her hands out, reaching for him. They dripped with blood also.

Christina spoke, "Ashe, you were born of both worlds. Your soul is unique. I placed my mark on you long ago and because of that, the time is soon to come when you must face the pain. In the fire of this pain will your true self be born. A part of your pure soul that you have shared will be the implement of the Final Choice. All of the children must come together and what was once complete will be again. The door stands ready to open. When yours stands before you, you must go through. It is your destiny."

The woman in the shadows wept. She whispered one word, "Don't". In that single breath was the loneliness of being alone. The essence of the absence of the soul. A soul which only Ashe could provide. Ashe and one other. The people cried for their salvation and the voice of a child answered, saying, "I am."

Mara awoke suddenly in the dark, a scream almost at her lips. Her heart beat rapidly and sounded as if it would burst in her heaving chest. She was afraid but did not know why. As with all other strong emotions, her fear made her lose some of her self-control. With Ashe sleeping beside her, her eyes blazed with the color of rubies in the ebony stillness.

The end times foretold by prophets both new and old began. The Armies of the Beast roamed the world. Death walked in the form of a man. Atrocity begets atrocity. Man set upon man and the beasts of the earth set upon each other. What we had wrought upon ourselves went beyond the horror of any demons we could conjure. The Earth was ravaged from sea to sea. As the tears of Heaven fell upon her, she simply gave up and died.

Micah and the Council discussed the situation. Twelve hours were left before the bomb would detonate. They could evacuate but where to? The world was in chaos. Legion ruled it with an iron grip. All support had been cut off to the Order. To breathe a word of Dominion was certain death. Switzerland still remained technically neutral as always but even they could not help. They had been cut off as a country and it would just be a matter of time before they were attacked. The Vatican was under the leadership of a new Pope who had sided with Legion. The Council agreed that their old comrades had been infiltrated by the evil around them. The Enemy had captured the throne of St. Peter.

The Order was far from defenseless. They still had a very well entrenched intelligence system and many pockets of resistance existed around the world. They needed coordination though to be effective. Without Sanctuary, it was feared that no central coordination could be conducted.

Even now, strike teams from the Order and a rebel group of priests who had broken with the Vatican were assaulting Enemy strongholds and targeting Legion himself. The prophecy of his ascension was being fulfilled. No longer the benevolent diplomat, he was the proclaimed King of this Earth. His evil grew every day as he feasted on the fear and death. His hunger was never sated, only the death of billions of humans would begin to do that.

Micah spoke of the refugees streaming for Sanctuary. Thanks to the underground levels and the stockpile of provisions, the number was not a problem yet. But now, it seemed that they were pouring into the path of destruction. As the television showed the horrors of the events unfolding around the world, a knock sounded once again at the gates of Sanctuary. More survivors, hero's young and old, made up of all races, genders and faiths. Those that would not bow down to the Beast and accept his mark. He had heard the countless stories from the weeping survivors at the end of their dangerous travels. Stories of courage and of choices made. Sometimes of the ultimate choice. His mind wandered as the Council still spoke among themselves. A choice made. A father's choice. What would he have done?

An elderly woman had told Micah the story a few nights ago upon her arrival. The stories seemed to cleanse them somehow and Micah would always listen as if he was chosen to sit in the confessional and hear the words that purified their souls.

The woman, once a real estate agent, had lain in the ruins of the factory, hiding from the government agents and the predators that stalked the streets of the city. Going on seventy, she was still "fresh meat" for the creatures that walked on two legs.

As she lay in the dark, she heard weeping. She looked through a pile of rubble and saw a man with a boy lying close together. Both had the Curse. The father in the latter stages with the boils and the fever. The boy, perhaps five years old, beginning to sweat with the fever. They spoke of their loved ones, Mom and sister Ruthie. They spoke of the good times and their love for each other. The woman listened as the father talked. Much of the time it seemed as if it was meant for himself as much as his son. He spoke of the sickness and how he knew it would not be long before he passed. What would become of his son? There was no cure without the mark. Tears rolled down the man's cheek as he thought of the vile creatures that would have his son if he was left unprotected. His right hand lifted and the Colt forty-five pistol gleamed in the dim light.

She could see him explore the depths of his love and with his fever-wracked brain as he struggled to think of any other options. His son fell silent and softly patted the man's stubbled cheek, as if to say it's okay. The pistol raised. The man's eyes blurred with tears and his hand shook. Crying as if his heart would burst from his sunken chest, he let the gun fall. He shook his head and held his son tight. The old woman cried for the man. In the midst of all the horror she had seen, glowing like a candle in the darkness, was the pure love of a father for his son. As she imagined this soft glow, she realized that it began to brighten.

A soft blue hue, which grew with mounting intensity that, blinded her old eyes. The woman saw a figure in the light. The figure of a woman with honey blond hair and eyes the color of the sea. The figure held the man and his son in her embrace and softly whispered, "This day you will be with me." Then a whisper of a voice told the old woman to go, her destiny lay elsewhere. As the woman walked away in the night, she heard the sound of shots. Two of them. Perhaps the sound of death. To her, certainly the sounds of rebirth.

A beautiful vision sparked through Micah's brain. That of a lush garden with a beautiful waterfall. Nearby played a small golden haired boy, laughing with his father. Close by, sat his mother and sister. There were other figures nearby playing and laughing. He could almost recognize his Sarah and Jerrie among the company of the family whose love had risen above the price of their souls.

Micah returned with his thoughts as Gabriel spoke, "There may be a way. We must go to the past to have hope for the future."

Micah walked with Gabriel and Ashe to the Hall of Valor. It would be the last of many walks together.

The Book of Hans

On that frigid Christmas Eve, Hans Thielemann had waded through the blood of his comrades. The battle roared all around him like a great beast. Weary to the point of exhaustion, he literally fell into the foxhole. When his eyes cleared, he saw the American soldier. They both drew weapons and Hans knew he would die this night. He thought of his daughter. He would never see her again. As his finger tightened on the trigger, a blue glow covered both weapons. In wonderment, Hans slowly released his pressure on the trigger. The American sat back against the wall slowly sliding to the ground. Hans sat down, every breath as precious as the kisses of his sweet Erika. They shared the silence and a meal, both men lost in thoughts of home and warmth. The foxhole seemed to glow with a soft hue, which lulled the senses. Hans drifted into a much-needed sleep. He dreamt.

The Beast led his army, ravaging the world before him. None could stand in his way. The horror and misery that followed him burned into Hans' soul. The death of thousands in the ovens was not enough to satisfy the Beast. The death of millions would follow. As the Beast conquered the world, his legacy would be the power of the atom unleashed on humanity. A power that could be used for so much good could also be used for the consummate evil. The Beast must be stopped. Hans saw the true face of the Beast and he knew him.

Hans crawled out of the foxhole before the morning light broke, leaving the American a small thank you for sparing his life. Perhaps, he could one day repay the debt. As he wandered through the now silent battlefield, he looked up and saw the brightness. A shining symbol. A beacon to his destiny. Dominion.

Hans walked the bomb-ravaged streets of Berlin two years later. He had returned home in the duty of the Order. His team spread out over the city block. All five of them. All had volunteered for this dangerous mission. They would most likely not return. With the help of sympathizers, close to the Man, Hans now had access to the bunker. He prayed that he would not be too late. The Beast had been cornered. His army broken not only by conventional Allied forces but also by a parallel secret war which had been fought in the shadows. With the end in sight, the final plan would be to detonate the prototype atomic device. It had been built in secret and the countdown would commence soon. There would be no victory for the Allies, only death.

As Hans and his team slipped down the passageway, another figure watched. The immediate future of his world lay in the hands of a few humans. The blue eyes burned.

The team burst into the room. The Beast screamed in rage and his minions moved to battle. The Order stood their ground. Soon to be a very bloody ground.

That day as the bombs fell above, the battle raged deep beneath the ground. Sweat and blood poured as the men fought the unholy. Death walked the bunker. As Hans fought shoulder to shoulder with his friends, his eyes fell on the device. A timer was already attached. "Oh my God, it's active", cried Hans. His friend turned just in time to be impaled through the chest by a barbed talon of the Beast. Hans instinctively reacted and his dagger, blessed by a saint a thousand years before, found the heart of the Beast. Vile black blood dripped from the wound as the last of its breath completed the silence.

Hans looked around the bunker that looked as if it had been splashed with buckets of blood. He himself was covered with the thick copper scented substance. No one moved, human or other. He watched as the timer counted down. He bowed his head. Hans had received one miracle in his lifetime; he had lived to see his daughter again. Hans raised his head in defiance and asked for another. No, he demanded another.

The creature stood before him, like no other he had ever seen. Hans had seen evil. He had fought with it up close and personal. Here before him was…beauty. The tall being with eyes of liquid blue fire and pure white wings spread behind him. Hans had not truly known what it was that he had fought for. Not until now. He fell to his knees.

"Rise, my friend", spoke Gabriel. "You have done well. Your prayers have not gone unheard. I have been sent to see that your efforts are not in vain." Gabriel told him of ancient times when civilizations had risen and fallen. Man had made their choices even then. To strive towards the stars while creating unimaginable destruction. "Now, sits before us, that which has not been seen before and hopefully will never be again."

Gabriel stepped towards the device, which pulsed with a quiet menace. His eyes blazed with blue fire. Hans watched as the air around Gabriel charged with power. The wings spread and curled inward as Gabriel surrounded the device with his body. The wings formed a solid cocoon. Hans breath came rapidly as the very fabric of time and space rippled. Gabriel's essence faded with the bomb.

Gabriel floated in the womb of creation. With him, he carried a malignant tumor. The clock counted down. In this place was everywhere. The birth of his soul had begun here. Time meant nothing in this nexus of souls. A second or a thousand years could be the same. This was the place from whence he came to the Son of Man on that night so long ago. The beginning of his journey with these beautiful humans. He remembered the vision of a strong man dressed in bloody armor from his ancient memories. A man that gave everything so that Gabriel might live. The debt would be repaid this day.

On a desolate landscape, Gabriel stood with the harbinger of death. Another world or dimension? He did not know. Only that the device could do no more harm than already had been done in this place. The counter struck zero and the fire began the fission of particles so small yet so powerful. As Gabriel was engulfed, fission became fusion with the purity of Gabriel's being. In the dust of a strange world standing on the brink of eternity, Gabriel died his true death.

Gabriel floated above his ravaged body. In wonder, he looked at the charred skin and withered wings that were once him. Into the tunnel of blue light he drifted, then propelled rapidly towards the end. He stood in the place, enveloped by the warmth of the love from the being before him. A being who was familiar as well as a stranger. Gabriel stood waiting with the patience of a child before his beloved father.

The Father spoke, "My child, your selflessness has saved the ones you lived among. The purity of your compassion transcended the small world in which you lived. You have chosen your friends well. Even now, he weeps for your sacrifice.

Hans wailed at the sight of the body. So strong in life and so very fragile in death. The air had shimmered and Gabriel's body had appeared. The device was nowhere to be found. As Hans wiped the blood from his own wounds, he sat quietly in the corner. His thoughts would not form and his world had stopped as if frozen in this moment of time. Even the bombs overhead were silent in his grief. True, the Beast was defeated. It would be the first of three as foretold. The second would be defeated in the desert fifty years later. The true story would not be known to the world, as the events of this day would not. The military would classify it higher than top secret and formulate a believable cover story. Suicides were always good stories. The world could believe in monsters that self-destruct.

Hours passed. The shelling had ceased. Hans eased his bruised and torn body up and walked to his fallen comrades, saying quiet farewells to his friends. At last, he came to Gabriel with tears streaming down his face. As Hans brushed the hair from the open eyes of the fallen body before him, a gust of air smelling of honeysuckle blew softly across his own face. A wing moved; then a hand. A hand that clasped the outstretched hand of Hans. A strong firm hand pulsing with life. Tears of joy flooded the face of the young protector.

The Covenant of Gabriel

"You have done well, all of my children. Your courage and faith have defeated the first of three. Gabriel, you will return to your place among man. Not as strong as before, but everything for its reason. This promise I will make unto you. Though your old eyes will witness much destruction in the end times, you will be the guiding instrument of salvation to a world that cries out for help. I will send a special one to seek your guidance. Teach well Gabriel, for the choices made will determine the Final Choice. Go with my love."

Hans would serve the Order with honor for many years. Of all his battles, he would never forget that single day. The fear he felt and the courage he saw. The beauty and love that immersed his soul in that long ago place. He would smile at the time of his death, knowing the fight had been worthy. He was not afraid to go home.

The swallow flew the currents with her mate, drifting and diving above the hamlet set among the trees on the hillside. As her mate dived from the deep blue sky, littered with the white wisps of clouds, the fireball engulfed his tiny body. She rose upward riding the thermal currents of the explosion until the heat burst her body into flames.

The tactical nuclear weapon had been fired in the small village about fifty kilometers outside of Frankfurt, Germany. A skirmish between the armies of the Beast and the forces of man. The blood bath had started.

Shannon Gzar sighted the crosshairs at the base of the man's neck. As she slowly squeezed the trigger, the rest of the team led by Jack Dalton got into position. As the silenced shot whispered death to its target, the team moved forward. In practiced movements, the team entered the compound located on the outskirts of Casper, Wyoming. Glowing, slitted eyes opened in the darkness. It smelled the approaching humans. Not the ones who surrounded it with their already rotted souls, the other ones. The Enemy. Gunshots shattered the quiet cold morning. Screams of the dying sounded. It slithered forward from its hiding place, to feast.

At Sanctuary, the Security Chief slowly approached the device. Erika Thielemann slowly looked at it from all sides. She had dismantled many bombs during her service to the Order but never one such as this. She knew she was the last line of defense. As she lit a cigarette, she squatted before the device trying to merge her soul with that of the machinery before her. She closed her eyes trying to visualize the components. The clock ticked. Twelve hours and counting. The young lady, who carried the name of her mother before her, thought of her grandfather and felt she might see him soon.

Micah and Ashe greeted the new refugees. A group of twenty had arrived at the doors of the compound. Ashe looked on with tears in his eyes at the new arrivals with so much pain evident on their faces. As he looked deeper, his heart lightened. Yes, there was pain but also hope and determination. The leader of the group came forward and shook hands with Micah and they embraced as old friends. Ashe stared at perhaps the oldest human being he had ever seen. The man had to be at least one hundred and twenty years old. He looked to be in amazing shape and his eyes twinkled with intelligence. Strong looking, his only infirmity was that he limped and walked with the use of a mahogany cane. Standing beside him was a beautiful blond haired girl and the most magnificent animal that Ashe had ever seen. A German Shepherd which stood quietly beside the two, as a friend and protector. As Ashe's eyes met those of the dog, he could almost hear a whisper in the depths of his mind. "Protect the Child."

In the dimness of the chapel, Gabriel sat in his special place designed to allow for his wings. As he communed with his Father, the curtain behind him parted, revealing the blade of an ancient dagger. The blade rose as crimson eyes burned.

Legion snarled as the last human uttered its final breath. It was not enough he thought. Five had not sated his hunger. He had fed on their fear and the carnality of their flesh. It was over all too soon for his satisfaction. He threw the limp body of the woman away from him; scarcely hearing the skull crunch as it hit the blood smeared wall. He bellowed for his servants to bring forth more entertainment for him. And they had better hurry or they would serve in their place. While he waited, he stepped onto the balcony. As he waited in anticipation, a red laser light appeared on his forehead. In the silence of the palace, the Beast roared.

As time ebbed and flowed around them, they readied themselves. The eyes of liquid blue watched as the world died. The time of the last had arrived. Man had wrought his own destruction. Evil incarnate walked the planet and fed upon the chaos. The Gates of the Lost would soon be unleashed. The Protectors, who the humans called archangels readied for war.

On the erected stage in the middle of the capitol building complex, a man stood alone. Surrounded by thousands, watched by millions courtesy of modern technology. The man stood alone in the sea of dark humanity. His voice had been heard and feared. Now, he would be silenced at last. Perhaps his voice, but not the message it had carried. He smiled to himself. His son and daughter were safe for now. Legion's forces had taken everything else that mattered to him. He was ready. He did not fear the end for he knew it was only the beginning.

As the modern guillotine fell in the presence of millions, Peter Beck smiled at the moment of his death. The executioner could not understand. What remained was only a body, a shell to be discarded. Peter's soul soared to his destiny.

The smoke hovered over the blasted rubble of the compound and the smell of cordite permeated the air. Bleeding and torn bodies lay strewn, looking like the broken dolls of a child's temper tantrum. The buzzards had already started to feast on the freshly dead flesh. Soon they would be so bloated; they would not be able to fly. As the earth soaked up the crimson stains of its victims, the cold sleet and rain began to fall.

Jack and Shannon huddled under the parka with their backs pressed against one another. Jack inhaled the rich smoke from his cigarette and passed it to Shannon. He enjoyed the warmth of her body so close to his. The quiet was blessed after the noise of war and death. After the screams of agony had seared the western plain.

The battle had been one of the toughest he had ever fought. It had lasted over six hours with both Dominion and Enemy engaged in close quarter combat. In the end, their forces had been victorious but not without a price. They had lost some good men and women in order to breach this encampment. Legion's followers had been well prepared and deeply entrenched here. The high ranking members of Legion's forces, his "princes" had been waiting for his ascension to eclipse the world, then the princes would take their rightful places and rule the underlings of the conquered globe. These men and women had sold their souls for power long ago. If CNN had been filming, many of the faces would have been recognized. Shocking? Perhaps, but power is a persuasive vice and seductive to many.

A few more moments rest and Jack would radio the operation report into Sanctuary via satellite uplink. Shannon leaned her head back against Jack and talked to him in that smoky voice that he loved so much. "So, when are you going to make me an honest woman Mr. Dalton?" Jack chuckled softly, reaching back to touch her cheek. "Soon", he said, "As soon as this is over." Shannon thought this extremely funny saying that they could serve Geritol at the wedding then.

The inhuman scream cut off Jack's smart reply. Except that the scream was indeed human. Eddie's scream ripped from his throat as the creature impaled him on one of its many talons. The mouth, with rows of teeth from a child's nightmare, ripped Eddie's body in half during mid scream throwing them right and left as so much discarded garbage. The beast had come from beneath, bursting through the boards of the basement, rising like a leviathan in the splintered wood. In the space of seconds, it had killed five more of the team members without mercy. Return fire from Sanctuary's forces pounded into the flesh of the demon. Black blood flowed, hissing like acid as the beast screamed in pain and rage.

Shannon moved forward with a portable rocket launcher and fired just as the tail of the creature whipped through the air behind her striking her in the side. The crunch of bones could be heard in the cold afternoon air. Jack roared with rage as he drew the dagger of St. Thomas and threw himself at the horror before him. As he grabbed the throat, pulling it back the talon closed over his face and the world grew dark. The wind whispered, softly blowing the dark hair over Shannon's still body.

Half a world away, Ashe entered the dark paneled study at Sanctuary. There, Micah introduced him to the leader of the last group of refugees that had arrived. The man stood with the assistance of his cane, shaking Ashe's outstretched hand in a firm and warm grip. "I am Theo Dmitri Salinas, at your service." he said in a rich baritone voice. Ashe immediately felt drawn to the warmth and humility of this man. Ashe thought he embodied the word "grandfather" with his genteel looks and manner. Ashe looked into Theo's hazel eyes and saw great strength and compassion. But there was also great sadness buried in those beautiful eyes. Theo continued, "I am so glad to meet you young Ashe. I have heard so much of you from my close friend Micah. With that and what I've read of your mother, I feel you are family to me. Ashe's excitement was immediate when his mother was mentioned. Theo explained, "I never met her but I know much about her. I am the last of the Oracles. My counter part died earlier this year, killed by the Enemy. It was she who chronicled the service of your mother to the Order. My comrade had prepared, hiding her writings well including those of your mother's. She protected their secrets with her life. I recovered them per her instructions and have had them in my possession since. Due to the increasing hostile situation in the States, I remained there until now. Now the chronicles, I and my charges are where we belong." He waved his arm to encompass the room and all it stood for. "In this place," Theo whispered, "This Holiest of Holy. This Sanctuary we call home." The dog named Saint quietly showed his agreement by lying in front of the fireplace in peaceful sleep, with his nose resting on his curled tail. He dreamt of the Child.

The dagger wavered and held. Gabriel said, "Child, if thou do this, do so quickly but know the price is that of your soul." Mara spoke softly, "My soul is already damned so what does it matter?" Gabriel's slight cadence filled the small distance between them. The distance of eternal life and death. "You know this not to be true or you would have already plunged the blade into me, which is what you were sent to this place for. The fact that you have not bespeaks of the love that you did not know you had in you. The love for Ashe and that of your unborn child." The dagger fell. The silence was broken by the clatter as it struck the floor. Crimson tears dripping down her cheeks, Mara was enfolded in the great wings and love of Gabriel.

As the world crumbled in the ashes of destruction, a small glimmer of light struggled from the depths of darkness. A light for all creation. A light known as *Jarred*.

Jack spit the bile out of his throat. He crawled from the coils of the abomination that lay in death around him. Its vile life had been vanquished by the blessed dagger, which lay plunged into its black heart. Jack stumbled over to Shannon's body, lying face down in the blood-splattered ground. His tears fell as he cradled her head. "Stop twisting my head around you big badass teddy bear", she whispered, "you're hurting me. I feel like about ten mules kicked the hell out of my ribs." Jack's tears turned to cries of joy as he hugged his reason for living to his chest. She smiled gently and looked at him as she brushed his hair back from his grime-streaked face. Her eyes widened and she gasped, "Oh, my God." Shannon looked into the eyes of the man she loved with all her heart. Into the dark brown eyes beneath hair, that had turned pure white in the space of a few seconds. The seconds of a lifetime.

As Theo and the young blonde walked the corridors, they spoke in whispers. He said, "I know its hard not to go to him but you must wait. Secrecy is his only protection now. Soon, it will be time for him to be revealed. You must be patient." Ashe approached the pair and was introduced to the girl. Rachel Beck. Ashe's compassion and concern was immediate. "I have heard of your father. He was a great man, I am so very sorry for your loss. My prayers are with him and your mother. Where is your brother, Joshua?" Rachel replied, "He is safe, for the moment anyway. He will join us soon." After saying their good byes, Ashe continued on his way in search of Mara.

Mara was talking with Gabriel in the chapel as she sat close beside him. She talked and Gabriel listened, speaking small words of encouragement as she struggled to bare her soul. The words of his love helped to heal her spirit as she related what had been. Her eyes focused in the distance, she said, "I was born of a human and demon conception. I survived the birth, which is rare. My mother did not. They raised me, the ones you call the Enemy, except that I grew up thinking of you by that name. Due to my unique genetic makeup, it was thought that I might have more resistance to the relics used in the initiation tests here. They thought that I would have the best chance of surviving those tests and infiltrating Sanctuary. So, I was picked as the perfect assassin. My primary target was you. Micah next, if possible. Without your leadership, it was felt that the Order would be disorganized and easy prey. I did everything perfectly except...I fell in love. Ashe's soul is so pure; I'm drawn to it in a way I don't even understand. In his love, I found a home and safety. Now, it is over. The Order will execute me or banish me. Either way, I die."

Silence passed for a few moments. "I think not, my child." Gabriel spoke, "You have proven yourself worthy of our love. Ashe's love will keep you safe. Even Micah, in time will understand. You are very valuable to the Order now. With your knowledge of the Enemy, there can be a future for all of us." Ashe walked into the chapel, seeing Mara and Gabriel. Gabriel leaned over her, kissing her gently on the cheek. "I will leave you and Ashe alone to speak for awhile. Then he must come to the council chambers. Our time is short." Mara's teary eyes looked into the bewildered ones of Ashe as she said, "Come my love, we must talk." Talk they did. And cried as well. And their love for each other only grew with every tear that fell.

Two hours later, the Council of Seven had met in the crisis room. Erika had briefed them on the situation of the bomb. Micah had revealed to them Mara's true background and the events as she related them to Gabriel. After some doubt and concern, it was agreed to abide with Micah's plan and accept her as a new ally. After all, she had Gabriel's highest recommendation. Even Micah silently felt puzzled by Gabriel's unwavering support of her. He acted as if he knew a secret, which he either could not or would not share at this time. Plans were laid for a final effort to save the hallowed place they stood in. A deactivation team led by Erika would begin the process of trying to defuse the bomb. Her backup would be Gabriel and Ashe, at their request. Micah did not know why, only this had occurred after Gabriel and Ashe had spoke at length in private.

The team stood surrounding the device. The timer showed two hours and counting. Erika and her team began their delicate work while the others watched. Gabriel and Ashe because they knew they would be the last hope should this attempt fail. Micah, because he wanted to be there and Theo, to chronicle the events of this day, should he live to tell it.

Erika thought of her grandfather Hans as she began the task before her. Gabriel thought of Mara and the hope she would bring. Ashe thought of his many blessings. Mara and their child, along with his family here at Sanctuary. And thanks to Theo, he thought of his mother's life. He had read her book last night.

His soul had always known her instinctively. Now he knew of her…and his father.

The Book of Samantha

The wind blew against the canvas of the tent, the sand sounding like the skittering of a million tiny beasts. The woman lay in great pain, surrounded by her attendants in the birth of her child. As the contractions grew in their frequency, she closed her eyes. She stood upon the mountain looking down on the cities of the world. Flames reached to the heavens as millions cried out in agony, their bodies infected with horrible diseases. In their pain, they all pointed their misshapen hands towards her and cried as one, "Thou art the one". Her eyes flew open as the tiny body slid from between her blood-slicked thighs. Later, as she held her newborn son in her arms, she looked into his eyes. The eyes of his father. In the soft crimson glow of those eyes, the woman silently slipped into insanity.

The soft Scot accent of Samantha Duncan sounded like music to the ears of the children as she read them stories of hero's. She read of hope and faith that urged them the realization of their dreams. Deep beneath the stone walls of Sanctuary, she taught them the knowledge of the future. The future that they would make.

As Teresa Silovitch watched the classroom, she thought of how the beautiful raven-haired woman had come to them long ago.

Samantha had been abandoned at an early age and raised in an orphanage in the low-income section of Glasgow. Educated by the Catholic Church, she had excelled at her studies and was an excellent candidate for further scholarships, as the visiting Bishop had told her. Right before he tried to molest her in the darkness of his chambers. The young woman-child struggled with the large man until, her hand in panic clasped the first thing she touched. Silver letter opener with a very sharp point. Two heartbeats later, the bishop lay gurgling in his own blood with the letter opener skewered through his throat. Samantha fled into the night. The long night of being a fugitive.

She had survived on her own wits for the next five years. A Protector, on a mission in London, had stumbled across her when she helped him in an alley fight with agents of the Enemy. She had been given sanctuary. A routine physical disclosed the extra genetic component that marked her as the Order's family. Samantha began her training at the age of seventeen, excelling in both academics and close combat. Her athletic grace belied her quick intelligence. She completed her training, ranking the highest in her class. She had worked as a teacher to the children at Sanctuary because no openings had occurred in the Protectors. Until now...

In a battle with the Enemy, the Order had lost a Protector three days ago. The Council had met. Along with the recommendations of Teresa and Gabriel, Samantha would be initiated into the Order, if she accepted. Teresa sighed. She loved Samantha like a daughter. In all of her year's service to the Order, she had not seen as bright a light as that of Samantha Duncan in a long time. She would make the formal invitation to her in a few minutes but for now, she was content to watch the young woman with the gift of compassion, teach the future to those bright young eyes.

Five years and many missions later, Samantha was a seasoned battle veteran now. She was summoned before the Council and briefed on the biggest mission of her life.

Gordon Elias, the head of the Council, gave the briefing. "It was foretold in our time that the Beast would feed three times. The first was during what the secular world called World War II. The second is upon us, the war in the desert. The United Powers thinks that they have beaten back the threat of the Beast. In reality, our intelligence indicates that he is only toying with them to buy time. There is death buried underneath the sand, awaiting the time when it will destroy all of humanity. You, with the other Protectors and a support team, will be inserted into the palace of the Beast with the help of our agents there. You must make a final stand and destroy the Beast and the death he has created in his laboratories, once and for all. "What of Gabriel?" one of the Protectors asked. Gordon explained that Gabriel's assistance would not be possible this time. "He is on a very important mission of his own. To protect a young man in the United States. Already agents of the Enemy move to harm him and prevent him one day from leading a nation to the stars and a friend to his destiny. He did say he would try to intercede on our behalf and attempt to send help. May our thoughts and prayers be with him."

The team readied their gear and flew off into the night. In the east, a great storm moved across the desert. In its fury could be heard the howl of the Beast.

The Book of Samantha

She dreamt of the light coming forth unto her. She felt the warmth and peace, as she smelled the odor of honeysuckle. She felt love in the great presence that surrounded her. The light faded and she was alone in the dark caverns choking with fear. The fear of being hunted. The Beast stalked her with fiery eyes and a surgeon's tool. The tool that would rip an unborn child from her belly. His soft, chafing voice whispered, "Come unto me Child. Thou art mine."

As the plane engine changed pitch, Samantha awoke with a start. Shaking off the remnants of the bad dream, she checked her battle gear while drinking a mug of steaming strong coffee.

Six hours later, the Protectors and their support team were inserted into the capital city. They made their way into the palace via a secret passage known by the sympathizers. This was to be an assassination mission. Silenced weapons were the order of the day. They would eliminate the palace guard, destroy the Beast with sacred daggers and destroy his legacy beneath the sand with good old-fashioned C-4 explosives.

The team took out the perimeter guards with no problem and made their way to the inner chambers deep beneath the massive palace grounds. Samantha and Teresa, side by side, with their H&K submachine guns moved quietly through the narrow tunnels. Samantha spoke through her throat mike to one of the other team members, "It's too quiet. I've got a bad feeling about this." "Me too, "he replied.

The shots rang out from all sides as they entered the antechamber. A hundred weapons against twenty. The Order's forces had walked into a well-planned ambush. Five members fell during the initial onslaught of fire, including one Protector. Then began a deadly game of cat and mouse in the lower chambers of the palace. During it all, they could hear the cackling of the Beast above them.

As Samantha and Teresa turned the corner in the lower quadrant, a man stood before them. Tall, perhaps almost seven feet and muscular with shoulder length brown hair that was highlighted by streaks of honey gold. Samantha raised her rifle and began to pull the trigger. "Don't", he said. "My name is Michael, Gabriel sent me to help." "Good", Samantha said, "Right now, we need all the damn help we can get". As they turned and ran she couldn't help but notice that she could not see his weapon.

The hunt was bloody as human and unholy alike, hunted for the Order's team. Small, quick and vicious battles erupted in the narrow confines of the below ground lair. A day turned into five. Five into twenty and twenty into a month. Back home, friends and family waited. Without much hope, only faith.

As Samantha, Michael and Teresa shared their meager rations, taken from the supplies of one of their dead enemy, they spoke in whispered voices. They had killed many of the enemy in the seeming endless war but more were still hunting for them. They had some contact with the other teams that had split during the ambush but decided to stay separate for now, for safety reasons.

The three spoke to pass the time. Michael had related how Gabriel had contacted him and asked for his help on this mission. No, he was not a member of the Order, however he had many friends among them and from time to time, would help if needed. Samantha had found Michael to be soft spoken and good-natured despite the hardships they had faced. Despite her doubts, he had proven himself in combat time after time in the last month. You would have thought that he invented warfare, he was that good. The only thing that still bothered her, was that after all the battles, she still could not tell exactly what weapon he was using. Must be a knife or a small caliber silenced pistol. She would have liked to ask, but considered that to be rude and dismissed it. No matter how hard she tried to watch him during battle, there was too much confusion and he moved way too quickly. As for Teresa, she was totally in love with the man. Of course, she was about twenty-five years older than he looked. But to hear Teresa talk, the few moments they had to themselves, the man was "better than sliced bread", well nigh perfect in her book according to Teresa.

They had found a way to the upper chambers of the Beast. They had met up with the other surviving members of the team, ten in all, not counting Michael. They prepared for an all out attack. They knew that the last month had weakened them considerably and they must move quickly in order to overcome the creature, which masqueraded as a man. A creature who would unleash death upon their world on an unimaginable scale. The clock was ticking...

The team was attacked just outside of the Beast's room. The Enemy's number had been deleted severely. What was left fought with the desperation of a suicide mission. The battle enjoined while both sides closed in close quarter combat. Samantha had lost sight of Michael during the bloodshed. Her, Teresa and another Protector fought shoulder to shoulder with what was left of the palace guard. They had wondered why no replacements came forward. Above the ground, they could hear the cries in the streets of the city. The revolt of his enslaved people had begun.

The chamber doors flew open with a terrible stench spewing forward. What came from the inner room was a being born of Samantha's worst nightmares. Part dragon, part snake and maybe something else. Maybe everything else. Its eyes blazed with crimson intensity. Samantha believed those eyes must be like looking into the heart of twin nuclear explosions. The aura surrounding the Beast moved as if it was a living thing unto itself. Samantha could feel the emanation of hopelessness and rage from its blistering pus ridden body. The Beast joined in the battle. As it screamed, the deaths began.

They fought with valor. The Protector to Samantha's left went down, his right arm ripped from his body and his chest split open by the creature before them. As John Dalton went to his rest, his last thoughts were that of his wife and newborn son, who they affectionately called Jack. As the blue light surrounded him, he willed his love to survive to reach them in their memories. A talon slashed across Samantha's left shoulder. Screaming in pain, she emptied a thirty round clip into the belly of the Beast. Teresa was trying to get into position with the dagger. Between the two women, there was hope. A tiny hope to be sure, but hope nonetheless. Teresa did not see the tail arching towards her exposed back. The tail they had not seen before. That of a scorpion.

The tail whipped forward. Teresa felt no pain but she could not move forward. She didn't understand. Her brain was sending messages to her hand but it wasn't responding. Samantha froze in horror, staring at her longtime friend. Teresa's eyes looked down.

The stinger had entered her back shearing her spinal cord and exited out her chest. She was dead. Her brain just had not received the message yet. A tear rolled out of Samantha's eyes as she stared at the ones of her friend and mentor. There she saw peace, an inner peace beyond this world. Reflected in those eyes was a blue hue getting brighter by the moment. Samantha whirled around.

In the glow of a thousand suns, stood the being known by man as Michael. He was the same as before but much more. The chief Archangel of the army of the Father stood in all his glory. Massive white wings with crimson tips swept from his back. A mighty shield was held in his left hand that carried the Protector's symbol. His eyes burned a liquid blue, which had the intensity of a million gas flames. In his right arm, he held the legendary sword. Forged from creation itself, the Sword of Michael stood ready for battle.

The Beast and Samantha were separated by mere inches. Both stood in awe and fear. The voice of Michael ringing as if from the gate of Heaven itself thundered, "Fear this day High Son of the Liar, Destroyer of Dreams. These brave warriors have given their all. They gave everything that their frail bodies and beautiful souls had to offer and still you cannot defeat their spirit. I have been sent by my Father's love. Now the battle will end this day and you will return to the pit from whence you were born."

The Beast uttered a cry, sounding curiously like that of a wounded child, and threw Samantha to the side like a ragdoll. Michael closed in battle with the creature from the darkest reaches of Hell. It lasted less than an hour. Talon and sword with flashes of pure blue and deep crimson. As Michael's sword raised over it, the Beast sounded the shriek of defeat and raised its arms to ward the blow. Samantha dove forward, driving the dagger deep into the heart of the Beast. Its talons, even in sure death, closed around the head of the young Protector. The mighty sword sliced the air connecting with unholy flesh and with the sizzle of a lightning strike, the great creature's head rolled across the chamber coming to rest beside the pilfered tapestry of an enslaved nation.

In the days that followed, she rested in the shelter of the palace with her wounds. Riots jammed the city streets for the next few days until the rebel army breached the inner chambers. It was there, they found the bodies and heard the quiet story of one lone woman. Beautiful with raven hair now adorned with two pure white streaks from the touch of the Beast. The story from the new regime would say that rebels within the former leader's ranks had revolted, killing the dictator. The new leader made a sincere effort to learn from the mistakes of the past. He ordered all the biological weapons destroyed with the assistance of the United Nations forces. Being a good man, he tried. But being a good man, he was deceived.

Samantha returned to Sanctuary, to the home of her heart. In the days that followed with the bustling activity of having to replace their fallen comrades, the Council did not think to ask her who had tended her wounds and comforted her in the days before the rebels found her. As she gently rubbed her flat stomach in awe, she could already imagine the slight swelling begin. She knew she must tell the others soon, it was very important. But for now, for a few days, she would enjoy Michael and hers little secret.

Warrior. Teacher. Mother of Hope to mankind. May the angels sing her praise.

Ashe stood upon the hill with the others, watching as Erika and her team worked frantically on the device. The timer and detonator were the most advanced that she had ever worked on in her career. She worked carefully but quickly, time was running out. Micah, Gabriel and Theo stood by silently. In the crisis room inside the fortress, the Council of Seven waited in silence.

Mara sat and waited with Christina, joined by Saint who had followed his instincts to the child he had protected so long ago. A time that was a bridge between life and death for the loyal animal with the purest of souls.

In the combat simulation room, the young man Levi ran through all known simulations of Order combat missions. He looked for the weakness he knew had to be there. His razor sharp dagger lay in the scabbard strapped to his right thigh.

In UN-1, Legion waited for word from Switzerland. Soon, he would rule the world without opposition from these puny rebels. Without their cursed home as a base, his armies would defeat them in the last great battles and he would remold this world into his Father's vision. No humans for starters. Well, maybe they would have to discuss that one thought Legion. After all, one had the desire for some fleshly entertainment, right? Legion's armies were poised to move in and wipe out any survivors from the bunkers underneath. Doubtful that there would be any, but it pays to be ready. Legion wiped the drool from his mouth as he entered the soundproofed bedroom. The woman tied naked to the bed, cowered in fear. As Legion's laugh screeched and he revealed himself to her, her muffled screams became the sound of the insane. "Okey, Dokey", he grinned, "Come to Papa."

Erika snapped the final wire, holding her breath. The timer read thirty minutes. The display went blank. Erika stared, dumbfounded at first. Then she screamed with tears of joy, "We did it! We did it!" As hugs and congratulations were bandied around, a small click sounded, drowned by the noise of the celebration. Micah looked down and saw the display relit. With horror they realized that a hidden backup system had been activated. The countdown read sixty seconds the blood red crystalline numbers. Fifty nine…

Gabriel shouted, "No more time. Ashe come here." As Ashe ran forward, he glanced over his shoulder, catching a glimpse of Mara in the window and mouthed the only words he could to her, "I love you." Micah and Theo said their final prayers as Gabriel wrapped Ashe and the device in his old but mighty wings. As the glow began, Gabriel whispered softly into Ashe's ear. "This we do for man. For our souls and for our home. Sanctuary must abide.

Time stood still upon the hilltop as the glow began like that of a second sun. Dimensions inverted and the air mass shimmered. The purity of two souls born thousands of years apart merged with the atoms of death somewhere in the womb of creation. With their cells accelerated beyond the speed of light, their lives passed before their eyes in the space of a millisecond. Or a thousand years in this place. Either was possible in this nexus of all possibilities.

On the darkest day in the history of the Order, Micah stood upon a lonely hill and wept with his friend Theo. They had lost both mentor and pupil. Past and future as one.

Sanctuary stood safe for now, Micah thought. But at what cost? He turned slowly back towards the fortress. He would tell Mara. It was the least he could do.

Seven months later

Micah sipped the whisky while looking into the beautiful face of Mara. Made even more beautiful by her pending motherhood. They had become close friends in the past months. He felt like a father towards her and she adored him as the father she never had growing up in the cold commune of the Enemy. It had been hard months. The Order always lived on the edge of violence. They knew of loss better than anyone did. No matter how many there were, they all hurt. But these had hurt like none before. Gabriel and Ashe would be remembered with all the love that they had to offer. Part of that love, thought Micah, would be that Ashe's child would be taken care of, no matter the cost. Micah vowed this as he swallowed the last of his whisky and thought of old friends in the firelight.

Inside the walls of the ancient fortress, quiet preparations were made. Mara prepared for the birth of their child. Theo finished his writings on the final days of the saviors of Sanctuary. The books and statues would soon be made ready. Micah oversaw the training underneath. They had prepared for years; soon the time of training would be over. Christina sat in silence, softly scratching Saint behind the ears in his favorite place. The time of her own ascension neared.

Alone, in the darkness he waited. All of his comrades had been massacred. It was left up to him. He lit a candle in remembrance of his father.

The Council met behind closed doors. Men and women, who had devoted their lives and that of their ancestors before them, to the protection of this sacred ground. As the ancient clock, which once belonged to a Pope, ticked the seconds away they finalized the plans all had known must come but had prayed for delay.

Shannon and Jack lay together enjoying the warmth in the velvet darkness they lay wrapped in. All of the Sanctuary teams had returned home. Now they waited, enjoying the rare moments of peace and togetherness. The present was real, the future unsure.

The General lay in a bloodied heap, not recognizable even as human anymore. Every bone in his body had been broken. Legion sat in a chair sipping his drink. As he looked at the remains in front of him, he felt remorse. The General hadn't been that bad. As a matter of fact, he had sucked up to Legion pretty well for an old army type. Oh well, no sense crying over spilt milk or blood for that matter. There were plenty more to replace him. At least Legion thought so. He would have to check with his aides and see whom he had not killed since he had been told of the failure of the bomb. No matter, soon his ground forces would have the cursed fortress surrounded. There would be no escape for the hated ones. Especially sweet, would be the death of his traitorous sister and the bastard child her belly swelled with. Legion's mood got better as he thought of the things he would do to her before he killed her.

Christina bowed her head as she heard the words of the Council of Seven. She concurred. "The time is at hand. I will enjoin at morning's light. I take your leave now to prepare." Micah entered the council chambers. Deep into the night, they spoke. It took time to convince Micah. In the end, with the absence of Gabriel, it was the only logical choice left.

As Mara lay in her bed, deep brown eyes watched her closely. Her constant companion for the last few months, Saint was never far away. He stared at her swollen belly and his thoughts wandered back to past years. Could dogs remember? He could. He saw the eyes of deep blue of his beloved One so long ago. He remembered the day of blood. He saw his death when the shotguns ravaged his leaping body. As his soul floated in that place, he remembered the Father. Father had spoken to him, not with words but with all. *"You are a special soul, my beloved. The tears of the one you loved with all your strong heart even now call you back. I have other tasks for you in time. There will be another. In your heart of hearts you will know when the time is right. Go now, with my love."* Had other souls touched the face of God? He had. The brown eyes closed and Saint dreamed the dream of all dogs. As he chased, his legs twitched.

Theo wrote the final words and wiped his tears away. All the years he had been writing, since that bloody Christmas Eve in Atlanta. So long ago and so many deaths since then. He had regained his soul from the fire of that time. His lifetime had been extended. He had wondered at the reason for this. Unlike Saint, he aged but it appeared to be at a much slower pace than his fellows. And that damned hip. Theo laughed to himself. He guessed that was just God's little way of reminding him not to get too cocky. Theo lovingly closed the books engraved with the names of Gabriel and Ashe. It was time to sleep and rest. And perhaps to dream of his beautiful Rose.

The Child dreamt of crumbling castles and toy soldiers scattered among the dust. Tears like rain fell from above. A star dissolved into the mist of reality...or is it? Home was so near, wasn't it? Faint voices calling. Somewhere in the twists and turns of the deep forest. Secrets to be found. Salvation or damnation? Or neither? Perhaps only oblivion waited.

The tanks rolled through the hillside and the armies massed. For the first time in modern memory, Switzerland was invaded. It was easier than Legion had thought. Not much resistance was forthcoming. Strangely, many cities had already been abandoned. No matter, the world was his. His armies swept across the nations of the Earth. Those that had not bowed down before him were destroyed to the last man, woman, and child. Whole communities had disappeared. Legion smiled. The weak fled before his coming. As his plane landed at the Geneva airport, Legion was content. Life was sweet. He smiled at Silas, his small unassuming advisor. Silas smiled back, the patient smile of a favorite uncle.

In the bowels of Sanctuary, Christina stood at the gate, accompanied only by Micah and Saint. The Council watched via video feed. Christina bowed her head in prayer. She turned to Micah and hugged his broad shoulders as he kissed her forehead whispering his blessing. Saint stepped forward. Her hand stopped him. "No boy. Here forward, I must go alone. It is what I was sent for." Micah stepped in front of her. "Christina, are you sure this will work? The words of the Old Ones say that you must be accompanied by a member of the Blessed." Christina thought for a moment. "That is the literal translation. However, without Gabriel among us, I will have to do the best I can. We have no other choice." She stepped forward into the circle of stones that were perhaps as old as man. The sacred heart of Sanctuary.

For a moment nothing happened. Micah saw the swirls of light first, then quickly gaining in intensity. As Christina slowly spread her arms, it was if a great wind blew in that confined place. Her blonde hair swirled about her shoulders. Her eyes closed in concentration, flashes of lightning sparked through the circle as the glow of a thousand suns rose. The very earth trembled as the ground opened up as if to swallow her. It was as if the whole of creation gathered in that small space focused on the diminutive figure which stood in the center. A tear rolled down Micah's cheek at the beauty he saw. Then he heard the scream of infinite pain. Christina's pain.

As the light enjoined her body, she felt the bolt of lightning enter her heart as if it sought all of her compassion. As the energy passed through her, it felt as if it traveled a natural arc. Suddenly the pain was there, beyond comprehension as if the energy had no where to go. No final destination. She screamed and prayed to the Father for intercession. The pain drove her to her knees. No! Her love for these people would be their light. That was her vow before the Liar in the desert. She had sworn her light would shine with hope in this world of darkness. She did not ask for intercession, she demanded it!

Micah fell to his knees as the heavens opened up. Saint howled like an animal gone mad. The air thickened as surges of power pulsed from within the circle. No weapon dreamed of by man contained the power emanating from this simple circle of stone. Soon, the convergence would leave the protective circle and burn this world to a crisp.

Looking above, Micah could not see the ceiling of the fortress. A swirling vortex of colors not of this world poured into the lower chambers. A portal? A great white light engulfed him. Shielding his eyes, he saw a figure floating into the center of the circle on great white wings. *"Gabriel? No. It's...Oh my God! Ashe."*

Ashe entered the circle in front of Christina. He had grown even larger and broader than before. His blue eyes pulsed with liquid fire. Adorning his back, completing him at last, was what had been taken from him long ago for his safety. The upswept mighty appendages were snowy white with tips of crimson denoting his heritage as the son of Michael. Ashe the Blessed. The final of three supreme gifts of the Father's love. As he moved towards Christina in that maelstrom, he smiled as he took the place that had been foretold in his dreams. As the bolts entered his chest, the energy connecting his pure heart and out of his back to the apex of his heritage, the elemental forming a perfect symmetry in the body of angelic and human.

As Micah watched, a circle glowed within the sacred ring as Christina held her hands out, she held the Earth in the palms of her hands. From them flowed the blood of the Seraphim and the Thousand Saints. To the source. The very human heart of a young woman with enough love for the whole world. An eternity rested in that place. Then all was as it was before. A young woman standing in the center of a stone circle, holding a parchment engraved with the symbol of the Protectors. Not quite as before. Standing beside her was the most beautiful thing Micah had ever beheld. Ashe Duncan had returned.

The Covenant of Ashe

"You have come to me before your time because of your love for your fellow man who raised you from childhood. You have repaid the debt in full for all that they have sacrificed for you. You will return to your world in your true form. You complete the circle of my promise of long ago. You will be the final Blessed One sent to the Son of Man. I promise you, from the love and courage of your heart, will come the Light. A

small shining light which will engulf the darkness and serve as a beacon to the Lost. In the way of things, this will be the last of days for man and the beginning of all that can be. Go, with all of my love."

The flowing blue eyes looked on with love at the return of their beloved. He was everything they had dreamed of and more. He had returned to his rightful home and a family of his own. Now it was almost their time. With mighty wings unfurled, Michael and Samantha waited with hands clasped, one unto another.

The time of rejoicing at Sanctuary was intense however short lived. The arrival of Ashe was one of celebration. Mara was beyond tears in her joy. She was also a little nervous when she saw him in all of his glory. She wondered that her darkened soul had not been burnt to a crisp in the presence of such beauty. She wondered if he had changed. Perhaps. But not in his love for her and their child. Tears of blue flowed down his face as he enfolded her in his massive arms. She shivered as she felt the great wings enfold her and her soul warmed at the love she felt curled in that protective cocoon. The celebration must end however; word had been received that Legion's forces had arrived. Legion himself would lead the battle to destroy their home. The Council of Seven had called for a full meeting. It was time. The hope of Sanctuary rested in the next few hours.

Christina stood before the Council and all that had gathered. Jack and Shannon were there along with Ashe and Mara. Standing with Theo was Rachel. Saint lay in his usual place beside the fireplace. Christina presented the scroll to the leader of the Council. As he opened the document, he spoke to the assembled.

"From our earliest times as advisers to this Order, we have known that this time would come. When the first Council was convened and given the power to dictate the policies and operations of the Protectors, it was done out of the love and desire to balance the power of this organization. A governing authority guiding the operations of the military style warrior priests was thought to be best for all concerned. Our wise forefathers knew that one day this would end. In their wisdom, they provided the means of this end but did not make it easy to obtain. Specific instructions were passed down for the accomplishment of this task. If those guidelines had not been met, it would have meant the destruction of those attempting it. This was to ensure the purity of the Order. No one man or woman could ever turn the organization into an instrument of his or her own agenda. The document I have in my hands my dear friends, is the sum of our predecessor's wisdom. They knew there would be a time when the Council must end. We believe that time is now. This is our Final Resolution.

The young communications specialist sat in his small room in the bowels of Sanctuary. A worldwide communications network was at his fingertips. Everything from high-speed microwave transmissions and satellite links to an old-fashioned telegraph network. The young man laughed to himself. The Order thought of everything. They probably had carrier pigeons hidden somewhere. His job was normally boring but satisfying. He coordinated the communication with all other Order enclaves. Since the time of Legion, the airwaves had been heating up. Coded transmissions back and forth from the outposts to Sanctuary. As he looked around, he noticed the safe. In it was one red folder with one sheet of paper. He had spent four years in the Air Force. He knew what it was that lay in there. Doomsday orders. A small shiver ran up his spine.

As the simple document was passed around the room, the men and women of the Council affixed their signatures, sealing their votes for the Final Resolution. As the leader of the Council, a man who had once been the president of a great nation, signed his name, it was done. As the silence descended, the thoughts of the gathered focused on the fact that for the first time since its inception, the Order had no leadership. This would change in the space of seconds. The leader nodded for the security personnel to open the door. As the massive oak doors swung inward, in walked the proud figure dressed in a white uniform of military cut complete with beret. On the left breast of the uniform and the crest of the beret was the symbol of Dominion. As they looked on, General Micah Sarentstein stood in all his glory.

The former leader spoke, "I introduce you all to the Commander of all Dominion Forces from this day forward. To ensure our survival, our resources will be under the direct leadership of a man who has devoted his life to combating the evil of the Enemy and protecting our home here at Sanctuary. General, the floor is yours."

Micah spoke, "My friends, we are surrounded by Enemy forces. Divisions of the unholy stand at our doorstep. They mean to wipe us off the face of this planet. I will not allow this to happen. We will implement that which we have prepared for over the long years of our heritage and all the sacrifices that have been made. The good men and women who disappeared from the face of the Earth, forgotten by history but not by us. Now, their efforts will be rewarded. In less than six hours, we will face our enemies. My vow before you and my God, is that victory will be ours."

As the machines of war surrounded the fortress, Legion relished his forthcoming victory. As he prepared to order his troops into the battle, he listened to the quiet words spoke into his ear by Silas. He nodded as his eyes blazed with crimson.

Colonel Jack Dalton, Chief of Operations, gathered his personal team together. Their assignment would be to protect the heart of Sanctuary. Christina and Mara would be there along with Rachel and Theo. They would be the last lines of defense if all else failed. As Jack left, he brushed Shannon's cheek with his lips wishing her luck and all his love.

In his small room, Aaron felt the strong hand of Micah on his shoulder. "It's time son." The safe was opened and the red folder removed. As Aaron felt the sweat trickle down the base of his neck, he entered the codes that would signal the end of the world. Throughout the great network, coded and digitized, sped the words: *The sparrow sings no more.*

It was the time for war. Blessed be the children.

The young warrior lay quietly, thinking of his home. His old home in a land faraway from this Sanctuary. He missed the warmth of the sun and the mild breezes that favored his island. He missed his family. All of them dead now, due to the vicious campaign by the Enemy. As he looked at the massive army before him, he uttered a small prayer. For his old family as well as his new one. He heard the whistle of the shell as it flew high over his head, striking the stone walls. The battle had begun.

In the frigid morning, the attack on the fortress was initiated with firepower that made the very earth shake. The defenders answered with automatic weapons fire and laser guided missiles backed up by mortar fire. Death walked among the battlefield as commanders shouted orders. Smoke filled the small valley while blood drenched the hillside.

General Frank Terrigan ordered Legion's forces to advance behind the tanks. He cursed as he looked at the overcast sky with snow starting to blow in. He would have really liked to have some air power backing him up but with the blizzard coming, he would do the job with tanks and troops. The tanks fired upon the ancient walls of the fortress. Walls, which were crumbling from the ferocious assault of the modern weapons.

Micah's troops had held the perimeter as planned. Now, as thousands of Enemy troops pushed forward behind the large battle tanks, Micah ordered his troops to withdraw. Though severely outnumbered, they had bought the time they needed. As they retreated through the gate of Sanctuary, Micah smiled as he looked at the titanium walls. Walls, which had been painstakingly added behind the old stone of the enclave over the years. They still held, even as the stone was smashed into the dust of centuries.

Mara lay on a pallet in the circle of stones surrounded by her friends and protectors. Christina and Rachel were there in attendance as well as Theo and Saint, who lay close by her side. The labor pains were beginning, seeming to keep rhythm with the pounding of the explosions above them.

Legion reeled in fury. "What do you mean the walls still stand? I want that cursed place leveled to the ground." General Terrigan stood in fear before the creature in the guise of a man. He shook as he related that his troops could do no more damage with the resources at hand. Unless they waited for the weather to clear when an aerial attack might be possible. The only other way would be for the troops to storm the fortress and look the enemy in the eye. Silas quietly whispered to Legion. As drool trickled from the corner of his mouth and his ruby red eyes glowed, his chuckle turned into the laughter of a beast gone mad. Legion looked at Terrigan and said, "Send the ground troops in. This day I shall feast on the hearts of my enemies."

Jack and Ashe spoke in the cavern housing the heart of Sanctuary. "It is time", Ashe said. "Move our people into the sacred ring and have them prepare the relic. I must go to prepare. Wait until all is as planned, even if you have to stare them in the eyes." Jack nodded his understanding. As Jack moved his people into place, he thought of Shannon.

The bullet tugged at a strand of her hair. Shannon ducked and rolled, bringing the Uzi up and letting a burst of the nine-millimeter rounds send her attacker into his bloody judgment. The man to her left cried out as he took a round to the shoulder, a fine mist of blood spraying the wall next to him. Shannon and her squad fought a hundred of Legion's troops at the very gate of Sanctuary. She quietly voiced the affirmation into her throat mike as the words from Micah sounded in her earpiece. Her team fell back as the hordes breached the sacred ground of her home. "Come on you bastards", she whispered, "It's a good day to die."

They waited for the signal that would soon come. Talking in hushed voices and silently saying their prayers for their comrades. They spoke of their love to their families and the hope for the future. The hope of their heritage as their fathers and mothers before them had spoken of. Over the long years they had waited. Soon, very soon the wait would be over. The careful plans and operations from the earliest of times would soon burst forth with the blooms of determination. A determination born of the ancient injunction of the Blessed Ones: "Protect"

Levi waited in the soft glow of the candlelight in the Hall of Valor. He felt his time was nearing. As the ancient dagger rested in its scabbard, he thought of its heritage. In a small village, so long ago. At the nexus of humanity's time…

The Book of Bethlehem

The cosmos whirled, billions of galaxies carefully choreographed in their eternal dance through the endless reaches of the universes in this dimension. Comets traveled their elliptical routes as the suns of millions of worlds rose and fell upon the faces of the beings upon them.

The eyes of the Creator looked from his home upon his children. He felt the love and sadness of each. He looked far into the depths of the teeming masses into a small corner where a galaxy, man would call the Milky Way, spun on its travels. Through the myriad stars and planets, which floated in the womb of space, His will reached toward a small sun that shone on the nothingness of a single planet rotating around it. A planet that once had enjoyed life and choices. A planet whose beings had succumbed to the quiet lure of complacency. A planet which had paid the ultimate price for its choice. The small sun burst with new energy. The energy of a million upon millions of hydrogen bombs. In the silence of space, the nova flared. The light would reach a small speck of dust rotating around its own sun. In thousands of years, according to the time of man's reckoning, this light would fall upon the world that man called Earth.

The three men sat around the small fire that gave them the much-needed warmth against the cold of the night. They thought of the task before them and made their preparations. Shiloh sharpened the blade of the dagger. The ancient weapon from a civilization that no longer existed. Rumored to have existed from the time of the birth of man, the blade honed from the very essence of creation that was a gift from the First Ones. Adam himself was said to have protected his family from agents of the Liar with this blessed dagger. As Caleb and Rabin prepared their own weapons, the men awaited the sign that had been foretold.

A short distance away in the small village, Mary lay against the straw as the labor pains began. Her husband and her friend Salia attended her. Mary closed her eyes as the pain washed over her. She whispered a small prayer. A prayer that was lifted to the heavens by the love of a single beautiful soul for the world that she lived in. A prayer for the soul that her frail human body would soon give birth to. The hope for the entire world she loved so much.

As he traveled through the night, his blue eyes shone with the wisdom of the ages. His time neared. He felt the weakness of his ancient body as he followed the currents. He could not do this alone; he was old and scarred from the many battles before. The future of the ones he had loved all of his life now depended on the humans. They, who in their lives had answered the call. A small whisper, which carried to the depths of their souls that, said, "Protect". Urial neared the glowing embers of the fire in the wilderness.

The molten eyes slivered the night. The beast moved through the silent streets. It smelled the fear of the pitiful beings shuttered in their frail homes quaking in their aloneness. Good, there was no hope. Only the loneliness and alienation of their lackluster lives that they so much deserved. Such was the legacy of his Father, then so be it for these puny things that took up the space of this world. Instead of the promise this night sought, only death and desolation would be found. The blood of the child would flow from the talons of the beast this night.

The Child dreamt. In the vast wasteland, a small glow lit the darkness calling him home. But a barrier was there. A barrier of blood. The blood of his mother lay spilled across his path. Had he not done this? All had been lost in the madness, fractured beyond repair. With tears burning like a billion flames, he turned away from the light until the flicker had been snuffed out. In his deepest slumber, the nightmares began.

Caleb the Oracle would write of the battle that night. A battle fought by a handful of human beings against the forces of nightmare. A nightmare which sought to snuff out the light of man.

Joseph's blood bubbled from his brow where the talon had slashed. Salia had plunged her dagger into the side of the beast. The roar of pain shook the rafters of the small building as Mary's final scream had escaped her throat and the cry of the baby could be heard. In the light of the star that shone above them, Urial descended. Shiloh and Rabin enjoined the battle. Blood spilled and stained the straw as man's future was decided.

The beast bled with hundreds of wounds to its body. Rabin lay dead. Joseph's right arm had been mangled and was useless. Still he fought to protect his wife and child. Once, the beast had been within striking distance of the child. As its talon fell, Salia placed her aged body in front of the child. It was her blood which stained the earth, not his. The beast again towered above the child and his mother. The baby boy opened his soft brown eyes and looked into the soul of the creature. A silent message was sent. Time stood still until the scream of the damned shattered the night as Shiloh plunged the blessed dagger into the heart of the beast.

Urial lay near Mary, dying from his wounds. As he looked into the eyes of the smiling child, he felt complete. From the beginning to the end, he looked upon the Alpha and Omega. He was tired. He could go home now. With the last of his strength, he stood and with his love blessing those he left behind, he rose towards the sky. The glow enveloped him as higher he went towards the brightly glowing star in the blanket of the night. Brighter and brighter until he merged with the light sent from his Father. The light of his home, so close now…

As they sat gathered around mother and child, a soft blue light shone in the darkness. The voice spoke to them. "Unto you a child is born. My love made flesh. You have done well, my beloved. This special child will become a man. A man, like you, who will know of the strength and weakness of your kind. If his faith is true and his choices are right, he will show you the path to your destiny and salvation. Do not despair, in your darkest days I will send another Blessed One to you. Stand fast and be watchful for the day. My love will always be with you."

The wind howled outside but inside it was warm as they looked upon the child. Soon, they would take him and his family to Sanctuary until his time would come. But for now, they were content to rest and enjoy this night of celebration.

O Holy Night.

The whirlwind blew the dust and crimson laden snow about. Smoke filled the battlements of the once mighty fortress. Bodies lay strewn like tiny limbs after the storm. Among both sides, it was a day of gluttony for the thing called death.

The labor pains intensified. Mara's brow filled with sweat as the birth neared. In the midst of death would be life. At least for a short time. Saint moved closer still to the woman as Christina waited and prayed.

Shannon's team was pinned down near the right side of the wall. Withering fire from the Enemy had stalled their movements to safety. She radioed in telling Micah they could move no further. They would make their stand there. "Micah, tell Jack I love him. I love you all."

Micah nodded silently as his headset went silent. He entered the communications room as the remnant of his troops fought the final skirmishes up top. The Enemy had made it to the entrance of the antechamber at the heart of Sanctuary. Only Jack Dalton's team stood between them and their final hope. Micah bowed his head. Had his plans been sound? Or was it just the dreams of a madman? Micah squeezed Aaron's shoulder as he leaned over and pressed the red button. That which had not been summoned in the history of man. The words went out as a whisper amplified to the sounds of a final trumpet. *"Let the earth bring forth each and everyone."*

Silas sat back at the rear of the battle lines and watched the carnage. If one could look past the unassuming exterior, you could perhaps just glimpse the slight crimson light that danced in his eyes. The flicker of hell in the eyes of a librarian.

Silas wondered when Legion had gone truly mad? Perhaps it had been the failed assassination attempt by the renegade priests. Technically, it had not failed. The bullet had shattered Legion's skull, penetrating his brain. It would have killed a mere mortal. Luckily, he had healed rapidly. Legion had never quite been the same afterwards. That was when he started peeling back the layers of the skin of humanity that he wore and Legion's true self was revealed. It was then that Silas had been summoned to make sure his Father's plans did not go awry. Silas thought of the priests, they were insignificant. They had all died appropriately horrible deaths. The last martyrs of the Throne of Peter. What bothered him was the signal that had been sent by one of them before he died. A signal which had been traced to this place. This cursed ground called Sanctuary.

Mara screamed and the child burst forth from her loins. A boy child with dark hair and liquid blue eyes that flashed with crimson sparkles, like lightning upon the face of the ocean. Tears poured from Christina's eyes as she held the tiny hope of the world in her arms. Saint moved to the child and held his massive snout next to the child's face, feeling the tiny breath on his fur.

The explosion sounded as Enemy forces breached the doors to the chamber. Jack racked his shotgun as he faced the inhuman creatures before him. The Beast called Legion snarled as the death began.

Jack's team circled the ring of stones and fought the Enemy for every inch of the room. As blood poured from the unholy and man alike, the very air charged with electricity. Micah shouldered his way through the bloodshed as the young man Levi leapt through the broken door with dagger drawn. He moved towards the blessed circle with fury in his eyes.

Mara's eyes stared at the ceiling above the circle. A ceiling that no longer existed. Instead a swirling vortex of colors churned above her. As she held her child to her breast, the light above moved towards her. Three stars moved in unison, towards the small circle of humanity.

The earth rumbled, the low pitch sound carrying throughout the desecrated countryside. Silas rose with a start. Why did the sound send fear into his dark soul? His thoughts raced to identify the sounds. In the back of his mind, random thoughts fired of the lost civilizations of history. The statistics of missing persons over the many years. People, who just simply vanished from the face of the earth. Single people, families and even whole villages had vanished in mystery without a trace. Ancient racial memories of man that spoke of whole civilizations that had disappeared, never to be seen again. Where had they gone? No one had ever found the answer. Lost in the realm of fantasy and far-fetched theories of vortexes and alien abduction, never to be thought of again.

Silas remembered a news show he had seen once about the underground cities that had been prepared by the Swiss government in case of nuclear war. As Silas paled, he wondered with horror if that had been the real reason after all? "Oh no", he muttered to himself, "How many were there?" Acting on animal instinct, Silas fled the battlefield as the very earth erupted.

The great tunnels opened in the countryside. Around the world, the warm nurturing earth uplifted as its children began their ascent. The men and women stood proudly as their battle tanks and vehicle upon vehicle poured from the hidden recesses. The well planned wisdom of the ancient protectors had culminated in the mighty army, which stood ready surrounding Legion's forces on the hillside as their brothers and sisters stood ready all over the world. As the clouds cleared, the bright sun broke through glinting off the dazzling white uniforms of the ones who had sacrificed so much before. The generations that had waited and learned while they prepared for the final battle which would begin this day. The sons and daughters of those who had gone before. The Army of Dominion.

The tide of battle had turned inside the compound. Shannon's team had linked with others and even now pushed the Enemy forces back into the reinforced walls of the fortress that would not give. Now, a mighty army surrounded Sanctuary. There would be no escape for the evil trapped inside.

Inside the antechamber, the Beast closed for the child. Jack and his team fought hand to hand with the spawn from a nightmare. Dagger versus talon, human will against the evil that surrounded them. Screams sounded as the blood flowed. Legion had almost made it to the circle. His human façade had fallen completely. What stood before them now was pure evil in the form of the Beast. Its foul odor burned like sulfur. Its seven heads had the fangs of snakes and its seven tails were that of a scorpion. In its molten red eyes were reflected the abyss of madness.

As it towered above the circle, Saint growled and positioned his noble body between the evil and the child. Micah leapt on the back of the Beast, emptying his Browning into one of the heads. He then unsheathed the dagger that once belonged to a sainted monk, and plunged it into the Beast. The scream of the Beast echoed in the walls of Sanctuary.

As Mara watched the stars descend the ground beneath her rippled and became transparent. From the depths of the heart of this sacred ground rose the simple relic. A relic etched in the forgotten script of the Seraphim. A relic that man had whispered of in awe down through the ages. That which he had called the Ark of the Covenant. It glowed with the essence of the Creator. A glow which had not been seen for thousands of years.

As the stars hovered above the Ark, Mara and Christina saw the outlines of the beings inside the light above. Mighty winged beings with burning blue eyes. The Blessed Three had returned. They smiled down upon their beloved ones as they took their place in the holy triad. Urial to the west, Gabriel to the east. At the apex, floated Ashe in all his glory with great crimson tipped wings unfurled. Their great voices sounded as one and the Ark pulsed. A mighty rumbling which permeated the very molecules of the air as the power of the Creator gathered in that small place. Christina bowed her head in the presence of her Father's unblinking eyes.

Micah was whipped to the side towards one of the creature's tails. He reacted and pulled his head back but not soon enough. The great stinger pierced his eye. As he hung limp, the creature threw him into the great well at the center of the chamber. Legion had been severely wounded by Micah's attack but he was still deadly and his putrid breath could be felt upon the face of the helpless child.

Levi had silently climbed across the rafters above the Beast. With a small prayer in honor of his father, Levi leapt to the back of the Beast. In his right hand, he held the sacred dagger. Now, the thing once known as Legion would pay. Legion howled with fear as the young man rode his back. Legion knew the whelp. His madness-fevered brain recognized the boy, who was now a man, from his days in Washington. Legion had known the boy as Joshua. Joshua Beck. Legion had feared his father, Peter above all other humans. Legion had been the instrument of death for Peter Beck after he had Beck's wife killed. The boy Joshua had vanished and been presumed killed by the plague. Joshua Levi Beck rode the Beast with all his might, slashing the seven vile throats with the holy blade. Every battle he had studied, every preparation he had made in his long exile was used to slay that which screamed in fear before his wrath. As the dagger plunged into the heart of Legion, the billion screams of the lost whispered to a death rattle as the obscenity lay in the stillness of its final death. As Joshua lay there, badly wounded by the talons, the light of the Ark burst upward.

The light of creation broke forth with the brightness of infinity. As it pulsed towards the glowing figures forming the trinity, it reflected forth and out through the halls of the ancient building and upward onto the blood stained grounds where Legion's forces were trapped between it and the strong walls of the fortress.

The damned screamed as the blue light washed over them. The screams of hopelessness. Where the beam found no love or compassion, it burned to a crisp the hollow shells of what once was. As the mighty Army of Dominion knelt feeling the love of the Father wash over them, the unholy felt the fires of hell unleashed on earth. As the twilight approached, there was silence.

The Ark dimmed and lowered back into the reaches from whence it had come. The three Blessed Ones merged into one and tears fell from Mara's face as the star ascended into the night sky. Fading, never to be seen again. A whisper in the depths of her soul, she heard her beloved Ashe say, "Forever my love."

As Theo helped Rachel over to her brother, he wept for his old friend Micah. It would not be the same without him. As Shannon ran into the arms of Jack, Christina softly stroked Mara's cheek brushing the tears away. As Saint lay curled next to her, she looked into the unusual eyes of her son and smiled tenderly, thinking of the future. *"My beloved Jarred."*

Epilogue

The Book of Many

I finish this document with a blessing of tears. Tears for the many that sacrificed everything so that we could survive. Tears for our loved ones. We all will miss them and they will be remembered, this I promise. Tears of happiness blend with those of sorrow. Happiness for Mara and her son. He is very special, this Jarred. I haven't figured it all out yet but I see the way Saint looks at him and how close he stays to the child. I'm happy that Rachel and Joshua are back together again. Already they are becoming leaders in our new army. Happiness for Jack and Shannon who married just this day in a quiet ceremony in Victory Chapel.

I am old, so sometimes my fears surface. I know that the thing called Silas has escaped. I fear that he will be a stronger adversary that we could imagine. Even now, Christina meets with her advisors and plans for the future. War has come. We have won the first battle but there will be many more to follow. I will say my prayers now, for outside of these hallowed halls, the wind whispers of death to come. May Sanctuary abide.

The Evil One summons the forces of its Father as the Gates of the Lost are thrown open, unleashing the sum of nightmares upon man. The sun darkens as the moon bleeds. Hell has been loosed on humanity who huddles in the still darkness of a small planet it calls home.

In the vast darkness, a small gem shines with the light for the future. A small home in the midst of a sea of ebony that will nurture he who will ignite eternity. A beacon of hope for those who seek its shelter. A place known as Sanctuary.

Book Four
Blessed Be The Children

The soft light shone as he inhaled the honeysuckle smell of his mother, kissing her cheek. His laughter rang as chimes turning in the wind as he ran to his brother. He slowed as he saw him sitting in silence. He had heard the words of anger between his brother and father. The broad shoulders were hunched as if in deep thought. The lines of worry etched into the beautiful face. "What is wrong?" he asked. That soft knowing smile that he knew so well was his reply. As his brother ruffled his hair, he said, "Nothing to worry you, my beloved." As he played, he watched the others. He listened to their talk as it floated on the warm winds. Talk of war to come.

A dream of falling into the precious darkness. The blood still flowed to the source of all that was. His heart beat in time with the thundering power unleashed far above him. A shaft of blue light touched his broken body. He felt the bones, which had been shattered. Left arm and right leg. At least four broken ribs. The blood dripped down his face. He floated in the warmth and listened to the voice. *"It is not your time, my son. Those that you love need you. I need you. It is your choice. I welcome you home if that is your wish but the children need you. You will bring the children together. Only you can end the nightmare that has come."*

His body felt leaden. As he opened his eye, the fire of pain engulfed his soul. He longed for the warmth and the love of the voice of his dreams. As he focused, his thoughts became one. Protect the child. With that mantra, he reached his good hand forward. To the wall and upward, every movement of the scraping bones feeling like the strike of daggers into his body. Each inch of the twenty feet was an eternity. Each breath stronger than the next. The pain fed his determination. Stone by stone fell away and as he reached the top and over, he passed out from the pain. The soft breath on his cheek awakened him as the tongue licked the tears from his face. He reached with his good hand and felt the warm fur as soft brown eyes gazed into his. As if from the womb of the earth itself, the rebirth was announced as Saint let out a triumphant howl. General Micah Sarentstein smiled.

The War Years

Mara sat alone in the library with the firelight dancing on the walls. She missed Ashe. Seven long years since he had left. Seven years of war. The quiet was a welcome peace. Tomorrow morning would begin the final battle. She thought of her loved ones and knew they were preparing. She held the soft leather volume in her lap. The chronicles of Theo, the last of the Oracles. A chronicle of the war years. Soon the chronicles would end. She sat by the warming fire and read of the past.

"The war years are upon us. We won the first battle with the creature called Legion. Now we are engaged with his legacy for the very survival of humanity. As the last, I will chronicle the next years the best my old hand can. Never shall we forget the bravery of those that have gone before nor the children who will inherit the results of our labors now. May the Father bless us and keep us. Yea, though we walk through the valley of death....".

"The return of Micah was a miracle unto itself. His homecoming was that of joy. How he endured the climb from the well with his injuries, we will never know. Legends are born in this manner as they now are throughout our Army. The young ones bathe in the glow of leadership that Micah exudes. His recovery took a while and the patch over his left eye reminds us of that which he sacrificed but our army is strong. Jack and Shannon lead their divisions as well as Joshua and Rachel. Christina has become quite the strategist along with the Council. Mara has provided excellent intelligence on the Enemy. These battles will not be easy. The world churns in the darkness of the Beast's evil, but we will prevail. We look into the eyes of our children and know that we must."

Private David Stichcomb stood at attention as Colonel Jack Dalton and General Micah Sarentstein walked past his company. A new arrival, David had just graduated from basic training and ranger school. He had arrived at the Sanctuary base unit just four days ago. He was proud to be with the home guard protecting the heart of his world. David's parents were just as proud of him. They worked for the medical corps. Because of his father's compassion and work, he had found a home with the Dominion forces. David thought back to that late night, when a stranger had arrived at their house. He told of the war that had come and said that David's father was in extreme danger due to his breakthrough research on the plague known as the Maryland curse. The protector had spirited them away in the middle of the night. A dangerous run down the East Coast and a boat to Bermuda base. Later, after completing training at Idaho base, the family was brought to Switzerland just before the great battle of Sanctuary. David was combat trained and cross-trained as a medic ending up assigned to a readiness group designed for rapid deployment from Colonel Dalton's division. David's chest swelled as he saw his hero's walk by and quietly thanked the protector who had risked his life for a family he did not know.

Micah stopped and spoke words of encouragement to the young men and women. Those who had survived the rampage of the beast. He honored their dedication and bravery. These children whose beautiful souls surrounded his essence. These children who would face the horrors of war and hell on earth with valor. The precious heartbeats of those that would give their lives for what they believed in and so that others might enjoy those freedoms. As he ended the tour, Micah looked upon the faces of those that he loved so much with a tear in his good eye. Blessed be the children, for they shall know war.

The child dreamt. The light was darkening. Rumbles of war surrounded him and he was afraid. His brother spoke in whispers to his mother and father. "They will not succeed. The choice has been made and we will protect that which is ours." The mighty sword in his hand, his brother left to lead the battle. For home.

Year One was that of desecration. The Enemy had enslaved the people at large. The men and boys were inducted into military service. The women and girls were forced into labor camps and war factories. Governments fell apart. Without the implant, no one was entitled to food or medical care. The world became a refugee camp. Reports from field units stated that unusual beasts and hybrid creatures roamed in the cities and countryside. They terrorized and killed the citizens except for those in the highest circles of power. Intelligence reports verified the existence of the abominations. Every horror of imagination from vampires and werewolves to insect type creatures the size of a man stalked the humans. Pitched battles with these creatures and the Dominion forces revealed that they could be killed. Some with ordinary weaponry, most with holy relics. The Maryland curse had killed easily a third of the world's population but new plagues and diseases cropped up here and there keeping the Dominion medical experts hard at work for vaccines and counter measures.

War is chaos and Death feeds upon the destruction. Silas was death. He sat in his tower and slaked his thirst on the rape of the earth. These beings were not worthy of drawing a breath, but even he had to give them hope. With promises of power and wealth, he held his empire together. With the mark of his Father, their souls rotted as they fought the agents of Dominion. He had summoned forth the legions of the damned from the very gates of hell. All manner of beast stalked the earth in search of prey. Every nightmare and mythological beast of man's imagination now existed in this plain of reality. Silas laughed, thinking that man was his own worst enemy. The nightmares that man could dream were worse than he could have summoned. Demons roamed the earth and every last one of them came from the minds of these insects that called themselves man.

Micah briefed the Council in the war room deep in Sanctuary. A worldwide map glowed on the massive screen backlit in green and red. "Our forces are in green, the Enemy in red. We have seven divisions whereas the Enemy has approximately twenty organized divisions. However, even though they are larger in force, many of their soldiers have been drafted and retaining loyalty is a problem. They fight mainly from hunger and fear. We have most of our bases intact and well concealed. Our intelligence has infiltrated many of the Enemy's units and establishments. We are sitting pretty well supply wise and know most of the whereabouts of the Enemy's stockpiles. Fuel, food and ammunition will be the priorities. After my discussion with the Council and Christina, I have developed our battle plan." Micah drank from the cup of dark coffee sat before him and continued, "We cannot, for the most part, win with direct confrontation of conventional forces. The Enemy controls most of the world government's assets. Our strength will be in guerrilla actions striking at the nerve centers of the Enemy operation.

We will take four of our divisions and break them down into small strike units, which will be targeted by incoming intelligence. The other three divisions will conduct limited conventional warfare on selected targets. Luckily, there should be limited if any nuclear exchanges. My congratulations to Captain Jay Johnson and his team. Over the last few years, his intelligence team infiltrated most of the world's nuclear sites and quietly rendered them incapable of use. In our intelligence estimate, it would take several years to place them back into operation. A few tactical weapons may still be armed but so far they have not been used. We have our bio-med teams working around the clock in case of chemical or biological warfare. Even the Enemy realizes that this is a two edged sword. Should something like that be loosed on the world, their own troops may not survive. In closing, there are only two major factors that we don't have the answer to. First, what I call the chaos factor. The creatures that now exist, hunt without remorse or restraint. We know that they can be killed but they seem to just be predators with no predictable patterns. We need to find out where they are coming from and hunt them down to extinction. That will be one of Colonel Dalton's primary missions. Second, we don't know where Silas has gone to ground at. Captain Johnson's intelligence unit is working full time on that. We need to find his lair and destroy him. We do believe he is basing most of the major activity out of North America, so that is where we will start. Colonel's Rachel and Joshua Beck will cover the North and South American operations, with Colonel

Shannon Gzar taking the European area. The other divisions will send strike units to Africa, Australia and the Middle East. Colonel Dalton's Rapid Deployment Division will trouble shoot any hot areas identified by intelligence and creature hunt. Any questions?"

A few minor operational issues were discussed and the meeting broke up. Micah met Mara in the hallway, accompanied as usual by Saint. "How's Jarred doing?" Micah asked. Mara's smile lit up the hallway; "He's fine. He is with one of Christina's aides, playing. He has grown so much. I think he's going to be the size of his father." Micah grinned and said, "Well, I want to see my godchild before I have to go back to the field."

Jack and Shannon sat savoring a cup of coffee and a cigarette after checking on their troops. Jack was gently teasing her about keeping her maiden name when they married after all the pestering she had done to get that wedding ring on. "Well, she said, "I figured one Dalton getting into trouble was enough. I don't want to take the blame by mistake when Micah kicks your butt for playing cowboy." Jack laughed softly, saying that he had calmed down quite a bit. "Yeah and I'm still a virgin", laughed Shannon. The talk turned to more serious tones as they discussed the readiness of their troops and missions. Jack said, "They all look so young and they're just itching for a fight. Sometimes I feel like I'm a hundred years old." She softly touched his short-cropped hair that glinted silver. "They will be fine. They are well trained and think the world of you. You know they are calling themselves "Dalton's Daggers". He smiled at that, then looked into Shannon's dark eyes with that Jack twinkle. "How about you and me go snuggle before we go kick ass tomorrow?" Shannon smiled back, "Well soldier, that's about the best offer I've had all day." The strolled off hand in hand. A fire of warmth against the cold called Death.

As Mara stroked the forehead of her son, she gazed into his blue eyes with flashes of crimson. Her love swelled and tears fell as she looked to the heavens and thought of the proud eyes of Ashe looking upon her. As her soft lips touched his tiny cheek, she felt his breath against hers. Her heart glowed as the blue light bathed her and her child.

Joshua and Rachel finished their dinner and spoke for a short while of their mother and father, especially how much they missed them. They then finalized their deployment plans with their commanders and went their separate ways. Joshua walked to the Hall of Valor and watched as Theo gently placed the statue of Ashe Duncan in its alcove. The mighty wings unfurled holding the tiny figure of a child in his strong arms. As tears washed down his aging face, Theo wrote the last of words in the book before the statue.

"Our beloved One who was sent to us in our time of need. The compassion of that child which saved our world with those who had forgotten the blessings of their children. Know that you will be remembered and loved by those lives that were touched by you and honored by your son who will bring light unto the darkness."

The liquid blue eyes flashed with flames as the armies met. Great wings unfurled as the battle ensued. The lines of demarcation had been drawn and now the blood of the First ran in the streets of Home. The Father wept at the sight of his children. His anger swelled as he watched the carnage. In a rage, he massed his energy to dispense his justice over them all. The soft voice of Mother whispered in his ear, "Be still my beloved. Our most sacred love is choice. We cannot take that away." His hands stilled at the truth, as the blue tears fell in sorrow for the fate of his children.

The young man and woman slipped through the alleys of the city. It was after midnight and to be caught without the implant would mean certain death. They had heard of a safe haven ran by agents of Dominion and were trying to make it there. They shivered in a small alcove as the footsteps of the soldiers faded into the misting rain. James and Darien breathed a sigh of relief. A little more than a mile to go and only six hours of darkness left. The brother and sister resumed their quiet trek through the back ways of the almost deserted city. Their clothes were torn and still stained with the blood of their parents who had been slain by the Enemy. Their parents had led a small resistance group of twenty on the south side of the city of Jacksonville, Florida. They provided intelligence and struck at Enemy targets through coordination with a member of Dominion intelligence. As the group had met the day before, something went terribly wrong. They had been compromised. Fifty Enemy agents had raided the basement of the building in the abandoned industrial area. Darien closed her eyes against the warm tears as she remembered the massacre. No mercy was shown as the men and women were slaughtered. James and Darien had been near by the hidden exit sliding through the trapdoor as the carnage continued above. Pure hate surged through James' heart as he thought of the good people that were lost to these animals that called themselves men.

As they turned the corner, the sound of a bottle gently rolling froze them. In the silence, the bottle came to a stop next to the foot of James. As Darien's eyes pierced the shadows, a darker shadow emerged from the alley. The silent scream echoed in her mind as her vocal cords locked down. It was not human.

The creature approached. For James, time had slowed and he could make out every detail of the abomination before him. Scale lined skin glowed dully in the ambient light. The misshapen head on the seven-foot plus body had the jaws of a beetle. They made soft ticking sounds as they opened and closed, seemingly in anticipation. The vicious claws of the hand and feet were at least a foot long. A barbed tale with a scorpion type stinger completed the nightmare before them. James looked around for any type of weapon. All that presented itself was the bottle at his feet. He grabbed it, breaking it on the pavement resulting in a jagged edge. With one hand, he moved Darien behind him and braced for the attack.

The shadows came alive around them and as Darien said her final prayer, they exploded into motion. Five red laser dots appeared on the creature and whispers of silent death erupted from the weapons. The creature staggered as automatic weapons fire struck its torso and head. Pus colored blood ran in rivulets as it twisted from the onslaught. The scream sounded like nothing James had ever heard before. A high pitched howl sounding like thousands of angry hornets buzzing. The five black clad figures closed in as the beast slumped to its knees. A flash of silver and the beetle head separated from the body. James and Darien stood in shock. The whole encounter had lasted less than fifteen seconds. A tall figure approached, removing the black facemask. The smiling eyes of Colonel Jack Dalton met theirs as he sheathed the long silver dagger while slinging the silenced H&K MP5 machine gun over his shoulders and walked towards them. "Wh—Who are you?" James managed to gasp. Jack smiled and glanced over his shoulder, "Just think of us as the friendly local bug exterminators." Darien leaned into James as the team led them past the monster and on to safety. She had not said a word, just stared at Jack and the creature. James chuckled at her whisper, "I'm damned glad I'm not a bug." James nodded, "Amen to that sister, amen."

Silas sat in the situation room of the White House in New Washington. He thought it was much prettier here than Old Washington had been about fifty miles south. Too bad that stupid terrorist had not managed to wipe out the whole city years ago. But for a backward camel jockey, he had not done too badly with the dirty suitcase bomb. Oh well, I wonder if the stupid bastard had wondered why the man who had sold him the weapon always wore sunglasses. Probably not, just as he did not know he was already dying from radiation exposure when the irritating American's hunted him down and killed him. As he read the reports before him, he decided these same types of annoying people were starting to piss him off.

The smoke hugged the ground of the battlefield. The acrid smell of cordite curled around Corporal David Stichcomb's head. He slipped down the muddy bank of the stream and made his way toward the tree towering over the bank. As he crawled through the snarled branches, he could make out the silhouette of the sniper that was pinning his squad down. The soldier wore the uniform of the New World forces. The uniform of the enemy. David estimated he was about ten feet away. He quietly raised his rifle and sighted down the barrel at a point just above the neck of the sniper. He let out a slow, silent breath as he squeezed the trigger. The bullet struck the soldier right at the junction of his neck and head, blowing bits of blood and bone upward. The silence was complete as the stream gurgled just as the blood did from the Enemy.

How many?, thought David. How many men had he killed? He pondered this through tired, combat weary eyes as his squad circled around him. The nineteen-year-old shrugged off the invisible weight and they began their patrol, looking for the next target.

Saint lay next to Jarred on the pallet. The child looked into the great brown eyes as his flashed crimson and blue. A small hand reached out to tug on the soft fur and a giggle floated in the air. As the great beast licked the face of the child, the soft voice could be heard, in his head only. *"Protect the child."*

War is blood. Whether it is deep crimson or shades of blue beyond human understanding. Home was torn asunder. As they fought one another, the brothers and sisters of each became the enemy. Mighty trumpets sounded the battle cry. The legions met and wielded their weapons. Territory was lost, then gained. Dimensions exploded and stars went nova. The Prince of Light screamed at his brother as the battle was enjoined. Hell was born, not in some deep subterranean chamber but in a place of light called Home. The Father wept as he held his beloved to his mighty chest.

Year Two of the war was that of horror. I had never imagined the evil that man could do to one another. As the world burned, they massacred each other in the streets and fields. With every weapon at their disposal, be it rocket or rock, they killed one another while Death slaked its thirst of the blood of the slain. My old eyes have seen much. Too much. I just want to go home. I've lived way beyond my years. Yet, I must continue to chronicle the death of our world. Christina comforts me with words of hope but they help little. The blood continues to flow and the flames consume this tiny planet we call home. I look up at the darkened sky and look for a sign. Any sign of hope. I am answered by the great silence.

We lost most of the Middle East region. There were a few nukes left and Silas made sure they detonated. Millions of screams were cut short in that second that the artificial suns rose from the earth. The air and water, a full third of it, went bad from the radiation fall out. Thousands more died as the sickness ate them from the inside out. Thankfully, most of our forces had been warned and had pulled out of the area. The dead zone would be hot for a thousand years. The tidal waves and earthquakes began as the earth slowly wobbled on its axis. The sick met death with wonderment in their eyes. They had never seen snow in the desert before.

As London burned, Shannon Gzar pulled her division in close. They had to make it around the city and they were fighting the Enemy for every inch of ground. She had spoken to Jack by satellite this morning and there was something he wanted her to check out for him. Sure Jack, she thought, no problem. Just let me figure out how to get these few thousand bastards and creatures out of my way. She shook her head and smiled as she gathered her commanders around her. "The things we do for love."

The decimated head separated quite messily from the body as the twelve gauge pellets shredded it. Colonel Jack Dalton racked another round in his combat shotgun. His unit had the farm outside of Denver surrounded. Howls split the air as the gunfire continued. Nothing human could make that sound. What Jack fought could not be considered human by any standards. He turned to his right as he heard the blast and saw three wolf creatures shredded by the claymore mine. Vampire and werewolf together. Who would have thought? These creatures did not go by the rules of the movies. "Damn good thing", Jack thought, he didn't think he could get that many stakes and silver bullets together. His forward scouts had found a nest of about thirty in the abandoned farmhouse. Jack watched as his team moved in for the clean up. There were only five of the creatures left. He walked over to the two young men he had lost in the battle and quietly read their names from the silver tags around their necks. He swore by his God, that he would remember them. Every last single one that had died under his command. Their memories would fuel his hatred for the foul beasts from hell until he found where they came from.

Rachel Beck fired the forty-five automatic again and again. The large grain bullets found their mark as the man's chest burst like a ripe tomato. Her left arm useless, she crawled back behind the rock looking into the small valley. For now they had the high ground. She had lost over fifty good men and women. A rifle round had shattered her left shoulder. No pain yet, just numbness. The army below had them pinned between valley and mountain. Mortars rocked their deadly lullaby as they flew from behind Rachel into the valley below. Bits of rock and body parts answered the deadly orchestra of Rachel's troops. She smiled as the Enemy below learned a hard, hard lesson. Watch your back. With Rachel's forces cornered, they had made two mistakes. They did not know her ability and they forgot she had a brother who was at their backs this instant. The sweet smell of victory turned into that of the putrid stink of death as the screams began and the true fires of hell waited.

Silas slithered to his corner and screamed in rage. The generals paled as the molten eyes glowed even brighter in its hate. Things were not going to plan. Not enough had died. He had fed on the fear and death and still it was not enough. He slammed the maps and papers from his desk. More plague. More nuclear weapons. That was what he needed. He didn't want thousands killed. He needed millions. Didn't these stupid sheep in front of him know that? His Father would not be happy until these insects were wiped from the face of what was left of this planet. Well, it was just going to have to get a little more right, that's all. As he looked at his weakest general, a smile grew. A smile wrapped around fangs with the burning acid of his home dripping from the sharp points. Maybe he would have to make an example. Yes, that was it. Lead by example. As he closed upon the face of the general, his chuckle was lost in the screams. The others fled as they heard Silas sigh, "Mmmm, crunchy, just like the cereal."

Micah and I spoke many times that year. We had destroyed almost two entire divisions of the Beast. I saw the confidence of Micah when he planned with Christina and as they discussed plans with their advisors, the former Council. I saw him stand firm in front of the young faces which stood proudly at his side. I saw the strength and tenderness he showed Mara and Jarred when they needed him most. I walked with my friend when he brought hope to those in the underground complex monitoring the world events. I listened with my old ears when everyone praised the bravery and fortitude of Micah. I became enthralled as everyone else and I envied him for being so strong.

I sat unnoticed in the shadows of the chapel, deep in the shadows of my own thoughts and memories. As I looked up from my introspection, I saw him sitting by himself near the candles, which burnt throwing a soft orange glow on his mighty face. As I watched my friend, I saw those big square shoulders slouch as if the world rested on them. As he ran a trembling hand through his hair, I saw tear drops falling from the good eye. In the silence of that place, the tears beat upon the polished floor. A heartbeat for every one, young and old, that had been lost. I left him in peace with tears in my own eyes. No, my friends, I do not envy Micah anymore.

As the beasts roamed the countryside and mankind fought their terrible battles, the First Beloved watched and waited with hope in their fiery eyes. The survival of all their dreams was vested in that small pocket of humanity resting on the tiny piece of rock floating in the vastness. Soon, the waiting would be over.

The child hid in the farthest reaches of his home as the symphony of battle sounded. The sound of swords singing and blood pounding out of the torn bodies to the beat of their hearts until the beat was heard no more. The screams of rage and pain blending into a serenade of nightmare. What is more terrible? The sounds of screams or that deep silence of the final death? Oblivion waits as tears from a child fall through the secrets of worlds unknown.

Year three, we lost our beloved. God, the tears burn. I feel the darkness falling around me more and more. I look into her eyes and I don't know what to say. I know he has gone forward to a better place, but that does not seem adequate. I look into those eyes and see the fury and sorrow. It echoes through my soul. I remember that look. I remember those feelings so long ago as I watched the life drain from my Rose sitting in the bloodstained seat of my Buick in a Publix parking lot on the south side of Atlanta. There is no comfort. There is no reason. There is only hope. The hope that she is stronger than I was. Despair and a bottle was my refuge. I felt helpless and alone. I look into her eyes and see the loneliness. He was her only one. I also see the vengeance blistering there, held by a tiny thread of sanity. Even Micah cannot talk to her, though of us all, he understands the best. She will have no mercy on every last one of them. I cannot. I guess it is up to God if he wants to. As she walks into the darkness, I am afraid. I know that the fury of Rachel Beck will be a terrible thing.

It happened three days ago outside of Dallas. Captain Johnson's intelligence unit had identified an encampment of the Enemy. The word was that Silas' Chief of Staff; a former senator named Franklin Covington was visiting the site. Joshua and Rachel met about twenty miles from the fortified complex. The brother and sister sat down to plan their attack.

Rachel thought of Joshua, as he looked that day. His sunbleached hair was almost golden with the deep tan from the Texas sun complimenting it. His division had just come in from Idaho where they managed to wipe out about a half of a division of the enemy troops.

He told her of the battle in a small Texas border town with creatures who were the size of a grizzly bear and looked like a cross between a dog and lizard. Regular bullets worked on them but if you got too close they spit acid venom which could kill in just seconds. Joshua's unit had found twenty in the town. The only human survivor died shortly after describing the massacre of the town's population by the beasts in their quest for human flesh, which was their main diet. There had been seventy-five men; women and children before the hellish creatures had overrun the town. Within twenty-four hours, there were none. As the flamethrowers burned their damned bodies, Joshua wondered what else waited for him in the gathering darkness.

Rachel was tired. It had been a long haul up from the Gulf of Mexico. They had found the enemy in pockets, hidden in the towns and countryside. The battles were quick and furious. There were no prisoners taken. The Enemy retreated until no options were left, then they killed themselves at the urgings of their leaders. Most of the leaders wore sunglasses, which hid their true eyes. They laughed as death surrounded them and grew stronger from the fear as the true vision of their reward reflected in the dying eyes of their troops. They were only fodder to feed the Master of their world.

The fort was large but the Enemy seemed lazy and secure. Their guards mainly ate or smoked at the main gate. Not a lot of traffic was seen coming and going. No perimeter patrols were observed. According to intelligence, there were about five hundred soldiers guarding the post along with the former senator. Rachel and Joshua decided that a conventional attack should work since they had two thousand soldiers plus their scout unit. After the commanders were dismissed, they met with the Scout team leader and made a couple of last minute modifications to the plan. Thus, Operation Hollow Throne was born. Rachel and Joshua enjoyed that time that only a brother and sister could enjoy, with quiet laughter over a cup of coffee. Both were at the point of exhaustion and retired early. Everyone was tired. The sentry did not notice the commander as she slipped into the small stand of pine, deeper into the waiting darkness.

The dawn was breaking, glinting silver from the approaching truck. The guard was tired, being at the end of his overnight shift. His eyes were bloodshot not only from the long stretch of duty but from the cheap vodka in his system. He was already getting a blinding headache and was counting the minutes until he could lie down on his bunk. As he looked into the truck, he noticed the cute blonde driver. Now, why couldn't they station someone like her with him on guard duty? She looked a lot more tasteful than the vodka. Then he noticed the Major in the passenger seat. Swallowing hard, he whipped out a quick salute to the officer whose eyes were as black as his skin. The Major returned the salute and handed a single sheet of paper to the guard. The guard barely glanced at the sheet, which had Washington, DC letterhead from headquarters. The Major's baritone voice softly explained that Supreme Commander Silas had sent a gift for his Chief of Staff. Today was his birthday. The guard just nodded, trying not to stare at the way the driver filled out her uniform. As he waved the truck through to the compound, he thought about calling the Chief of Staff's office and let them know. Then he saw his relief coming and said the hell with it, his head hurt. Twenty minutes later, he was in his cot thinking about all the great things he could do with that little blonde. He smiled at his little fantasy as his hand slid lower into his government issued boxers. That's when one of the first mortar shells blew his one-sided sex life and hangover through the wall. Hell was upon them.

The artillery opened up and the tanks hit from right and left. Squads had been designated for taking out the forward guard as the main column churned for the front gates. Accompanied by armored personnel carriers, Rachel and Joshua led the way. As the two thousand men and women surged forward, the morning sun danced reflecting the brilliance of white uniform and vehicle alike. All emblazoned with a symbol that meant hope from the beginning of time. A symbol forged from the blood of Michael himself.

From the air, it would have looked like a surge of burning diamonds washing over half the world consuming everything in front of it. The faces of the leaders, the brother and sister of whom legends would be written, led the dazzling wave. They glanced at each other remembering their youth. Now, weary and scarred from countless battles, large and small, their love swelled as it always had. For one another. For their mother and most of all, for their father. Both glanced upward not knowing that a slight chill had gone down each of their spines. As if a spirit of something had looked down on them in that moment in time. They felt the warmth of that spirit and felt love. The love of a father. The love of Peter Beck.

The Major and blonde driver drove to the rear of the complex. Julie Evans looked over at Charles Brady and smiled. "No problem at the first check point", she said. Charlie's bright teeth flashed against his ebony skin and he chuckled, "No, that idiot was too busy checking your boobs out." A sly smile crept across Julie's face as she unsuccessfully tried to convince Charlie that she had not ordered the smaller uniform on purpose. Charlie just shook his head and smiled. Julie and Charlie were with Dominion Intelligence, undercover operatives from Captain Johnson's team. They were use to finding humor in the most dangerous places. As they approached the headquarters building, security around the Chief of Staff would be tighter. Hopefully the documents had been well forged by their comrades and Charlie; the Major could sure look awful intimidating.

Sergeant Eric Stano lay in the darkness with his arms folded over his chest. Except for the slow rise and fall of his chest, you would have thought him dead. He thought of his wife and daughter who were back at Sanctuary in the underground base. Sheila taught classes to the kindergartners and first graders. Darcy had just gotten into kindergarten. Eric smiled as he thought of Darcy's already beginning complaints about having to put up with her mother as a teacher. He was due to rotate back to home base intelligence duties in a week. Seven long days until he could smell the sweet scent of his wife and the love of the bone crushing hugs of his beautiful daughter. Only seven days, if he could manage to stay alive that long.

The chief security officer was talking to the Major. "Well, everything seems in order. I'm just a bit surprised. We did not think Master Silas would know it was Chief Covington's birthday." Charlie just gave that knowing look to the security man and whispered that Silas knew everything. They agreed on that and enjoyed a smile. One of those, "don't you know it, we're all in this crap together' smiles. The security chief called six of his men to help unload the seven foot crate while he went to present the Major to the Chief of Staff.

As Charlie entered the building, the men begin bitching about the weight of the crate and bosses in general. Julie gave them a cheerful smile and bragged on their physical prowess. To a man, they puffed their chests out a little more and as they entered the cool shade of the building, asking Julie if she and the Major were staying for awhile.

The former Senator Covington sat in his private quarters with his bathrobe open. The fish belly white color of his layers of fat contrasted with the burgundy of the robe. Little puffs of hair, or what was left of it, rose from his scalp as he wiped the last traces of cocaine from the Hitler mustache that he had adopted in tribute to a true hero of his. The one that he thought to emulate when he was rewarded with his kingdom. A groan escaped his bloated lips as he dug his hand in the young girl's hair whose face was in his lap. She could be no older than fourteen and whimpered when he pulled her hair painfully. Her whimpers seem to make him more excited. Fine, she thought, the faster, the better. A knock sounded on the door.

Covington was closing his robe as he answered the door. His face was florid, whether from excitement, cocaine or both, who could tell. "This had better be important", he growled to the security man. Charlie, standing a little behind him could see the young girl quickly putting her clothes on. He hid his disgust and smiled at the newly appointed King Turd. The security chief showed the orders to Covington who looked a little confused and then smiled. Finally, Master Silas had recognized all of his good work for the cause. True, he had only been directly responsible for the rape, murder and mutilation of a few hundred meaningless people. But, just think. With his own kingdom, he could get the ovens and the medical experiments going again. Just like his hero, Adolph. Now, the Master had realized that Frank Covington was just the man for the job. "Oh, what a glorious day. Now I have two presents. Who would believe it!" Charlie smile faltered at that statement, it sent alarm signals along his spine although he did not know why.

Captain Ann Warren had volunteered her Charlie Company for rear guard action at the fort. They would provide protection to the rear flank of the Beck's combined command as they stormed the city. Warren led her troops down a short ravine, which would come out just to the right of the fort. When the gate was breached, her company would take up positions. As she walked among her men and women and lined them up in the deep defile, her eyes darted about. When asked by her second in command if she was all right, she replied she just didn't feel too well. Probably not, a rotting soul will do that to you.

Captain Warren told Lieutenant Sanders to go ahead and move the troops into the ravine to get ready. She went to the rear of the column. A young private spoke to her quietly with excitement in his voice. This would be his first combat mission and he was looking forward to meeting the Enemy face to face. As he spoke, Warren looked down at his chest. So did he. He was puzzled by the small red dot just above his sternum. He was still surprised as the silent rounds shredded his chest in two seconds. He fell silently with wide open eyes still fixed on his Captain's. The eyes of a woman damned. One hundred and ten soldiers died in the Texas dust of that gully that day. None ever managed to get off a shot. Warren walked slowly through the shattered bodies and spoke one word into a tiny radio, "Done".

The Major presented the red envelope to Covington. The large crate was wheeled in and raised to a standing position by the sweating men. Julie stepped unnoticed to the left of the room and waited. Covington opened the envelope and saw the words elegantly written. "I wish you a very happy day of birth my loyal servant. My present is symbolic, I'm sure you will want a larger one when you set up your palace as His Most High Ruler of the Southeast." "Shit, "thought Covington, "I would have thought at least half of the old United States. What the hell, it's a start." He thanked the Major and directed the men to open the crate. The security chief seemed fidgety and as the men worked on the crate with pry bars, asked Covington about the pending ambush. "Oh yes, there is that. Go ahead and see to it. Kill every last one of the bastards." The chief left leaving only eight security personnel in the room. Covington's gaze was fixed on the crate, which was now opening. He did not see the look of alarm between Charlie and Julie.

The guard dozed at the gate, propped against the guard shack. Thunder woke him up. It had not rained for over a month. Thunder getting closer. He looked up and had time to scream as the armored personnel carrier plowed into the gate rolling through brick, mortar, bone and blood. The courtyard erupted into fire as tanks fired into the buildings and bunkers. Machine gun fire raked in a decimating arc. Crimson splashed the dry Texas soil. Rachel and team split to the left while Joshua went to the right. The tanks and mortars grew silent as the soldiers closed for close quarter combat.

As a faint explosion was heard, the front of the crate fell. Covington stared at the small gilded throne. A smile sprang to his face. He would have to get a larger one, but this one would start. His eyes began communicating with his brain. There was his throne. Why is someone already sitting in it? A mannequin maybe? But why is he wearing black? Why do I see the glint in his deadly blue eyes? Why is he pointing that strange skinny pistol at me with the sausage like appendage? Covington's questions stopped as the burning began in his throat and the blood came gurgling out. It blended with his robe well.

Eric had fired two shots from the silenced Browning Woodsman. The .22 caliber slugs hit Covington in the throat and chest. As Covington fell backwards into his bedroom, Eric swung the gun left and fired twice. The two guards eyebrows raised in surprise as the small red holes appeared in their foreheads while the expanding hollow nose bullets blew their brains out a big hole in the back. Charlie and Julie pulled mini-Uzi's from their jackets and killed the remaining six guards. Charlie stepped into Covington's room. Covington was dead. No doubt about it. Eric's shots had probably done it. The young girl sitting astride his pale belly stabbing the dagger into the flabby flesh over and over was probably just window dressing. Probably.

Rachel looked up as she heard the whistle overhead. The explosion flattened her with the shockwave and killed three of her soldiers. It had come from behind them. Lying beside her radioman who had half his skull missing from shrapnel, she screamed into the radio for Charlie company. For Captain Warren. The silence was broken as the whistles continued.

The jaws had closed. A classic ambush. Most of Rachel and Joshua's troops were inside the walls when the Enemy closed from behind, underneath and from the flanks. Warren had brought the carefully laid plans to the Enemy. The Ann Warren who had never had much of a love life. Who had been targeted and seduced by a member of Enemy intelligence. First, it was only little unimportant things they wanted to know. Then a little more and then more. She didn't realize that the smell she sometime dreamed in the dark was that of her own soul. Now she had murdered. It didn't matter that she hadn't pulled the trigger.

The carnage lasted less than an hour. Death feasted well that terrible day. The dust of the fort quenched its thirst with the blood of the young. Five hundred and more of our bravest died that day. It would have been much worse if not for Joshua Beck.

Joshua ran along the right wall with his personal company. Mortar shells were landing everywhere, killing Dominion and their own troops as well. The Enemy did not care if they had to make a few sacrifices. Joshua sent Billy Thompson into one of the towers with instructions to visually locate the mortar positions and call him. Joshua screamed into the radio for Rachel to rally what was left of her troops and secure the left wall. He would the right. The Dominion soldiers outside were trying to move to flank the rear ambush, but were meeting heavy fire. Joshua had an idea, but he needed to get to the front gate. And there were a whole lot of nasty folks in between.

The private sat by the brick wall with his rifle in his right hand. His left hand was trying to hold what was left of his intestines inside his belly. He did not hurt only felt numbness. He saw an enemy soldier charging towards him with a long bayonet screaming. He wondered why all the screaming. Just lay down and die. That's exactly what the soldier did after being stitched from crotch to eyebrows by the young privates rifle rounds. Too tired to hold the rifle any more, the numbness had spread. Soon it reached his eyes. Numbness became darkness.

Sgt. Carrie Griffin had emptied her rifle and used all her grenades. She pulled her Beretta nine-millimeter pistol and carefully selected her targets. Her squad surrounded her but all they could do was protect her with their bodies. They were all dead. Carrie thought how nice it would be in her small quiet town in Northern Ireland. It was green there, not dusty. Green grass as far as you could see. A small farm with her husband and children. Only they didn't exist any more. The Beast had exterminated them. As the smoke cleared a little, she spotted an archway about twenty five yards away where some Dominion troops had taken cover. Reloading her Beretta, she made her run. Halfway across, she was lifted in the air by some invisible force. The rocket had been fired by an asshole that couldn't hit the tank he was aiming at. But he managed to hit Carrie's left leg. As she lay in the dust, she looked down and saw it was gone. Not the dust, her leg. She still needed to get to that archway and keep fighting. But she needed to rest a minute. Just a minute, then she would go. Where in the hell was her leg anyway? She tried to open her eyes. She could smell grass. Green grass like that of home with fresh tilled dirt. Carrie smiled. She could almost make out the words of her husband. *Love you. C'mon, Emma and me want to show you our house.* Somewhere in the darkness, Carrie found the light that shone on her farm.

Julie, Eric and Charlie made it over the side wall, fighting their way to the front. When they got to the ravine, they found Charlie Company. From body to body they went with tears blurring their way. They were just children. And they had been massacred. They found Sanders at the front. He had wounds to the head, torso and legs. But his right hand grabbed Eric's ankle as he stumbled by. Eric listened to the whispered words and held the man's hand until his eyes glazed over. Eric bowed his head and wished his comrade a safe journey to his new home. Julie softly touched Eric's shoulder as he bowed there. She flinched at the fury in his eyes when he raised his head.

Rachel and Joshua's remaining troops had held on the right quarter of the compound. Joshua was screaming to be heard over the satellite link with the squadron leader. Joshua shouted the coordinates and said that all friendlies would be inside the compound or to the back of it. It would be open season on the front and sides. The squadron leader replied that they would kick in the afterburners but it would probably be at least twenty to thirty minutes. "Roger that Avenger," said Joshua, "just burn'em to the ground." He contacted Charlie via radio and told him to move what was left outside to the rear of the compound. Charlie acknowledged and began gathering up whoever was left alive. He didn't notice that Eric had slipped off and Julie wasn't talking about it.

"We have got to get the front end of the compound closed", said Joshua. Rachel did not see how because enemy soldiers were streaming in. Joshua looked around and pointed at the two stone towers bracketing the entrance. He told her he would take care of it and she wanted to know how. He smiled and said, "Remember Jericho?" Joshua ran to the back of his unit and found Deke, the explosives expert. Together they put together two satchels. Joshua slung them over his shoulder with the charges behind his body. Then he picked up his Uzi and began working his way up front.

The three jets screamed across the crystal blue sky. As luck would have it, with only twenty aircraft in the Dominion service, these had been close by on another mission. The wing commander pushed his bird knowing that minutes counted. His partner flew right and a little back of his wing. The third jet was not as fast but would do what she needed to do.

Joshua stopped by Rachel's position and emptied two clips into the human wave before them. During a lull in the firing, he told her to give him five minutes and pour everything they could toward the front gate. With a quick kiss on the cheek, he ran through the smoke. At the last minute, she reached for him. A premonition perhaps? A whisper of his sleeve touched her as he disappeared. The tingle of electricity ran to her heart. She sent the word to everyone. Five minutes. Until salvation. Unknown to her, until sorrow.

As he made his way toward the gate, Joshua picked up three survivors who had been pinned down. A quick briefing and they were with him, moving in a loose triangle, firing to all sides to open the path. The burst of machine gun fire lifted Dickson off his feet to the left of Joshua. A gush of blood sprayed from the multiple hits in his femoral artery. Jackson bringing up the rear checked him, but he was already gone. Jackson moved to left flank. Joshua smiled at the young black man as he moved up. He had trained Jackson. A young man born into this world in the poorest district of Los Angeles. No one thought he would be anything more than a two-bit hood. When war had broken out, Jackson had joined the resistance and found his way to the Dominion Army. He was one of the very best squad leaders they had. On Joshua's right, Sahid fired his M-16 in a sweeping motion. The young Jordanian was not wasting bullets. Ten enemy troops fell from his withering fire. Joshua saw the burst of fire too late to warn Sahid. The rounds caught him at the jawbone and took most of his head off. Joshua pushed on. They were twenty yards from the gate.

The bullet took him off his feet when it hit his shoulder. Blood splattered Joshua's uniform. By the time he got to his feet with Jackson providing covering fire, the pain had begun. It felt as if his left hand was on fire. He and Jackson took cover behind a small concrete ramp about ten yards from the gate. Joshua looked at his watch. Ten seconds now. 9.8.7.6.5.4.3.2. he began his sprint as all of the Dominion troops opened up with a withering fullisade on Rachel's order. Bodies were blown apart at the gates by forty-millimeter grenades. Bullets rained their death as bodies were shredded by the projectiles. He saw the grenade bounce and roll to a stop just in front of him. He pulled up short and that was when the AK-47 round shattered his knee. Joshua lay there, staring at the grenade. From his left he heard Jackson coming at full speed like a fullback and saw him hurl his muscled body onto the explosive just as it went. Bloody parts rained down on Joshua, as he realized he was still alive and just feet away from the gate. He crawled forward. The pain was excruciating. He still crawled. Jackson was a good man. He was not going to die in vain. Joshua reached the base of the left tower. His leg was totally blown and he knew he was close to passing out from blood loss. He pulled the two satchels around to his lap and lay against the stone tower. "I love you sis," he whispered. Then he closed his eyes, and pulled the pins.

No trumpets blew, but the walls fell just as well. Bodies were crushed by the tumbling stone towers in a cloud of dust reddened by the sinking sun. The enemy outside massed and wondered why Dominion would close themselves inside. Then they heard the roar overhead as the jets came out of the sun. The men froze as the napalm enveloped them sending them screaming into the fires of their own hell. One that would burn even hotter. The survivors were retreating enmasse when the third party of the Avenger Squadron lumbered onto the scene. The captain grinned. I may not be as fast as those fancy flyboys but I am more feared. The gun ship was known by technical names, but most knew it as "Puff The Magic Dragon" because of the awesome firepower it wielded. Firing thousands of rounds per second, it simply wiped out anything in its path. Right now, about a thousand enemy troops were in that path.

The captain targeted and quietly gave the order to fire. A tidal wave of lead poured on the retreating soldiers. Then there were none. Silence sounded in the twilight as the fires of the napalm slowly burnt out. The buzzards would not go hungry for days.

Rachel stood by the gate as her and Joshua's troops conducted the mop up operation inside the fort. Already, the tanks and personnel carriers were being brought forward to move the rubble so they could get out. Covington was dead. Fifteen civilians had been rescued including the young girl. Rachel's assistant quietly relayed the information back to Sanctuary and gave orders. He didn't want to bother Rachel right now. She just stood there and stared at the rubble. She didn't know when the tears began. As she felt the salty tears flow down her dust encrusted face, she thought she could smell a whiff of honeysuckle and a sudden short breeze felt like a kiss upon her cheek. As she looked into the sky, she could have sworn she saw something. Something beautiful soaring through the clouds. To home. The rains fell as if heaven were crying with her. The rains mixed with her tears and cleansed the blood of the children, which lay scattered around her.

She stumbled through the pouring rain, sliding and falling in the mud. As she got up, blood flowed from a small gash in her forehead. Cursing, she wiped the blood away and walked through the blood soaked ravine. A shadow moved into the waning light. Warren screamed. "Oh my God, Eric you scared me to death." Then she ran to him heaving great braying sobs, "Oh Eric, they're all dead. Everyone of them." She hugged him with her arms around his neck as if she was drowning. Her muffled voice came from his chest in the cascade of the rain. "They were just children and they were massacred." She snuffled a little for dramatic effect and said, "It was a real bitch." He whispered in her ear, "Yes they were and yes you are." He tugged the back of her hair so he could see her eyes when he pulled the trigger of the Browning held below her throat and blew her brains out of the top of her head. What he saw her see in those final moments would haunt him for a long time. Reflected in those eyes were the long dark tunnel into hell. Eric let the body drop. He was going to see his family. He walked into the rain. He needed the rain. It would cleanse him.

We said goodbye to Joshua Beck standing on a small hill overlooking Sanctuary. The sky was blue that day and the wind rustled through the leaves in the small grove. I feel as if I've lost a part of myself. I watched him grow from a boy into manhood. A hero like his father. All the lives that we were saved that day, we owe to this brave young man. We also think of the other brave souls that perished that day. A day of betrayal. A day of courage. We have said goodbye to many on this small hill including Gabriel and Ashe. I look to the sky and I'm sure they mourn with us. We turn and head for home. Micah holds Jarred to his chest. Jarred's words are tentative but clear as he raises his eyes to Micah. *"I am the one."*

In the darkness of the forest where nothing lives, he wanders alone. Memory of blood running in rivulets to the source of all that could be. A name not remembered. The shattering like glass of things which swirl in the crimson glow. If only he could find the way. The darkness is silent but the voice is not. "I am the one."

The before had been so beautiful. Beings had tried to describe it but the words could not fulfill the vision. Home. Where the light and warmth came from. Only the One knew of its beginning. The One who filled it with his children and their laughter. The streets were filled with all of them. The First Beloved and those after moved through the plaza and among the squires reaching to infinity. The garden at the center was lush with grass and gentle slopes, which led to the great waterfall. The source of which returned to the One in its brilliance of millions of colors. Colors that are known and those only dreamed of. The family had gathered there for great occasions of joy. Father, Mother and the Beloved had loved there. That was before the war had come. War which had spilled the blood of brother and sister in the garden and streets of Home. The day Mother's blood ran in rivulets across the feet of the youngest is the day Desolation reigned, fed by the fires of a Father's fury loosed upon his children.

Year four, devastation marched upon the face of our earth. The cities have become the great tomb of the slaughtered. From large to small, they burn. Perhaps the fires will cleanse us from the evil that had entrenched there. A once mighty world whose great people had traveled to the stars has become a wasteland where a fraction of its once mighty population live in the shadows of this immense cemetery that we called home.

It seems that the cities were the worst if you could make a distinction between city and countryside. We had become soft with our luxuries and technology. We ignored our home dying from our misuse of her resources and the rape of her bounty. As the earth gave way to drought, the great forests died. The animals died with them. Man streamed into the cities to live off of the salvage of the billions who had perished. Even leftovers are eventually depleted. So it was. The streets were territories where predators marked their turf. There were the creatures that hunted in the cities for the human flesh to satisfy their hunger. Or not. Some killed just to enjoy the killing. Then there were the ones that called themselves human. I think not. Whatever lay behind their rotted souls was the putrid smell of pus and rot, not man. When they had taken everything there was to take, they burned, just to see the destruction. Maybe they did us all a favor. The great cities are gone now for the most part. My home, Atlanta was once raised from the ashes. This time, I don't think she will make it back to us. New York, Chicago and Los Angeles are no more. The other great cities of the world are bathed in flames. No more Big Ben. No more Eiffel Tower. They melt inward as the flames are fanned by the roaring winds. The coastlines have changed now. The tilt of the axis after the nuclear detonations caused massive tidal waves. The dust encircles our globe and winter is permanent.

I often wonder what it would be like to be able to see from the old space station. Could I have seen the great waves wash over the land? Or see the flames, which burn miles into the sky? Or would I see what I see here? A dead planet encircled in gray, rotting from within. If I had been one of the astronauts who had been abandoned, I think I would have turned my dying eyes towards the stars. I would have looked at that crystalline clarity until the darkness stole over me. Looking out there. Somewhere. For Home.

Christina sat with Mara watching Jarred play. He had grown so fast. Intelligence gleamed in those flickering eyes. He was like other children. He laughed and cried, sometimes both at the same time. But Christina saw something else there also. Mara poured another cup of coffee and looked at her son who sat on the carpet playing with his favorite toy. The one "Papa" Micah had given him. Mara said, "I don't know what to make of him sometimes," nodding towards the toddler. "I know", Christina replied, "but it's hard to put into words. He's just a child, but when I look into those eyes it's like looking into something ancient. It's as if there is a knowledge there, just waiting for the right time." "Exactly," Mara said. "He walks and talks like your everyday four year old and then out of the blue, he'll say something so cryptic it sends goosebumps down my spine." Then they both chuckled, each realizing they did not have the massive amounts of experience of parenting needed to be so dead set sure what was normal for a four year old. Add in the fact that the young one under such close scrutiny had human, angel and demon blood in him and you might expect a few surprises.

Talk turned to the war. Christina brought Mara up to date on the campaign. They had gotten close to Silas' headquarters in DC but he had fled with his advisors. Rachel had returned back to that part of the world and had radioed yesterday from the former Canadian wilderness. Colonel Xian Ling, who had been Joshua Beck's second in command had taken over the young hero's former division, was currently in lower South America chasing Enemy troops.

Micah was attending a planning session at Sanctuary with the War Council. Christina had finished with her presentation and had come to Mara seeking some peace, quiet and companionship. Mara asked how Micah was doing. Christina told her he was doing pretty well considering. She was afraid he wasn't getting enough rest. If he wasn't in the field with the troops, he was in the underground complex checking on new trainees, reviewing intelligence and constantly reinforcing Sanctuary security. Silas had not tried again after the massive failure of the attack at the home of the Dominion forces, but Micah believed it would only be a matter of time.

Shannon and Jack had their divisions together getting ready to mount an attack against a major Enemy fortress outside of old Frankfurt, Germany. Christina said that she was worried about the weather there. It had been snowing pretty steadily for over three days. She was still waiting on a status report to see if the operation was still going forward. Knowing Jack Dalton, she figured it was. They both laughed knowing very well that not much could keep Jack out of a good scrap. He was learning though. In another joint operation with Shannon's group, Jack had taken a pretty nasty bullet wound in the side. He kept fighting; ignoring his medics until Shannon slipped up and shot him in the butt with a hypo filled with enough morphine to knock a horse down. After the battle, Jack's personal team fell on the ground laughing every time the story was told. Jack's cussing only increased with every telling. Shannon just kissed his flushed forehead and whispered she would make it all better later. As soon as he got some feeling back in his ass. She ran before he could grab her. Later that night, Micah told Jack in a serious tone over the satellite link that he was only eligible for one Purple Heart. Getting shot in the ass by your wife didn't count. Micah hung up with a chuckle as Jack began one of his famous cussing streaks.

As night fell, Erika Thielemann, the Security Chief dropped by to say hello and check in on Mara. Erika checked in quite a bit and always ended up playing with Jarred. As Christina watched the young woman throw the boy into the air, both of them giggling, she smiled. All Erika had known was fighting. She had grown up in the service of Dominion and had never taken the time to have a family. But there was always hope.

She had heard rumors that Erika was quite fond of the young communications sergeant here at base. He'd better be serious though; Erika was one woman whose fondness was not easily obtained. And one that you definitely didn't want to get on the bad side of. Not if you didn't want to sing soprano anytime soon anyway. You know that woman scorned line right?

Christina went to hug Jarred goodbye. "Bye Aunt Christina", said the young boy as he squeezed her in his arms. "When you come back, I'll tell you about my friend." "What friend? Christina asked. "My friend that lives in the forest. He'll be here soon. I'm calling him." With both her and Mara's eyebrows raised, Christina said, "Sure, hon. I'd love to meet him. What's his name?" A sly smile crept over Jarred's face, "You don't know but I do. I know his secret name." With that, Jarred's eyes focused in the distance somewhere way beyond what the adults could see. A shiver went down Christina's spine as she kissed him on the cheek with that faraway look still there. As Mara walked Christina to the door, Jarred's unheard whisper floated on the air, *"Thy Secret Name."*

A little ways off the cold Scotland shoreline, David Stichcomb drank the last of what passed for coffee. He warmed his hands against the fire that he had built. Already ice mixed with snow had begun falling against the small shelter he had made next to the cave with the rest of his team. He looked at the bronze glow that the lieutenant bar gave off held in his hand. The matching one was still affixed to the other collar of his uniform. He wished his mom and dad had been there to see him get promoted. They would have been proud. He had told them this morning on his weekly satellite call. They had been ecstatic. Their son was an officer now. Now he stared at the bar in the waning firelight. Yes, I'm an officer. A battlefield commission, but a commission nonetheless. David had mixed feelings. He had been accepted to the Special Operations Group last year after completing the most bone wrenching, muscle pounding and brain stretching training he could have imagined. He had heard that Micah himself had developed the course based on the best of Israeli, British and American Special Forces training combined. All David knew was that whoever came up with that course must have been just a little shy of insane. But it had kept him alive. The young man who had fired his first combat shot a little over four years ago was gone. In his place stood a tough man who had been transformed into a nightmare for the Enemy.

David's eyes closed in the warmth of the fire and he dreamt of his last battle. It was real all over again, except in Technicolor and slow motion. He had all the time in the world to see what had gone wrong. His team with Lieutenant Jerry Powers in charge had been inserted at night on the coast of Scotland. Their target was an Enemy company about five miles inland who was working trying to get a nuclear weapons station back on line. Powers laid out the battle plan. The station was believed to be staffed by thirty soldiers and five scientists who were working to get the missile system on line. Powers' ten-person team would split. Staff Sergeant David Stichcomb's team would approach the complex from the East Side where the main entry was located and terminate the occupants. No prisoners. The Enemy had already made their choices. Jerry would come in from the other side with his team. Explosives would be set and then the team would extract back to the coast for pick up. No questions were needed. The two teams moved out.

David slipped through the darkness. His black uniform and face paint blended with the shadows. His four teammates followed close behind in practiced movements. All carried Uzi machine guns except for the rear. She carried the explosives and had a Colt .45 automatic in her left hand. Within a mile of the complex, David held his hand up and the group stopped. On his orders, they lowered the night vision goggles lighting the darkness to their eyes in an eerie green glow. The checked for booby traps as they crept forward through the thick woods. They found many. This was the worst part on the nerves. Looking for tripwires and pits. Moving yards, sometimes inches at a time. They reached the fence and located the guard tower. David placed his face inches away from the fence and could hear the quiet hum. It was electrified. They were preparing to dig, when Sandy, the explosive expert, tapped David on the shoulder and he grinned. They were smart enough to get the power up and running but hadn't gotten to the basics of housekeeping as far as security went. Just behind the guard tower a large tree stood. With a large limb sprouting from it over the fence. A limb large enough to hold a good-sized man. David's team crawled down the fence line.

David moved along the length of the tree limb inches at a time watching the guard sleep. Every time he would twitch or snort, David stopped. He glanced at his watch. Still five minutes ahead of schedule but the clock was ticking. The guard's head was lying to the side with drool dripping from the right corner. He screamed when the sharp knife raked across his throat while David held his forehead back. Screamed and screamed. But no sound came except for the whistling of air through what was left of his windpipe. As the dark got darker, the flow of crimson mixed with drool down the front of the Enemy's uniform. David let the limp body slide to the floor as he switched off the power lead to the fence. Within a minute, his team had breached the perimeter and was moving towards the buildings.

Powers' group arrived a few minutes later, found the fence okay and cut through. They approached the building from the other side killing two sentries, on the way in.

Death came in the whispers of silenced shots and along the razor edge of knives as David's team worked closer to the control room. So far, so good. David along with his team met up with Powers and the rest just outside the operational room. Sharky, the electronics whiz came forward with a card attached by cable to a small black box with a digital readout. He slid the card through the electronic lock, watched the red numbers run and stop. He then slid the card through again and the door hissed open.

Four men and one woman along with five security agents were in the room. As the agents brought their weapons up, they were mowed down by the silent chattering of the automatic weapons guided by red laser dots. Blood, bone and brain matter slid down the wall like paint thrown by a manic artist. Two of the scientist pulled handguns and were blown apart by multiple hits. Two others ran for the door where they were met by Corporal John Sparrowchild. Sparrowchild ended their flight with two well-placed shots through the forehead. The young Apache smiled as he pulled their heads up by the hair to see if they were dead. David had a fleeting vision of John honoring his ancestors by scalping the traitor bastards.

The woman scientist had been wounded in the initial firing and was now on her knees in front of Jerry Powers, begging for her life. Her lank brown hair hung down over her eyes as she wept. Through snot-filled sobs, she cried, "Please don't. I've got a husband and kids. They made me do it." Before David could shout, Jerry bent down to say something to the woman. His head jerked up. David stared. Something was wrong. Something about the shape of Jerry's head. As Jerry slid to the floor, David saw that it was part of Jerry's brain on the end of a long dagger, which the woman had shoved through the soft underside of the young officer's throat. A dagger carried by the Enemy High Command. As the woman's head flew up, David saw the crimson eyes and fanged mouth as the sickening laughter poured forth.

David fired at point blank range watching the bullets tear into her dancing body. Yet the laughter went on and on. The Uzi empty, he pulled his dagger and slammed it into the open mouth of the thing before him. He heard teeth breaking as he shoved, throwing all of his weight behind it until he saw the blade exit her throat just above the collarbone. The red eyes bored into his and she shrieked with laughter still. David twisted the hilt and drove her backward, pinning her to the floor with the blade. He motioned for Sandy and the other explosive operator to set the charges. As Sandy placed one next to him on the machinery, he held out his hand. She knew. She slapped a block of C-4 into his hand along with a detonator. As the thing squirmed on the knife blade, David was so close to her face, he could smell the stinking breath, the breath of death and decay. He watched in horror as maggots crawled out of the hideous mouth as if they knew their host was not long for this world. He looked into the molten eyes and thought for a moment he might slip into insanity. Instead he slammed the C-4 into what was left of the mouth and stuck the blasting cap in. Taking Jerry's body with them, they ran for the exit. At the fence line, David turned and flipped the switch on the detonator. "Bitch, have a free ride to hell". And so she did. The glow showed as the flames still burned five miles back. The glow turned into eyes. Eyes of blood red filled with the fury of almighty evil.

David woke up sweating in the freezing lean-to. As he sat in the dark smoking, he looked again at the Lieutenant bar and thought of his friend Jerry. Jerry had been the best, except for the soft spot in that heart of his which had caused him to hesitate. Jerry was a decent man who had shown mercy in a war. A decent man who had left a wife and son behind defending what he believed in. David crunched out his cigarette and pinned the bar on his uniform. For Jerry and for all that was right, he would show no mercy.

The child sat on the ragged stump of the tree and screamed in anger. He looked for the stars, which did not shine on the landscape of twisted wood and darkness. One path had led to another and another and another. Then to nowhere. Voices calling. Closer then farther away. As the tears fell in the crimson twilight, the words came floating from somewhere on the angry winds: "I know...."

The Sacred Books tell the story but only part of it. They know not of the war that raged that day. A day that lasted moments or millennia, it depends on your perspective. What is sure is the end. In the end, he and his were vanquished. If only the rest had been so clear, the agony may have been avoided. If only it had been known what the end would mean. For in truth it was a beginning. For the child resting in the blood of the mother. The heavens wept but they knew not why.

Year five was that of insanity, or so we began to think. It was a strange year. The war went on with savage skirmishes the world over. We were close to Silas many times, but he managed to slip the noose. He would sacrifice thousands as he made his escape; it did not matter to him. We lost many fine young men and women and we mourned every one of them. More poured forth from the underground bases to take their place. To spill the precious blood of their young bodies to fight for the last bit of humanity on this whirling bit of dust in the vastness of the seemingly unfeeling universe. The weight of their sacrifices weigh heavy on each of us that send them into battle. Micah ages before my very eyes. How long can one man cope with this responsibility? I don't know. I just pray that it is long enough. Christina speaks to us with soothing words. She is the keeper of the faith. Even her words begin to sound hollow to me. Is that right? We knew we were destined to enter this darkness. There is a reason for the path we follow. My old mind knows that there is a greater wisdom at work here than I could ever understand. My heart, which has, beat long past its due feels the despair as I ask the great silence when it will end. There is no answer. Perhaps that is why we are all dreaming. Vivid dreams, which we cannot discern the meaning of, but we know there is a reason. Maybe we are all going insane together. Maybe this is the answer we have waited for and just don't want to hear it. Where do the dreams end and reality begin? Somewhere there is an answer, I hope.

With their permission, I have documented these dreams. I don't know if it will help but I feel I must. If not for us, then perhaps for those that follow.

Mara told me that due to her unique nature she has never dreamed much. She watches Jarred as he sleeps beside her and he twitches and talks in his sleep. According to her, much of what he says she does not understand. A few words come through. Some appear to be the dreams of any five-year-old she said. As countless mothers before, she watches her beautiful child sleep in innocence. She feels the soft breath upon her face and watches his eyelids as those mysterious eyes move rapidly back and forth, entering the domain of dreams. The fear stalks through her heart when she sees that small smile and hears him whisper, *"I know. I know Thy secret name. I am the one."*

The dream Mara remembers the most is that she had of Ashe. In the dream, Ashe is as we last saw him. He stands in a cavern by a river, which runs to an unseen source. His mighty crimson tipped wings are spread and he is holding out his hands. He holds them as if he's waiting for Mara. She looks down at her own hands. She is holding baby Jarred. She looks into the eyes of Ashe and watches as the blue tears streak down his face. She does not want to let the baby go. She stares at Ashe. Each tear is a laceration across his beautiful body but still he waits with hands out. Mara looks down and sees red rain falling upon her child. It is the tears of her own washing him. She places Jarred in Ashe's hands. The blue tears of Ashe mix with her own splashing the child with the purest of red and blue. Ashe walks to the river and plunges the child beneath its waters. As Mara screams, the river runs red with blood of her son. She screams again as Ashe lifts with the great wings and rises out of sight. She plunges into the river where there is only darkness tinged by crimson. Jarred is gone. Swept away by the strong currents to the source that she cannot see. Mara sinks deeper into the darkness. Into the forest at the bottom. Into nothingness. Then she awakes.

Micah has many dreams born of his life before and after Dominion. We would call them nightmares. Most he will not share with me but after talking of the others, he told me of one, which he has had several times recently. Micah is only human and he bears the weight of the world on his shoulders. I listened to my friend and I held my tears until he had left. I hope my friend will find his peace someday.

Micah stood upon the mountain looking into the blood-drenched valley below. Millions lay dead. Bodies torn and mutilated by every weapon known to man. Strange beasts lie among the dead. He looks at his right hand and sees the old Browning handgun, which he has carried for years. It is black with cordite. He feels the heat and drops it, hearing it clatter down the scorched rocks. His left hand drips blood on his boots. Not wanting to but having to, he walks down the rocks into the plain below. Micah walks among the dead. For a moment, he considers he may be dead. Maybe this is a warrior's hell. These are all the people he has killed. As he steps through the carnage, no living thing moves. Even the scavengers are dead. There is nothing left. This was the final battle. No one survived. Except Micah Sarentstein. He wanders among the corpses. They are Dominion and Enemy both. He checks for life but knows that there is none. Death is his only companion on this journey. And it is a journey. He knows this. The journey that will lead him to the end.

He walks on through the valley littered with those that he loved. He sees Jack and Shannon in death. Mara, Christina and yes, even me. Saint lies dead with his jaws around the throat of the Enemy. Still Micah walks. Time does not exist. Numbers do not calculate. Millions. Billions. Dead. But Micah lives. He is broken but the blood still pumps to the heart and the brain wills the legs to move forward. The legs follow their orders and Micah wades through millions whose open eyes meet his and ask why he did this to them. At the end of the valley, in the shadows of the forest someone waits for Micah. As he approaches the small figure, Micah stumbles. A small hand catches his and holds him.

He looks into the face of his saviour. He would almost say that it is Jarred but there is something very different about him. The same and not. *"We must hurry Micah. We have to go into the forest. Time is running out."* Micah stares at the darkness amongst the thick trees and he is afraid. Something is waiting in the forest. Something that knows his heart. Something that knows the guilt he carries for the wrong choices he has made. He tries to pull away from the small hand but it is strong. *"Do not be afraid,"* the small voices says, *"It does not matter what is behind, only what is from now. I have to go and you are the only one that can take me. Hurry! He is coming."* Micah looks over his shoulder at the bodies. Reaching into the deepest part of his soul, he takes a step forward. Then another. And another. Into the darkness with a small hand in his.

Christina sits in the ancient circle at the heart of Sanctuary and closes her eyes. Vision or dream? She does not know. She is in a forest. She sees neither light nor stars. She makes her way by a reddish glow. The paths turn and twist deeper into the depths of the trees. The paths converge, turn around on each other and stop in dead ends. It's like a maze. As she turns the bend, she sees a small boy sitting under the canopy of a great tree. He is crying. The sobs break her heart. She touches his shoulders and he looks into her eyes. He has no eyes. There is only ebony in the sockets. But he smiles and asks if his mother sent her. Christina says that she does not know, but that she will help him find her. His smile fades. *"You cannot. She is dead. You are not the one."* Christina pleads with him to let her help but he only turns his back to her and walks deeper into the forest which is as dark as his eyes.

Well, that is about it. I'm sure others may be dreaming but I have not been told. Jack, Shannon, and Rachel are in the field with their troops. If the dreams are the same in the battlefield, I have no way of knowing. I'll close now.

I know. I didn't include my dream. I don't really want to but I guess it's only fair. It's just, given the context of the others; my dream does not make sense. Also, I believe my old mind may be cracking. It might be the first signs of insanity. Hang on a second, my hands are shaking so bad you won't be able to read it.

There. A good dose of whisky. Just one glass mind you. I haven't had a drink in. Well damn, I don't know how long, that's how long it's been. Back to the subject. Dreams.

Mine is simple and that is why it scares me. If you analyze the others, there are so many symbolic possibilities and tangents. I could probably do an intricate study if my speciality was psychology.

I guess I've stalled enough. I only see two things in my dream. I see a man that I know only from old photographs that Rachel has. I see him on a world with three moons beside an ocean I can't describe the color of. I see him nailed to a cross. A man named Peter Beck. That's it. That's my dream. Yeah, there is the other thing. I try to wake up and not see it. I believe my mind is going. I see...I see the face. A face I think I do know but I don't. I think it is the face of....God. Weeping. Tears of shimmering blue.

This ends my chronicle for today. It is late and I'm sleepy. That one glass of whisky was a strong one. I needed it. No, perhaps I didn't but I enjoyed it. Now, I'm going to put these old bones to bed. Tomorrow is another day.

I give Saint a scratch behind the ears as he lies beside my bed. He is staying with me tonight instead of Jarred. Good dog. I think maybe that I need him more tonight. As I rub his soft fur, I can see his legs twitching while he sleeps. I wonder...

He stood over the fallen one with the mighty sword raised for the final blow. Liquid fury poured from the blue eyes as the pure white wings spread, looking down into the face of the vanquished. Screams for mercy rang out from her as she ran to her beloved. The child screamed and hurled forward. In the midst of the storm of battle, one small piece of stone was all that it took. As the small one stumbled into the mighty arm, the error was slight. Only that of a measure of breath. But just as true as if it had been aimed. As the mighty and small lay there, rivulets of blood ran from tiny to great in just moments. Across their feet and wings in a dark crimson flow. It flowed to the source of all. The light became darkness as He approached. First anguish, then rage followed. No mercy was shown that terrible day and the children were lost.

Year Six was one of mystery. In the twilight of man there was wonderment. From our home to the farthest reaches of the scorched earth, we heard the stories. Wrapped inside those words of awe and astonishment was a tiny sliver of hope. Hope for the future of man and his children who knew nothing but war. In the midst of all the horror we beheld the miracle of the faith at the core of our essence. The faith that warmed us against the coldness called Death.

Private Andre Bennett lay in the foxhole outside the small village in the countryside of what had been Austria. He shivered against the chill in his bones trying to warm himself from the small fire he had made using a can of dirt soaked in diesel fuel. It was not just a physical sense of coldness but one of the soul as well. For his young years, he had seen too much death and horror. The smoke still lingered on the battlefield, fed from the pockets of fire left from the battle. The silence was a blessed relief after hours of explosions and gunfire. And of the screams. The screams of soldiers, their bodies shattered from the weapons of both sides and those of the inhuman creatures, which had hunted among them. The night sounds of the woods were so different from the pulse of the city life of Paris which Andre's parents had spoken of with fond memories. The laughter and joy of a city before the Beast had come.

Now, they had met the Enemy in this small village. He did not even know the name of the ground that he had fought for. The battle had been fierce. Led by a young German captain, Andre's company had been assigned to clear the village. The first shots were fired on the edge of town. Andre's best friend since basic, had pulled him down to cover as the bullets chipped the plaster from the building next to him. They had fought street by street, clearing every building. Small arms fire and grenades were the order of the day. Andre had watched his squad leader ripped apart by the heavy rounds of a fifty-caliber machine gun, fired from the second story of what used to be a police station. The rest of his squad fought their way to that floor and tossed a grenade into the room, which rained body parts and ruined metal.

In the pre-dawn hours, the gun smoke intertwined with the morning mist, which carried the smell of cordite and blood. Andre would remember the copper scented smell mixed with excrement of the dying, even in his dreams. The worst was to come. As Andre's team entered the torn door of an abandoned bakery shop, they saw one of the creatures they had heard about. Whatever they thought they had been prepared for, they were wrong. The nightmare was muzzle deep in the bloody flesh torn from the chest of its victim. The beast looked like some kind of ape except for the barbed lizard like tail and the six inch fangs which dripped with bits of bloody pulp from the soldiers chest. Andre stood frozen with fear as the red eyes of the beast met his. He could hear the crunch of bone as the monstrous jaws snapped down. He didn't know who fired the first shot but then all five of them let loose, their fingers held down on the triggers until the ammunition was gone. They screamed as they fired. Even the sounds of empty clicks on the spent magazines were drowned out by the screams that went on. The creature spun as it was struck by hundreds of rounds of ammo. Pus smelling blood poured forth from the entry wounds as pieces of fur and matter blew out the back of its hideous body. The screams from it were high pitched like that of a child. When it was over, there wasn't enough left to identify it, just a lump of flesh remained. That was enough. The five young men would never forget what it looked like. The reloaded their weapons and moved on.

Throughout that endless day, they saw many more creatures. From small bat-like flying forms with poison stingers to something roughly the size and shape of an elephant. An elephant from a child's nightmare with rows of sharp teeth, its hide adorned by small parasite sucker creatures. When a rocket launcher brought the abomination down, the surviving parasites crawled off seeking a new host.

As the day turned into twilight, the battle wound down. Dominion troops were clearing the last building where random shots here and there were heard as the mop up continued. Andre and his friend sat with their backs to a small stone wall on the edge of the village. They had their ration packs out but Andre did not feel much like eating. He did manage to swallow a little bit of processed cheese and crackers. His friend had finished his meal and was leaning back against the wall enjoying the last of his after meal cigarette. Andre saw the snake first crawling tentatively along the top of the rough stone. Except it wasn't a snake, it was a tentacle. It had to be at least a foot in circumference with a blotched purple color along the top and pale white on the bottom, which was lined with reddish suckers oozing a clear liquid. Before Andre could react, his friend screamed in agony as the tentacle wrapped around his neck.

His hands grabbed it as it began tightening. Andre was on his feet with his knife out before he knew it. As he hacked at the exposed limb on the rock with his left hand, he tried to help his friend with his right. The screaming rose as the suckers sank into the flesh of his friend's neck. As Andre's hand touched one of the suckers, the agony was immediate. The liquid was acid. He brought the dagger down on the appendage with both hands as it sliced until striking stone. As the knife bit into the ancient rock, Andre glimpsed the owner on the other side of the wall and recoiled at the single eye and wide open beak of the thing which looked like an octopus with spider legs. His friend's screams had turned to whimpers. As Andre reached down to help him, the head rolled off, landing in his friend's lap with open eyes staring into Andre's. What was left of his neck, still dripped with acid as the tentacle twitched with nerves not yet realizing it was dead. Andre fell to his knees and heaved what little of his lunch he had onto the face of his friend. As he cried for his friend, he heard the terrible slither of the rest of the tentacles dragging the ground as the creature retreated into the darkness. Andre would always remember that sound.

So it was, that a weary young man fought sleep because of the nightmares that he knew waited. But even beyond the terror lies the need for the body to rest and soon Andre was asleep in the waning glow of his small fire in a foxhole which should have held two. Now he was alone wrapped in the blanket of his sorrow.

The beast smelled the human even before it saw him. Crouched among the brush, its snout twitched at the scent of flesh. The padded feet moved forward with razor sharp claws digging into the soft dirt. The cat-like yellow eyes lit the darkness as the anticipation caused drool to drip down its massive jaws. The shaggy head stayed close to the ground as it closed on the foxhole.

Andre snapped awake as the heavy body landed on his. He smelled the foul breath as he stared into the burning yellow lamps above the snarling mouth filled with fangs. He heard a whistling sound and the heaviness was lifted. The yellow eyes turned sideways and then upside down, dimming as they fell at his feet. The head rolled to the side of his foxhole. Above him, Andre could hear the thrumming that sounded like the beat of mighty wings as the body disappeared into the darkness. With revulsion, he grabbed the decapitated head by the mane of hair and threw it as far as he could, then slid back into the foxhole resting against the earthen wall. He would never be able to get back to sleep. With no one to watch over him, he could not allow it. But his body did not listen to his mind. It needed rest. As his chin nodded on his knees, he dreamt of the lights and laughter of a long ago city loved by his parents. In the dream he smelled the scent of honeysuckle as he was young again and played with his best friend. And in the night, he was not alone. The eyes watched over the boy and he was safe in his bed surrounded by Mother Earth.

The Special Operations squad moved silently through the darkness on the approach to the cabin nestled among with pines. In the wilderness of western Colorado the snow lay unlit by the moonless night. Lieutenant Michele Johnson held her hand up and the team halted. Ten men and women dressed in black halted as one with silenced Uzi's held at port arms. Johnson surveyed the cabin with night vision goggles and did not see any movement. She motioned for her second in command to come forward. Master Sergeant Juan Sanchez huddled with Johnson as they spoke in whispers. "I don't see anything moving," Johnson said, "not even sentries. That's strange isn't it?" Sanchez agreed saying that he would think there would be some kind of security around the cabin, which hid the entrance to the cave complex behind it. Sanchez said, "Well, I guess we go but let's split up in case they've been tipped off." "Okay," Johnson replied as she pointed at members of the team splitting them into two groups. She took one group to the right; Sanchez went to the left. The only tracks in the new fallen snow were theirs.

Lieutenant Johnson had received the call from Colonel Rachel Beck the evening before. Intelligence had been received that an Enemy enclave was hidden in the cave complex. The primary purpose of the group was to finish the development of a chemical weapons delivery system to be launched against Sanctuary. The information that was relayed was that they were very close to completing it. Johnson's orders were to locate the specific entrance and to destroy the complex. An over flight of the area by Dominion reconnaissance had detected traces of activity using thermal imaging. About thirty-five enemy personnel were believed to be inside. Johnson's team had parachuted in HALO (high altitude, low opening) and using the data gathered by the imaging had located the cabin about four this morning. Surveillance had shown no movement for the last two hours. As the dawn crested the Rockies, the team moved in on the cabin.

Sanchez and his team breached the entrance to the cabin. Three bodies were there. Cold bodies, which had been sliced from top to bottom. Johnson's team entered staring silently at the carnage. They moved to the back of the cabin and found the door leading into the shaft standing open. Weapons ready, they filed into the corridor. At the first intersection was a dead security officer lying in the congealed blood most of which had poured from the neck which no longer supported a head. The team moved forward with their nerves singing like high-ten-sion electrical wires. At various checkpoints, it was the same. More dead. No bullet holes only great slices from a large blade. The door to the control room hung by one battered hinge as if some mighty force had simply kicked the three-inch thick metal inward.

With a collective drawing of breath, the entry team hit the room. Two to the right with weapons up, two to the left and one on his belly facing the center. No shots were fired. Nothing moved. The white tiled floors were red with the blood of those that had worked in this room. The room smelled of death. The horror frozen on the faces in the rictus of death gave testament to the bloodletting, which had occurred. A man's head lay in a bowl of liquid, slightly green in color as if he was examining the chemical effects closely. His body lay three feet away. Whatever had happened had been quick and decimating. Clipboards were still gripped in the frozen hands of rigor mortis. A woman still had her glasses perched on top of her head as her body lay across the counter split apart from her right shoulder to her pubic bone. The bathroom door stood ajar. A pair of feet could be seen from beneath the stall, as a magazine from the New World lay askew next to them. One of the special ops troops nudged the door open with the barrel of her rifle. Inside was a man who had taken the last crap of his sorry life. His eyes remained open in astonishment as his head had been cleaved from his skull to his neck. Along with the blood smell, lingered the scent of the man's unfinished business. Well, the soldier thought, he could finish it in hell. She left him sitting there on his worldly throne.

If the missile had been near completion before, it wasn't now. A melted lump of metal stood on the rack. Michele could not imagine the amount of heat it would take to do that. There was nothing left to do here. She slowly backed her team out of the death. The scene would be etched in her mind of the blood splatters decorating the gleaming white tiles of the floor and wall. As she reached the door, only she could look back into the room. The floor, walls and to the ceiling. She stared in awe above at the blood drawn symbol in the center of the ceiling. She did not know how she would describe this incident in her report but she would have no problem describing the symbol keeping watch over the crypt of evil before her. It was the same as rested on the left breast of her uniform. A sign of hope amidst destruction. Michele's team faded into the forest as the sun broke over the mountains.

The small apartment was lit by candlelight. The candles were stuck into the necks of old beer bottles surrounding the young girl. Marie lay on the thin mattress; her sweat glistening in the glow of the candles which flickered around her. She shivered a little as she drew the old wool army blanket tighter around her shoulders. The contractions hit again and tears fall from her dark brown eyes. They were coming closer together now. It would not be long before her baby would come. She was afraid, as she lay in the shrinking pool of light alone with her grief and the small life fluttering inside her swollen belly.

It had been tough but they had survived. She had met Frank in the small mid-western university town where a small resistance cell had formed among the students and some of the adults left alive. The ones that had refused to bow down before evil and accept the implant. The group had been small, only twenty or so. They were not very good fighters but they could gather intelligence. They had taken care of one another and somehow there had always been enough food to share and some place to stay warm. She thought she might have fallen in love with Frank the first day they met. He did not have the pretty boy looks you might call handsome but his warm smile and light blue eyes were beautiful to her as they were fueled by his kindness and bravery.

His story was pretty much the same as hers. Agents of the Enemy had destroyed his family for nothing more than refusing to sell their souls for the price of the implant. His mother had been gang raped and tortured before a bullet finally ended her pain. His father had been forced to watch the horror and he screamed until his vocal cords ripped, drowning him in his own blood before they could crucify him. But they had hidden Frank well. The teenager had been hidden in an old bomb shelter that had been long forgotten by city authorities and did not show on any plat maps of the property. With words of love, his parents had put him there the day of the massacre. After that bloody day, Frank had emerged and left the small Alabama town. For five years, he had survived with cunning and courage on the back roads and the forest as he traveled north, where he found the small group of souls who loved one another. Where he had found Marie.

Marie had grown up in the college town where her Dad taught science to the young ones who had come seeking knowledge for a better world. She shared him with two older sisters and a younger brother. Their Mom had died of cancer when they were young. Perhaps it was better. She had been spared the horror of what had come. And come it did. Enemy soldiers and strange man-wolf creatures decimated the small city. The thriving people in this innocent town of fifty thousand were wiped off the face of the earth in less than two years. What remained were small pockets of survivors who had become extended family. Not only for survival, but also for that which every human craves: companionship and love.

Marie's survival had been more luck than anything else. She had felt sick that day and didn't go to school. Anyway, her attendance had always been great and this was her senior year in high school. She was entitled to a day off. As she lay there switching the channels on the TV, she noticed most were not even broadcasting anymore. Just the twenty four-hour news stations and she could not stomach the reports of war and terror which just seemed to run a continuous monologue of carnage and fear. Even the newscasters looked pale and frightened. She flipped the set off and decided she was hungry. She flip-flopped into the kitchen, still in her Winnie the Pooh robe. Well, yeah she was a little old for that, but it was so trendy. Blahh—. Plus it matched her dark green slippers her dad had given her. She went into the walk-in pantry and switched on the light. The pantry was her Dad's pride and joy. His favorite hobby was always building things. Anything to do with wood. He would spend hours in the little wood shop behind the house enjoying the music of the saws and creating something of his own from the rough wood, mastering the design with his own hands. Yep, Dad fancied himself a true carpenter. But he wasn't perfect and that little imperfection probably saved his daughter's life.

The tie to her robe had caught the doorknob and pulled the door shut when she entered. After picking out a loaf of bread and some peanut butter, she turned the handle and pulled. She promptly sat very unladylike on her butt looking stupidly at the doorknob still held in her right hand. The bread had smashed under her right leg and the peanut butter had bounced into the corner. Ah, the wonder of plastic. She got the giggles as she realized how stupid she must look. Raising up she tried the door and found that it would not open. Great, she thought, she was going to look like an idiot when she had to beg one of her vicious siblings to let her out. Winnie the Pooh robe and all. She waited.

Not long though. About fifteen minutes later, she heard the laughter of her two sisters as they arrived home from college. She hesitated, not looking forward to the ribbing she was going to take for this predicament. Then the front door crashed in and the screaming began. Mercifully, Marie fainted shortly after the rape and sodomization of her sisters began. Marie woke in darkness. The bulb had either blew or the power had been cut. It took a few moments to clear the confusion of why she was lying next to the crack of the pantry door. Then she remembered. Not being able to get out. Then the laughter. Then the screams. Her face was sticky with peanut butter as she lay there listening for any sounds. All was quiet. Then she heard the refrigerator outside the door kick on, and then the light flickered back on. Her eyes adjusted after a few moments and she stared at the crack at the bottom of the door. She watched in shock as the blood flowed into the tiny room. It was not peanut butter on her face after all.

Her brother saved her. He was only fifteen but he had been a hero that day. In the blur that followed she remembered his young strong arms dragging her from the pantry. He tried to turn her head away, but she glimpsed the bodies of Becky and Christi spread eagle in the kitchen. Her mind recoiled; remembering the blood drenched thighs of Christi on the kitchen table. And the auburn hair of Becky as it hung over her face. Her nude body had been tied to the counter bent at the waist. A blood slicked rolling pin protruded from her anus. Marie passed out again. She vaguely remembered Johnny getting her to her room. Somehow he had a gun in his hand. Dad had hated guns. She didn't know where Johnny had gotten this one but it was a big revolver and it looked deadly. She knew Johnny practically dressed her. She wasn't much help. She kept telling him she had to clean up the peanut butter and bread. It was in the pantry. It was all over the floor. She had to clean it up before Daddy and Mommy got home. That wasn't right was it? Mommy was not coming home. There was more than peanut butter on the floor. Johnny whispered comforting things in her ears as he helped her pull her jeans, T-shirt and shoes on. She didn't have the energy to be embarrassed at her brother seeing her nakedness. They left the house with Johnny supporting Marie most of the way. Brother and sister ran for their lives into the darkness, which had settled over their quiet little town.

Sometime in the next weeks she came back around. Johnny had protected her and they had joined up with a large group of survivors at the chapel on the university grounds. Her Dad had been killed, Johnny told her. Government troops had entered the class and separated them, student and teacher into two groups. Those with implants and those without. The group with the implants was told to report to City Hall. After their departure, the commander gave the order to open fire on the remaining. They left the dead there among the books that spoke of peace in the future. So it had gone. The seeking of knowledge and peace had been replaced by the reality of survival. They fought for survival every day. They hunted food and shelter and they fought the Beast. Six months ago, Johnny had died. The young man had been killed; fighting to protect the ones he loved and for what he believed in. There are no age requirements on heroes. They all stand tall.

Frank had loved Johnny like a brother and Johnny had proudly been the best man a year ago at the small quiet ceremony celebrated among the survivors as Frank and Marie sealed their vows of love before their only family now. And now nine months later, the fruit of their union was ready for arrival. Frank had gone to get help. And had disappeared. Marie hugged her swollen belly as the contractions began again and the tears flowed down her face.

Marie screamed as the birth began. She screamed in pain and in fear for her child. She could not do this by herself. Her love for the tiny soul she carried soared up and through the soft blue light bathing her tormented face. The young woman closed her eyes as peace washed over her and listened to the voice whispering of the wonder of birth in her ear. Her breathing steadied as she was enveloped in the sweet smell that reminded her of honeysuckle fresh on the vine.

The door slammed open and there stood Frank with two men and a woman dressed in black. She recognized the symbol on the breast of the uniforms. She had seen it before. Her love swelled forward. Her man was safe. He ran to her hugging her to his heaving chest. His heart pounded like he had been running a marathon. "I'm so sorry," he said, "We ran into some problems but I found the good guys." With a glance at the Dominion woman, he added, "and gals." She returned his smile. "They've got medical training. They can help. We'll be okay." Marie smiled at her husband who was talking so fast that he was on the verge of babbling. She raised a finger and placed it tenderly on his lips to shush him. Frank heard the tiny cry, as Marie opened the wool blanket next to her. Frank gazed with love into the blue eyes of his daughter. His healthy, beautiful daughter.

They would have to go soon to the safe house. But for now, this small group celebrated the birth of life in the midst of a city of death. Frank and the team bowed their head in thanks and wonderment as Marie spoke of the beautiful young woman who had come in her time of need. In the warm blue light, her hair shone like honey and her eyes could only be described as that of the great expanse of the ocean. When the child had burst forward, she had smiled with the knowledge that only a mother could know. The miracle of birth itself and the renewal of light in the darkness of the world. Marie closed her tired eyes as she held her daughter tight against her chest feeling the tiny steady beat of that heart against hers. And in the desolation around her, she held the promise close that had been told to her. Her daughter would know peace. As she drifted towards sleep, Frank asked her if she had thought of a name. "Mary," she murmured, "I think that is a beautiful name." Mother and child slept in peace as the eyes of another mother watched upon them.

Do you believe in miracles my friends? I do. I have seen and heard of too many not to. But how big of a miracle must we see to believe? I sit here and watch my old hands write the words which form from my brain fed by the depths of my soul and heart. I feel the blood course through my body feeding it the oxygen and nutrients it needs for survival. I feel the beat of my ancient heart with its paper-thin walls as it co-ordinates the functions of this shell I abide in. I can touch and feel the texture of my paper. I can smell the fragrant smoke from the burning hickory wood as it warms me against the chill. I can hear the laughter of my friends. I see the hope and wonder in their eyes. I love the noble beast that sleeps at my feet while I finish these thoughts. All of these are miracles to me. Perhaps they seem small but are the greatest of the gifts we have been bestowed. Yes, I believe in miracles and mysteries. As I look into the eyes of the child at my elbow, I see the deep blue lit by waves of crimson. Eyes are the windows to the soul and in these young-old eyes, I see the destiny of man. This miracle will be the greatest of all.

Their heritage was marred by the day of rage and blood. The rebellious ones carried the blackened burns of the Father's anger. Crimson adorned the protectors with the blood of the Mother. There was desolation, guilt, and hopelessness in that place where there had never been before. In the fury and the tears, no one heard the child.

Many of us have gathered here at home. Sanctuary. For many reasons, we have returned to our heart. One is for practicality. There are no major battles to fight at this time. We have faced the Enemy and have been successful more often than not. The more intricate detail is however, that Silas has destroyed much of his own. In his rage, he has massacred thousands of his own people. I know we will face him soon but for now the lull holds. We must plan carefully for that day.

The other reason we gather is to celebrate the seventh year of our loved one, Jarred. He has grown and is a handsome young man taking the best of both from his mother and father. Already he grows strong but is quiet and has Ashe's soft way of laughing. Except for his eyes, he has the dark coloring of his mother. Those eyes that I could get lost in. The quick charm of the child lights up those blue eyes and if you look long enough, you can see the ripples of crimson flash like lightning over the deep sea. He is a good-natured, if mysterious, child and spreads the warmth of his love throughout his extended family. Especially Micah when he is home. Jarred never strays far from his godfather or Saint who like the good dog he is splits his time between the old man who loves him and the others that need him.

Jack and Shannon had just returned from England and were set on making this party a big to do. After all, one's seventh birthday is a big deal. Especially to the seven year old. And so it was. A beautiful party with all our loved ones there. Except for Rachel. She sent her gift and best wishes, however remained in the field looking for someone to fight. She has never been the same since the death of Joshua. I have seen the reports from the field although I think sometimes that Micah and Jack try to protect my old heart from the daily horror. Rachel is feared now. If not before, the Enemy realizes what they have loosed upon themselves now. The fury of Rachel Beck is legendary. I don't think enough Enemy blood can be spilt to sate her thirst for the vengeance of her brother's death.

Micah, Jack and I sat in the office enjoying a very old Scotch that had found its way into my hands. Micah and Jack spoke of the war. Jack was telling Micah he wanted to go back to England as soon as possible. "I think", Jack said, "that I may have a good lead on where the creatures are coming from. I might be wrong but the initial data looks good." Micah opened his mouth to ask a question when Jarred walked into the room and closed the door behind him. "It is time Uncle Micah, we must go now."

Earlier, the celebration had been pretty traditional with the chocolate cake, which was Jarred's favorite and the blowing out of the seven candles by the guest of honor. Jarred was just beginning the monumental task of opening all of his presents when Mara and Christina came in the room carrying a small wooden box decorated with a single red ribbon. As Mara set it down in front of the smiling boy, she told him that this was a very special present. "It is from your father," she said. "It has remained in safe keeping as his instructions were until your seventh birthday. Now it is time." Jarred's eyes sparkled as he gently untied the ribbon and opened the box. Inside lay a small necklace with a pendant engraved with the symbol we all knew so well, that of the Archangels. It shone in the light reflecting silver in his young eyes. Inside, along with the pendant was a letter from his father, our beloved Ashe. The letter was that of simplicity surrounded by mystery. It read, *My Dearest Beloved, it is the time of seven. The ones that love you so much have protected you. Now is the time you must return that love. For all of those now and that have been, your love must be a beacon shining in the darkness. You are the One now. My love will always embrace you. Love, Your Father.* Our eyes were moist with unshed tears as he lowered the silver chain over his dark hair and the pendant lay against his chest. With wonderment, we watched as the pure silver beat with a blue pulse next to the small heart where it lay. Saint went to the boy and sat at his side with his mighty head held high as the crimson flashes crept across the blue eyes we could only guess at the mystery, which lie behind them.

Micah got down to eye level with Jarred and asked him what he meant. Jarred said that they must go. All of Dominion to the place. We would leave by the light of morning. "Where to?" Micah asked. As if in a trance, Jarred slowly turned and pointed at Jack. "He knows." was the reply. Jack dropped his glass of scotch in the silence.

The War Room was full. The Council of advisors was present as well as the rest of us. Micah and Jack along with Shannon sat at the head of the long table. Mara and Christina sat beside me. Micah explained the situation to the council. "From a military standpoint, we are pretty much at a stalemate. We have destroyed much of the Enemy's capability but Silas is still well hidden and his soldiers number in the millions. To draw Silas out, we must offer him the ultimate prize." To their horror and surprise, he told them what he thought the prize was. Mara burst into tears.

Christina spoke to the gathering. "I have been in the circle and have meditated, listening to my heart for the instructions of what we must do. I agree with Micah. As unbelievable as it may sound, I think it is the only way to end this. In the beginning it was faith that led us to this path and in the end it must be faith that we follow. All of these numbers and battle plans are worthless against the evil we face. The best we can hope for with all our strategy and planned operations is to hold the darkness at bay. It will take faith and love to drive it from our world. Our Father has been kind but for the choices we make there have always been sacrifices needed. Though my heart breaks with that knowledge, somehow I know deep within, that now is the time for that sacrifice."

The debate among the gathered went on. To put everything at risk based on the words of a seven-year-old troubled them. In the end, it was those words that decided it. The great oak door swung inward as Jarred entered with Saint at his side. Jarred walked to the front of the table as Saint sat beside the child who stood with shoulders squared, his young eyes with the ancient knowledge falling on the all.

"It is my time now. In my dreams, my father has shown me what must me done. All but twenty including the council must leave at morning light. In the plains we will meet our enemies who will try to destroy us. They may be successful; I have no way of knowing that. Only that this is the way we must face them. This will be the final battle. All will either be lost or won but the time has come. It has been called many names but Armageddon will suffice. The blood that is spilt will wash this earth. The Enemy will come. They have no choice. They will come for me and only my death will satisfy Him. I am the One. The wolves will seek the lamb but I know their true nature and because of that they fear me. In the midst of this darkness, I have been chosen to be the spark that ignites eternity. To light the path unto home. Let it be done."

And so it was. As the sun crested over the mountaintop, we left our home leaving only a couple of dozen behind. The council and a handful of security and communications personnel who would have no one to protect or call if we failed. The call had gone out to all the units and enclaves. They were moving by air, land and sea as we were. My old hip ached as I climbed into the Land Rover beside Christina and Mara. As the massive convoy pulled out, I looked at Sanctuary and feared it would be my last glimpse of that which I had loved so much. We turned toward our destination, England. Where we would make our stand in the shadows of the ancient monoliths called Stonehenge.

As I write these words, I wish I could say that they were filled with hope. I cannot. I look at the faces of the ones I love around me and I think of death. But then, I look at the child that leads us and there is a whisper of faith in the words that he spoke. That is what it will take. With all our technology and weapons, it will be the faith of a child that will decide our place in this great cosmos. And the faith of another as he has led us through these dark times. The keeper of the faith and wisdom of a mighty man who even now holds the tiny hand of the child's in his great one. Micah Sarentstein. With a warrior and a child rests our greatest hope.

Silas sat in his great War Chamber. More or less in human form, his burning eyes gazed at the leaders of his forces. He sneered with disgust at the way this mighty army had been decimated by the actions of the pitiful band of rebels with their puny god. They sat in silence after Silas' tirade about their incompetence and stupidity. No one dared to point out that Silas had caused the death of millions of his own soldiers and civilians left in his territory. It did not matter to the demon. The death was all that mattered. The death of these insects who sat before him. Silas began his revelation.

"I have dreamed of my Father and know what must be done. Even now, the puny armies of our enemies move towards the fields where we will destroy them and drink of their blood as it stains the ground where they will gather. All of our forces will go there immediately along with any civilians who can carry a weapon. If they refuse, kill them where they stand. In three days time, I will feast upon my victory and receive the pleasure of my Father's blessing."

One of the Air Force generals spoke up, "I don't know if it's a wise idea to put all of our forces in one place———". The general's words were cut off as the bright red bolt of flame from the hand of Silas engulfed him. His screams ended quickly as what was left fizzled into a pile of burnt dust. "Any more opinions?" inquired Silas. There were none. A few moments later, the orders were sent out worldwide. And the exodus began.

The terrible beasts and abominations walked, slithered and crawled towards the place as if pulled by a sense of migration that they did not understand. One thing they did understand, there would be plenty of flesh to feed on. The horrors were returning home.

The eyes of the others watched as the humans made their way through the wastelands and ashes of the world. Their weapons were ready and soon the long wait would end.

Home lay in ruin, as the Father wept with his mighty head held in his hands. He looked upon the one whom was a part of his essence and the tears fell upon her body. In his grief, his sons and daughters were dispersed waiting in their own regret and fear. The little one had run amidst the blood and sadness into the forest of insanity. As he held the face of the one he loved, He felt the slight breath stir beneath his trembling hands.

Micah listened as Jack and Shannon detailed the information for him during one of the breaks. "It's weird," said Jack. "Just thinking about it makes my blood run cold. Of all the places on earth, he picked this one. Shannon and I have been charting reports of the creatures' movements and from what we found they all lead back to one place: Stonehenge. If you believe in certain places on Earth that are strong in mystical energies, then this is one of the most powerful. No one ever really figured out what the purpose of the structure was, but we think we know now." As Micah looked at where Jack's finger lay on the map of the English countryside, Jack said in awe, "I think that is the gateway into hell."

Captain David Stichcomb was in hell right now. He team was fighting on the coast of Dover, England. An Enemy unit had fired at them from high up on the cliffs whose whiteness was now stained with red. Added to that, they had been attacked by creatures that had come out of the ocean searching for human flesh. The firefight lasted the better part of the day but they had succeeded in destroying both. As his team made camp on the top of the cliffs, David held his steaming mug of coffee in his hands as he gazed at the dark waves as they rolled inland from the eternal expanse of the ocean. He shivered slightly as he bundled in his sleeping bag and slipped into the sleep of the weary. His dreams were filled with the sounds of battle and the vision of smoke, which hovered over the river of blood. At the end of the river, stood a child waiting. Waiting for him.

The quiet of the Virginia morning was shattered as the rocket blew the building into a thousand parts of wood, debris and human flesh. The division of soldiers moved into the Enemy camp as the other troop barracks were blown skyward. Colonel Rachel Beck led the charge as her driver tried to steady the armored SUV while Rachel fired deadly rounds from her Uzi with her right hand and chucked anti-personnel grenades with her left. He glanced at her face, which sent shivers down his spine. Such a beautiful face to be filled with the frightening fury there. Her teeth were drawn into a snarl as she reloaded and grabbed more grenades from the front seat. All he could think of was avoiding the potholes and being glad that he was on her side. He turned the windshield wipers on to scrub the blood and body parts from the window and drove on, as the compound became the sight of slaughter. Less than an hour later, the airport next to the compound had been secured and the troops had loaded on to the transports which, after refueling, had taken to the skies. Soon, they would meet the others. Rachel sat quietly among her troops, cleaning her weapons.

Colonel Lian Xing's tanks ran point through the silent outskirts of London. No one challenged him. His division would camp soon and get some much-needed rest. They had traveled far and fast to meet Micah's deadline. He was glad for the lack of battle right now. He had an idea that there would be more than enough waiting for them when they arrived.

In groups small and large, the civilians came from their hidden homes and camps. An unknown force seemed to be pulling them as one. Many died as they made their dangerous trek. The men, women and the children of the world moved to the source that drew them. In their dreams, he spoke. *"I am the One."*

In that mighty circle of stones, a low humming could be heard. And if one could listen closely, you could almost hear the cries of a child.

We had arrived just hours before dawn. We encamped on the slopes surrounding the valley just opposite of where the circle of stone pillars sat in silence. And we were not the only ones. Thousands gathered with many more on the way. The sight of it all staggered my old mind. I thought I had realized the vastness of the forces that our leaders had amassed but to actually see it in one place was something else. The mighty weapons of war encircled our camp. Tanks, armored personnel carriers and transports. Mobile mortar and rocket platforms aligned beside them. The airplanes had landed just a short distance away in a flat area that had been quickly readied by the engineers. Everything had been brought from the field hospitals to the often forgotten but necessary mess tents and toilets. Tents and pre-fabricated buildings quickly sprang up to shelter the crowds of civilians who were beginning to show. We seemed to have brought plenty of extra equipment. I don't think Micah was surprised that the others had come.

Micah had found a natural cave, carved over the centuries into the hillside. The engineers enlarged and reinforced it. Here, he would place Christina, Mara and myself with the children. He assigned a young captain and his Special Forces unit to secure the cave. Jack and Shannon had left with a scout unit to make their way to the great stone circle. Jarred sat outside the cave entrance with his arms around the great neck of Saint and stared at the great stone monoliths as the sun dawned over the valley. I looked into those strange eyes and sought the answer for what he looked for. If there was one, I could not fathom it. We waited.

As the sun burnt off the morning mist, the day warmed. Eyes stared upward in wonder as the winds blew and actually cleared some of the polluted air out of the way. For the first time in a very long while, we sat entranced, watching the pure blue sky with the cotton candy clouds. Throughout the day, more arrived until our end of the valley seemed it could hold no more. From the flatlands to the slopes, there were people and the utilities of war everywhere. As we looked to the other end of the valley near Stonehenge, we saw that we were not the only ones here. The Enemy had arrived.

Jack and Shannon met with Micah and Christina. They poured over the technical read outs, which were much beyond me but in essence said that something strange was going on inside that stone circle. The electro-magnetic and radio spectrum analysis indicated some type of energy source. Jack's guess was that it was a portal of some type. A place where dimensions met and somehow co-existed. As if a rip had been made, allowing the cross over from one to another. He believed that this was the focal point from where the creatures had come. He showed Micah his battle plan. If it could be opened, then he also surmised that it could be closed. And that was exactly what he and Shannon wanted to do.

Reports were received from the scouts on the perimeter. Enemy forces had made no hostile moves yet; they seemed to be settling in just as we had. The scouts had sighted terrible beasts gathering in the hills above the Enemy and us but again, no aggressive moves had been made yet. The scouts had seen some of the creatures in small skirmishes among themselves but they had not come near the humans.

We sat eating our meals by the fire. I could hear the sounds of readiness. Quiet discussions of battle plans and the clink of weapons being cleaned and vehicles being fueled. Cigarettes and pipes glowed in the dark as small groups sat and whispered to each other in the eerie silence. I don't know what people think during these times, only mine. I thought of the path that had led me here and wondered if I believed in predetermination. When had my long journey started? Was it the night my wife died? Or had events been set in motion even before then. I look into the face of my friend Micah. Where had his begun? I guess I do believe some things are determined. But, I also think we make choices along with way. Those choices chart our way through the numerous paths and tributaries that we call life. And death. I look at the stars and think of the worlds there. They have no concern over this tiny planet we call home. We have made our choices and if they were not the right ones, I don't think those so far away really care at all. I guess all we can hope for, is that the Master who made us all still cares. I think he does. Even for a scared old man huddled in the darkness on the edge of the destiny of the world.

Silas sent a short note to Micah. Four words until destruction. *"It begins at dawn."*

They searched for him but the twist and turns of the forest were great. If only it had been known that such a finite line existed between that of dreams and that of nightmare. The First Ones gathered as the reality of nightmare approached with the terrible sound like that of a child crying in the night.

How does one describe the end of the world? That, my friends, is the question of questions. The answer is simple. You cannot. The human mind cannot process the scope of the destruction and horror. It has certain fail-safe devices and filters to try and shield us from that which would drive us mad. Even with those blessed mechanisms in place, we still see too much. How do we cope with the insanity? Some don't. Some fight until their last breath. I just cried until the tears ran out and kept writing. God help me, I bear witness to what no human should have ever seen.

In the early morning darkness, Micah spoke with Jack and Shannon. Their divisions would have a single mission. Drive forward to Silas' command that had been centered just before the entrance to Stonehenge. Destroy it and the portal. Micah would remain with Jarred and the other children. They must be protected at all costs. Rachel and Colonel Ling would lead the combined forces straight up the Central Valley while Jack and Shannon ran the right flank of the slopes towards Stonehenge. The seventeen aircraft that were left would hit whatever came down the valley on the left side.

Silas met with his leaders. No more fancy battle plans and statistics were needed. He had over two million soldiers and civilians plus the creatures that seemed to be on his side. They would simply overwhelm the rebels by their sheer numbers. Their orders were simple. Slaughter the upstarts down to the last man, woman, and child. Silas then met with the head of his Special Services unit. Steven Uris had once been a captain when there was a United States army. He had been convicted of having raped, tortured and killed twenty-seven women on military bases where he had served. Those were only the twenty-seven bodies that had been found. He had been convicted and sat on death row when the world fell. His unique talents had been useful to the Beast and he had risen through the ranks of the Enemy forces. Now, he held the rank of General and commanded the most feared troops of the New Order. The old Nazi SS would have looked like boy scouts compared to his men.

Silas had not slept well the night before. He was assured of his victory but this damned dream had come to him and he had not been able to shake it. He had stood alone in the blood of millions staring into the far end of the valley. All were dead except for he and one. A tiny figure walked towards him. In his dream, he trembled at the approach of the small boy with black hair and the strange eyes. As the child stood before him, his gaze drowned in the blue and crimson swirls of those eyes and saw the truth mirrored there. And he screamed, until blood burst from his throat and ran in a river to the source of what was. Silas' molten eyes flew open in the dark. And he was afraid. None of this he told to Uris. Just gave him his orders. They were simple. Find the child he described and bring him his head. The smile of the General could not be contained as he bowed and left the tent of his King.

The dawn broke over the hills, the golden rays shimmering in the green valley and slopes. Engines revved, weapons locked and loaded while last prayers were said. As the mass roared toward the enemy, Saint howled, as did the beasts that poured into the valley. Like two mighty tidal waves of humanity and not, they met in the middle of the valley and the blood ran like nothing ever seen before. Or since.

In the darkness, he slept in the midst of the terrible nightmares. His cries were heard but so far away. He was so tired and lonely. Maybe tomorrow he could start again. Searching for that place he could not remember. The coldness burnt his skin like thousands of small flames. In the middle of the fortress of his dreams dwelt the nightmares that he could not wake from.

The sounds caused birds to fall from the sky, their tiny eardrums shattered. The tanks and artillery opened up as the whistle of mortar rounds sounded through the air. The explosions blew bodies into bits of bloody rags no longer identifiable as human. I watched as a young man was standing and the next moment only his boots littered the crater where he had been. Bright red boots, which had been black a millisecond before. A woman's head went careening down the slope as her body ran after it for a few seconds not realizing she had been killed. A red mist mixed with the smoke of the massive explosions and gunfire and a rain of blood and body parts drenched the valley. The scream of the jets overhead thundered as they brought hell to the left of the valley. Cluster bombs and napalm scorched the ground while soldiers ran screaming as the phosphorous burnt through their flesh and into their bones. The tanks and jeeps burned and rolled from rocket fire looking like the tiny toys scattered in the tantrum of a child. Except the tiny plastic soldiers bled the color of crimson.

Colonel Xian Ling called in more air strikes to his left. His command vehicle lurched as a mortar round missed it by a few feet. He watched as his soldiers closed for small arms combat. The sound of Uzi's, M-16's and AK-47's blended into one great roar. A ball of flame rose from just in front of his carrier and he felt the sickening lurch as it rolled. He crawled out of the side window with blood streaming down the right side of his face from a gash. His driver's head had impacted with the windshield and crunched inward. His radioman had been speared through the chest by a three-foot long piece of metal piping. It took a moment for Ling to realize that the young woman's heart was hanging on the end of the pipe. He rolled to his left as some demonic creature leapt for his throat. Emptying a clip into the man-sized thing, it went down. For good measure, he burned it with a frag grenade. He could see the face of the enemy now and he led his troops forward. He had been trained to win and focused all of his energy on that, ignoring his wounds. He was still focused when a rifle round shattered his left eye, blowing his brains onto the young soldier beside him. He would now find his victory in death.

The New World private had pulled the ring on the grenade arming it and pulled his arm way back to throw it just like he'd been taught. Except now his face was flat in the dirt and as he raised his head to look at his right hand, it was no longer there. He lay there thinking that they had not taught this in basic training. What do you do when the grenade goes off early? He found the answer in the darkness as his blood soaked the ground around him. You die.

Sgt. Eric Stano was a killing machine. He had off loaded after the rockets had disabled the vehicle he was on. Now, he moved in the smoke and confusion and had managed to get behind a company of enemy troops. He worked his way forward, back towards his team slicing throats and using his silenced Browning to sow even more confusion. He added a few well-thrown grenades to the excitement. A coward killed him. He had been running toward the back of an enemy soldier when the young man's nerve had given and he spun around to run back. The bayonet caught Eric in the chest. Looking into the wide eyes of the youngster twelve inches away, they were entwined in an obscene dance with Eric being led by the blade sunk into his organs. As his vision dimmed, Eric decided to end the dance. He pointed the Browning touching the forehead of the hysterical boy. He pulled the trigger and as the soldier was hurled back by the mushrooming round, Eric felt the blade pull from his body. As he lay there in the mud fed by his own blood, he thought of his wife and daughter. Eric's eyes closed for the last time.

The rockets and tanks did not differentiate between civilian and soldiers. The people who had come, drawn to this battlefield were torn apart from the blasts. One poor man whose bowels would not hold had run for the port-a-toilet. A mortar round made that his last resting place. Perhaps not the most dignified but he had not seen it coming. The civilians waded into the battle picking up weapons from the fallen. Thousands of smaller battles were fought on the stage amidst the larger. With enemy and creature alike. The outcome was the same for both sides. Death floated in the fine red mist.

Jack and Shannon inched forward behind the cluster of rocks. They and their personal teams had made it about two-thirds up the valley. The price had been high. Many of their dearest friends, who had fought along side of them for many years, now lay dead. But the goal was in sight. They could see the command tent of Silas. And just behind that, the entrance. To Hell.

Captain David Stichcomb lay behind the small boulders at the entrance to the cave with his H&K sniper rifle propped on the small tripod. He selected his shots through the powerful telescope and squeezed the trigger smoothly as the weapon rained death in the valley. His team was the last line of defense for Jarred. He had been hand picked by Micah and he would not let either one of them down. Another enemy appeared in the scope. Before the soldier could hear the crack of the rifle, his head had disappeared in a blossom of bone and blood. David moved to the next target.

Micah was at the entrance of the cave where Jarred and fifty other children huddled. Christina and Mara tried to soothe them moving around the little groups and talking to them. I sat at the entrance with Saint beside me and I watched the unbelievable destruction below me. Micah was calling in more air strikes. The left side of the valley was in flames but the Enemy's anti-aircraft guns had done severe damage. Only five of our planes were still up. The squadron commander told Micah they only had a few missiles left but had decided they were going to try and soften up the area around Silas' headquarters. Micah asked the commander what they would do when they ran out of missiles. The commander replied they had discussed that also. I saw a sad smile come over Micah's face as he told his old friend in the air good luck. And goodbye. I didn't understand until I saw the five planes turn in a v formation and head for the headquarters in the rear. Six remaining missiles flew. Four made it through the anti-aircraft rounds and found their targets. Machinery and men flew through the air near the headquarters but no direct hits were made. I saw something monstrous slither out of the tent and raise its obscene arms to the sky in rage. I knew I was looking at Silas. The five planes turned and dove. Three were hit with anti-aircraft fire or shoulder fired rockets. Two burst into fireballs. The third seemed to turn and aim for a battalion size group of enemy soldiers. And hit the group head on. I shook my head. I thought I could see the pilot giving them the finger through the glass of the cockpit before he struck the ground killing those below.

The squadron commander, Travis Shore looked at his wingman flying off his right. They had pulled up from the fireballs that had lit the sky. They spoke on secure communications and with warm farewells, turned the planes around. Both gave the thumbs up sign, then they dived. Coming in low, the air burst with shells but none struck. They were flying so low; no one could get a bead on them. Then the smelly spray fell on the gunners and they looked at each other in confusion. It smelled like jet fuel. As the horror of it dawned on them, it was too late. The planes crashed into the headquarters tent, igniting the fuel they had dumped behind them. The explosions bellowed with huge fireballs roiling into the sky, as the flames ran backward along the trail of fuel engulfing those caught in it. Silas screamed like those of the billions damned as the flames melted his skin and one of his eyes melted down the cheek of the beast like a foul teardrop. He ran half-blinded for the gates of home. Just in time to meet Jack Dalton and Shannon Gzar.

Jack and Shannon had inched the last hundred yards or so using natural and the dead as cover. Using special goggles that had been modified by Dominion scientist, he could now see the shimmering hole just inside the entrance of the stone circle. The theory was that a small, contained blast using proton enriched particle explosives would collapse the rift. He hoped the eggheads were right. He shifted the satchel of explosives behind his back and they continued to crawl.

From the right, came some type of six foot in diameter crab creature with razor sharp claws and fangs. Shannon lit it up with her silenced Uzi and watched as the bits and pieces flew apart. One enormous crab leg fell in front of him. He grinned at his wife and asked her sweetly if they could have seafood when this was over. He winced as she elbowed him in the ribs. Well, at least he hadn't suggested sushi. He motioned for his team to catch up with them and that was when hell broke loose. With fire, metal, and bodies raining down on them, he smelled the jet fuel and realized what had happened. He smiled and thought of those crazy flyboys. They had put on a hell of a show. As Shannon and he slid around the side of a large boulder, they faced the thing of nightmares. Silas in his true form.

Jack looked at the beast that towered above them. If you had taken a bat face, slapped it on top of a dragon's body and thrown a few scorpions, spiders and snakes in the mixture you might come close. Maybe. Yellow, foul-smelling blood poured from multiple wounds and one of the molten red eyes was gone. Just ooze running down its cheek. About half of it was charred and smoking from where the jet fuel had burned. Shannon opened up with her Uzi as Jack pulled his dagger. "You are one butt ugly son of a bitch," he said.

The bodies in the valley were piled so high that the vehicles could not move. Both sides had run out of mortars and rockets. Now it was down to hand to hand combat. As the war raged, battle lines disappeared. The fights were in little pockets amidst the creatures, which attacked all. The blood of the just and unjust ran thick.

Uris' team had moved to within a hundred yards of the cave. Bodies lay stacked like cordwood and he watched the Dominion Special Operations team led by Stichcomb as they killed anything that came near. He watched as the tall man with the eye patch lay down withering fire with a machine gun in his left hand and an old battered Browning pistol in his right. Uris pulled his squad leaders back and told them the plan. He made sure that the bulk of them thought they were doing a flanking maneuver. Not a suicide mission. Uris hand picked five men and started moving to the left.

The team opened fire with everything it had pumping round after round into the Beast called Silas. The creature screamed in agony as Jack and Shannon moved in for the kill. Jack saw Shannon stumble as a red blossom of blood appeared on her shoulder and belly. He whirled to the right and shot the soldier who had survived the fire bombing right between the eyes caving his face in from the heavy forty-five rounds. He saw Silas going towards Shannon and as his team continued to fire, he ran for the boulder using it as a launch pad to leap to the back of the beast. Jack fought as Silas reared and felt the burning in his side as claws dug deep into his flesh. Jack was pulled over the shoulder of the beast and felt his back break as he was slammed into the stone pillar at the entrance.

With blood dripping from his mouth, Silas leaned down to sink the sharp teeth into Jack Dalton's skull. Jack prayed for one more burst of strength as he reared forward and up, plunging the dagger hilt deep into the scaled chest of the thing before him. He felt the blade hit home and saw black blood burst from the wound as Silas' death scream deafened them all. The beast fell to the side and shuddered its last breath. Jack's team had moved in with flame-throwers to make sure there was not an encore.

Jack knew he was dying. Whatever had snapped in his back wasn't going to heal. He thought that his miracles had run out. With dizzying pain, he turned his head to the side and saw Shannon lying in the grass, a large circle of blood beneath her. He crawled to her and turned her head. Her eyes fluttered and met his. "Did we kill it Jack?" she whispered. "Yes, my love. We killed the shit out it." tears rolling down his face as he spoke to the reason he had for living. He looked proudly at their team. They had indeed followed him to the gates of hell. Now it was time for him to finish it. Shannon and he would finish the mission, together.

Jack called his second in command over and spoke quietly with him. The young man did not want to leave Jack. "It's time son. You've done your job. Now go and let me do mine. Get back to Micah; tell him it's done. Tell him that we love him. He was our father and so much more. Help him protect the child. That is what matters now. "Protect the child." With tears in his eyes, the young captain nodded and led the team back through the bloody battlefield toward the cave.

Jack and Shannon lay propped in the shadow of the great pillar of stone listening to the wind for a few moments. They stared into each other's eyes and there was nothing left to say. Not on this side of the mystery called life. Together, they crawled into the circle, Shannon leaving her lifeblood as a trail. Jack could only move his right arm and leg but that was enough. As they got close, they could see a faint shimmering circle. They did not want to focus on the images that flickered beneath the shimmer. They held each other close and tenderly kissed. As their breath intermingled, Shannon thought she could see a blue haze around them. Jack whispered he loved her and pulled the pin. The explosion rose to the sky as the ancient stones tumbled forming an ageless tomb for two beloved souls.

Micah saw the explosion as wave after wave of the enemy came towards the cave. Ammunition almost gone, they went hand to hand. I sat against the wall firing my shotgun seeing the blood splatter the walls as they breached the cave. The children were behind us with Christina. I saw our brave young men die feet away from us as the enemy just kept coming. Jarred had eased up against me with Saint. I was too busy trying to reload and fire to notice him. Micah looked to the right just as a rifle round struck him in the shoulder lifting him off his feet. I saw a man with the pure eyes of evil crawling through the entrance of the cave. Four others followed. I shot one, blowing his legs out from under him in bloody bits. One raised a machine pistol towards me and I realized, too late, at Jarred. Before he could fire, Saint bolted and leapt tearing the man's throat out. Mara ran forward, red eyes blazing and stabbed one of the men in the throat before a burst from Uris' machine pistol cut her down. I knew she was dead as I saw the bullets strike her chest. I was looking down the barrel of a rifle held by a man beside Uris. I saw my death down that long dark tunnel when the right side of his face disappeared in a spray of bloody splinters. Micah's Browning still smoked from where he had fired lying down. The evil glee shone in the eye of Uris as he aimed the pistol at the chest of Jarred who sat frozen beside me. I pulled the trigger on the shotgun just to hear the firing pin strike on an empty round. As Uris laughed and pulled the trigger, a hurling body knocked me aside and covered Jarred as the rounds fired. Micah had made it to his knees and held the Browning in a two handed stance to control the trembling of his wounded arm. The bullet left the barrel of the gun and sliced off Uris' face at the grin. The top of his head splattered at the entrance of the cave, while the body, still wearing that grin slid to the ground. I gently rolled the young captain's body off Jarred. The boy had not been harmed. Five bullets had struck the brave young soldier in the back as he shielded the child's body. His open eyes gazed heavenward which I knew had been his true path from this earthly shell, which I held.

Jack and Shannon's team had arrived just in time to finish the enemy who had been intent on assaulting the cave. All was quiet on the battlefield. With Christina holding Jarred tightly in her arms, I staggered to the mouth of the cave and stood with Micah. It was indeed the end of the world. Over three million people lay dead in that valley. The hideous creatures lay in death though I have no idea of their numbers. Micah learned of what happened to Silas and our loved ones from Jack's team leader. The survivors straggled in. Rachel was not one of them. She had been killed pulling a wounded soldier to safety. Saint lay dead from multiple gunshots. His mighty jaws were still clamped onto the throat of the man that had killed him. My tears burned. To the end, he had protected the child.

Micah sat on the boulder letting the medic patch his wounds. About two hundred and fifty survivors, including the young children were left. Micah limped over to Jarred and hugged him. We were his only family now. Micah raised the blanket, which had covered the brave young man that had saved this child of promise. He gently closed the eyes of Captain David Stichcomb. As he knelt beside the hero, his tears fell and I heard the words he whispered," Blessed be the children for they shall know war no more."

Epilogue

The small group of souls huddled together wait. They wait for salvation. They wait for the hope and goodness, which shall come from the sacrifices made this day. We have protected the children and most of all, the one child that will lead us. They wait while he and Micah begin their journey with my old body along to tell the tale. We walk hand in hand to the ruin of stones on the hill. It is there that we will begin and hope that there is an ending. I walk with my head held high. Though my heart is heavy with sorrow, I feel that the secrets of the child are at hand. And I think those secrets will be wondrous.

Book Five
Thy Secret Name

He walked across the strange field kicking up tiny puffs of pollen, which he did not recognize. His dress was that of a simple man. Tunic and breeches, that were laced with a soft leather type material. The same material that his boots were made of. The birds here, he did not recognize and he gazed with wonder that some had two pair of wings. As he crested the hill, he saw the city burnished in the setting rays of the twin suns.

Micah and Jarred walked hand in hand just a little ahead of me. We stopped at what was left of the entrance of the circle of stones, once called Stonehenge by man. There was not much left except a pile of rubble. Jack and Shannon had accomplished their last mission. The stones had fallen in a domino effect, crashing into the center of the circle and burying whatever mystical portal had existed. I saw the anguish in Micah's eyes and I knew he was thinking of his two closest friends lying dead under the tons of rock, which lay before him. My heart broke for him and I understood. I had loved them too.

I turned and look back the way we had come. The valley that had once been a lush green now lay soaked in the blood of millions. In the distance, I could see the white vehicles circled at the camp on the far end of the valley where we had left the survivors. Micah's orders had been explicit. If we had not returned in twenty-four hours, Major Johnson would take Christina and the remaining people back home to Sanctuary. From there, they would try to rebuild civilization. So few had survived the horrible day of death. I don't know if two hundred and fifty souls can make it work, but there is hope. And perhaps there are more out there. Somewhere.

Micah kneeled beside Jarred and I saw him wince. His right arm had been cleaned and patched by the medics, after he had been shot by the evil Uris during the battle at the mouth of the cave. Micah had survived as he always has. For the first time that I can remember, Micah is not carrying his old Browning pistol. I saw his eyes that day as he stood at the mouth of the cave looking at the destruction. He stood so long with blood running down his right hand, I was afraid he would pass out from blood loss. Then he simply dropped the weapon and I heard the clatter as it fell among the rocks. As far as I know, it's still there. Micah said that guns would not help us where we were going. I shivered at that statement because somehow I knew it to be true.

I joined them as Micah asked Jarred, "Well, we're here. What now?" Jarred looked around at the devastation and pointed to an area just to the left of where the entrance had been. Those strange eyes of his flickered faster as runners of crimson light sped across the deep blue background. "There," he said. "That is where we enter the forest." We walked to the patch of scorched grass and waited.

The air grew thick and heavy around us as if a storm were coming. It was, but not from above. As Jarred stood there in a trance, the pendant he wore pulsed with energy and we watched as the ground begin to shimmer and rotate like a massive whirlpool. A rotating mass that looked like it would suck our souls deep down into oblivion.

The vortex swirled with colors and images moving so fast as to be unrecognizable. Then the flattened whirlpool became an oval and rose from the ground. It stood before us beckoning, looking like a fun house mirror rippling at a thousand times normal speed. I felt my hair and beard rise as if a powerful wave of static electricity were washing over me. My eardrums felt a pressure just short of implosion. I didn't know if my old body would survive this. But then again, I didn't know if any of us would. We took each other's hands and stepped through. Into the darkness that was Hell.

Hell was not the flames that I had imagined in my childhood dreams and thought of during my adult years. It was dark and cold. That's not the total truth. It wasn't the pure dark of the absence of light. It was dim with a slight perception of a reddish tinge. We turned on our flashlights that we removed from our small knapsacks we had brought and the beams shone forth against the darkness. There was no reflection of light; the darkness seemed to devour the particles of light that went no more than a few feet in any direction. The light did not fade, it just ended as if cut off by a thick black velvet curtain. We stood there for a few minutes trying to let our eyes adjust and listen for any sounds, from the dark.

We stood there motionless trying to get our bearings. Solid rock was beneath our feet. We could see nothing above us or to the sides. The portal was no longer behind us. It felt as if we had been buried beneath tons of rock deep in the center of the earth. As our ears adjusted, we could hear what sounded like a breeze high above us. My heart thudded as I heard the slither of something or someone to my left. I turned my flashlight in the direction of the sound but the light only stopped short without revealing the source of the sound.

Micah cocked his head as I strained to hear what he did. It was a distant high-pitched warbling sound just brushing the edge of our hearing. Jarred stood with his head bowed as if in prayer or meditation. Then his eyes raised and turning just a degree to the left, begin to walk. His necklace glowed with a faint blue light that seemed to keep time with the beat of his heart. Here, he would lead. Micah and I followed. Our journey had begun.

As we walked forward, growls came from the darkness. From where, I could not tell. The sound seemed to echo in the space. Jarred walked forward unafraid. I wish I could say the same. I had seen the beasts on the battlefield. The thought of one of them coming out of the darkness with me unarmed was not a pleasant one. I jerked as my mind conjured up tricks making by body think that malformed hands and sharp claws were brushing against my skin. I finally got over my jitters after reminding my old ass that if a seven-year-old was unafraid, I could stop jumping at everything. That's when it grabbed me and I screamed.

It felt slimy as if it had just come from some subterranean swamp, which had never seen the light of day. My heart froze and I did not think it would ever beat again. Then it let go and went back to the abyss it came from. I had smelled the foul breath close to my face and heard the sibilant whisper, *"You are damned"* as it slithered away. I could have passed it off as the hallucinatory fears of an old man, except for the three red marks on my wrist. Left by long, dagger like claws. We walked on. The whispers were silent and no more talons reached for me in the darkness. It would soon be much worse than these puny little games. Much worse, indeed.

Jarred led us to a small entrance where Micah and I had to duck slightly to get through. When we straightened up, we could see a cavern, which seem to go on forever. The light was much better in here though tinged with the same red. Not the red you would think of as a color but more visceral. It was as if a fine sheen of blood floated on the very air before us. The flames were here. They spiraled upward from the very rocks themselves. A waterfall stood before us towering into the ceiling of the cavern. What flowed was thick and dark. I felt my gorge rise and I threw up a vile mixture of spittle and stomach acid as I realized what floated in the river of blood. Body parts. Millions of them as they bumped against one another drifting down the currents and swells.

We climbed down a twisting trail of rocks until we arrived at a wooden bridge that crossed the expanse. The bridge looked ancient, made of a wood that I did not recognize. The posts at the end of the bridge were adorned with two skulls of an unknown creature. The bleached bones were twice the size of a human head and horned. Vicious looking canines were prominent extending over eight inches. Jarred stepped onto the bridge as the boards creaked even with his weight. Micah and I followed close behind. As I tried not to look into the vile wash that swept under us, I believed I knew where the ancients had gotten their concept of the river Styx. They had not done it justice in their writings.

The first board that broke sounded like a pistol shot in the silence, and then the center caved in as we plunged into the bloody river. My screams were drowned by the crimson froth as the strong currents pulled us under.

The beings gathered around the one who looked so different from them. They listened with awe as he spoke with words that they could understand. Words which had never before been spoken by their leaders. Words that described love and peace from the One that had made them all. The crowd drew close to hear the words of the man and to touch him. Others fled in fear of the unknown. And the fear became hate.

My head burst through the surface of the thick liquid as my body was swept downstream. I saw Micah go under, then reappear holding Jarred above the churning fluid. I grunted as my ribs smashed against rocks that lay half submerged in the boiling blood. I took a great breath as the rapids sluiced through the outcroppings and propelled me faster. Those seconds that passed made every nightmare I'd ever had seem inconsequential. As I fought to stay afloat, I saw the flotsam that was swept with me. Half-rotten skulls and severed limbs jammed into the crevices of the rocks. Visceral trails of intestines and other internal organs floated with me in the red foam. Eyeballs rolled by me, one moment staring up and the other looking at the river bottom. My flailing hands struck severed fingers, ears and shredded flesh as I fought to survive the torrent that careened me through the carnage. I fought to stay conscious, not only from the lack of oxygen but from the shock of the horror I was immersed in. I tumbled over a large boulder and fell. It seemed as if I hung suspended for minutes before I plunged the six feet into the clear pool of crystalline blue water.

My pores opened wide, screaming for the pure liquid that I floated in. The pleasure was so intense it was painful as I was cleansed. I knelt on my knees in the shallow pool drinking great gulps of the cold water. I saw Micah and Jarred lying on a small beach a few yards away. Thank God, they were okay. I slowed down when my stomach cramped as if to reject the joyous offering of the water. It settled and I drank a little more as I waded to my friends.

Micah was washing his face in the pool when I made it to him. He looked at me and I knew I had not dreamt the nightmare. He had seen it too. We turned to Jarred who lay quite still staring upward. If not for the rise and fall of his chest, I would have thought him dead. Then I saw his eyes as they moved around the stone walls that encircled the pool. And I saw the wonderment in them. Micah and I studied the rock walls, which looked older than the pyramids. I did not recognize the script engraved into the mighty carvings in the rock. Along the top, were upright coffin sized indentions where beautiful white marble statues stood guard over us. Jarred stood up and pointed at one of the statues which came alive with the flap of wings and descended towards us. Mighty ebony colored wings that spread the width of two men.

The dark angel landed gracefully and stared at us with liquid eyes that shimmered with the purest red I have ever seen. His voice rumbled through the cavern, "You do not belong in this place. You must turn back and return to the world that you call home". Micah asked, "Who are you"? "We are the guardians of our beloved," the one before us replied. I stared into that cruelly beautiful face and could sense no evil, only the dispassionate tone of one whom might tell a stray dog to go home. Micah stepped forward and the air became alive with the thrumming of wings as at least twenty more of them took to the air. Ten landed, surrounding us. The others floated above us with black wings spread. The leader pulled a great sword and moved towards Micah.

Sapphire lightning flashed as thunder rolled echoing from the walls of the cavern. The red dimness gave way to the piercing rays of blue, which birthed from a vortex a hundred feet above us. The dark angels looked up and the sword stayed in the hand of the being before us as they came through. Ten of them. Angelic beings with wings spread and swords readied. It was the most beautiful sight I had ever seen. They glowed with a light within, feeding their blue eyes that were the color of a million gas flames joined as one. Eight had pure white wings. The other two had crimson tips on their mighty wings. Tears sprang to my eyes as I recognized one of the two. Ashe Duncan had returned. Ashe and the other great being with the red tipped wings settled next to us. Ashe smiled his small, secret smile but remained silent. The other angel was even taller than Ashe and he wore the crest emblazoned with the symbol of our home. I could see the resemblance in Ashe. I knew the being that stood before me had created that symbol. It was the symbol of the Chief Archangel of God's Army. Michael towered above us.

Michael spoke to the dark angel who stood before us. His voice, though soft, reverberated with great power. "Seth, you must let these pass. It is the only way." Seth argued, "It is not the way. These puny beings are only human. They can do no good. They will only die in great torment and it is my duty to protect those that come here by mistake, even if they are nothing but humans."

Michael sheathed his great sword and walked to Seth. Almost lovingly, he placed hands on the great shoulder and gazed into the crimson eyes. "My brother", he said, "You have done well since the Time of Sorrow that you have been here. You have done what our Father sent you to do. You have served as guardians of the gate and I know that you have searched for that which we cannot find. The disagreement over the humans is an old one. But now they come of their own choice. To lead us to our salvation." Seth shrugged Michael's hand from his shoulder in disbelief. He sheathed his sword as he paced with fury and frustration of the darkly beautiful face. "I can't believe it," he said, "The blood of our family was spilt over these pieces of clay that breathe. They are so weak they would have destroyed their world, even without the Beasts' intervention. Now, you say they can do what we could not."

Michael smiled a sad smile and raised in voice to speak with all of his brothers and sisters both dark and light. "It is because of our arrogance that we failed. We were the First and the first loved. In our arrogance, we could not conceive of a greater love that could encompass all. And in that time of selfishness, we destroyed what we loved the most. The humans that stand before you are frail. They are full of emotions that run in their veins from love to hate. The choices made by some have been self-serving but it is in the nature of the choice. The choice that we forgot in our arrogance that they have not. That the freedom to choose is the most precious choice of all. The responsibility for self-determination that has brought forth courage and love from the very souls of those frail beings that we looked down upon. And in that way, my loved ones, they are even greater than us."

Michael turned and looked at us. I trembled. What were we to these great beings? An old man, a scarred warrior and a young child. I felt as if we should fall to our knees in the presence of them. Michael looked at Ashe, who had remained silent throughout the exchange. Michael said, "Ashe. I believe it is time to introduce your son to our family." I fought the urge to giggle. And me at my age, I should know better. But, I had never seen the look of surprise on the face of an angel before. I thought Seth's jaw was going to hit the ground. I pinched myself quickly and grunted, seeing Micah staring at me wondering about my strange behavior. Somehow, I managed to swallow the laughter. With age comes wisdom, or so I'm told, and I did not think it wise to laugh at immortal beings circling you with drawn swords. Nope, not one damn bit. But it was funny...

The young boy walked into the great arms of his father and was embraced as the mighty wings folded into a great protective cocoon. The love that radiated from that embrace almost brought me to my knees. The love of a father for his only son. There is something special about the love of your children. Mine had loved me without question even during the dark times. I missed them so much. I never found them after the war started but I remembered the last letter they had written together. They had not bowed to the Beast called Legion. I knew they would fight to the death to preserve the goodness, which had come mostly from their sweet mother. Not only did I love them with all of my heart, I was proud of them. I saw the same in the face of Ashe as he held his brave son to his chest. Whatever Ashe had seen since he had left us, his love had remained. As the rest of the angels, both light and dark settled in a circle around us, Ashe turned and brought his son to Seth. "This is Jarred", said Ashe. "He is of us and you. The blood that flows in his veins is of the First and the Fallen. And of the humans that we call man. He is the One that we have waited for during the long night. He has made the choice of his own free will. The one that we have waited for so long."

I stood in amazement as I watched the molten red eyes of Seth stare into those of the young boy before him. He stared into the depths of those blue eyes that sparkled with the crimson reflection of his own contained in the tiny body of a human. I don't know if I could have withstood that piercing gaze. My old body may have been consumed. Jarred stood tall and proud with his father's hands on his shoulders and the communication of his eyes passed between Seth and him without words. In the silence of his family, Seth wept tears of crimson as he knelt before the boy.

They brought their sick and lame to him as he spoke long into the night. His touch upon their malformed limbs and blinded eyes burnt with a blue flame. Cries of wonderment and thanksgiving lifted to the heavens as their loved ones walked and saw the stars in the firmament and beheld the wonder of the moons for the first time. In the government palaces, worried voices spoke in whispers of what should be done. The world must be rid of this evil menace.

Michael and Seth held conference. It was agreed that the boy would be allowed to follow his path. As the great winged beings stood honor guard, we walked between them into the entrance of the forest before us. Ashe walked with us to the archway as we looked inside at the dark, twisted trees bathed in the dark red light. He hugged his son as if not wanting to let go. Finally, he stood because he knew he must. "This is as far as we can go," he said, "Where you tread now, not even the mightiest among us have been able to penetrate. The Father has marked all of you. None other than the one you seek can harm you. You will be afraid, but remember that our love walks with you. From the time before remembering, we have waited. Our hope rests in your courage. The children must come together once again." With that, he kissed my old cheek and held me like a child as I trembled. He embraced Micah as his earthly father. As he kissed Jarred on the forehead, I saw the blue tears began to fall as he rose into the air where Michael and the others joined him. They entered the blue vortex. Seth and his entourage returned to their places as before. We were left alone to go forward into the stillness that lay before us. With sure steps, we entered into the dominion of the damned.

Not much was said as we walked through the winding path before us. I was too overwhelmed by the sights to say anything. I jotted down notes in my battered journal, which had survived somehow through the ordeal of the river. After a little, we rested and ate. I didn't know how long we had been here. Our watches had stopped when we stepped through the portal and in this place I felt time had no meaning. I wondered what had happened to the ones we had left behind. Had it been a day? Or a year? I could not tell. I think time moves differently in this terrible place. I looked at the forest that surrounded us. I wondered if the bent and torn blackened trees had ever been green. I didn't think so. Their twisted trunks and limbs curled and arched as if not knowing the direction of the nourishment they sought. It reminded me of nightmares I had as a young child.

Some adult in my life, I believe it might have been my Aunt Susan, had wanted to read me a bedtime story. I might have been four or five at the time. Unfortunately, she chose *"Hansel and Gretal"*. The story had terrified me. I wanted to scream for her to stop reading the horrible story. But I had been taught that grown ups knew best and to mind my manners. As she kissed my forehead when she finished, I slipped into the darkness of sleep. This was like the terrible forest of my dreams and my fear as the evil witch who wanted to devour me chased me. I woke up my parents screaming. Maybe adults did not know best after all.

Micah sat looking into the winding paths leading deeper into the dark forest. One could get lost in here forever, he thought. The paths branched and turned in a maze of no form or reason. He looked at the trees and scrub that looked as if it had been burnt and mutated. He had seen this before. On the edge of the blast zones from the detonation of atomic devices which killed millions including his wife and daughter. He shook the thoughts away as he looked at the child beside him. He drew upon that strength which was deep within his soul. Whatever they faced, he would do as he had done for so long. Protect the child.

In his lair, the Beast awoke and smelled the scent of the humans who sought to face his unholy fury. As his terrible eyes searched the darkness and his strength swelled from the damned before him, he felt what he did not know. The fear of his black heart as they approached.

They came for him, as he knew they would. His time had been so short among these beautiful beings. He could see the path clearly. That which lay before him. In their fear, he would face the accusations in a formal but quick trial and sentence would be passed. He knew what the judgement would be. His words would survive though. Already they spread like a fire that could not be extinguished. In the alleyways and in small groups that met in secret in their homes, the words were repeated in excited whispers of hope. At some point in time, they would be written and passed down through the ages as the sacred writings of the Teacher who had come to them in their time of need. Peter Beck would be remembered as the saviour of this world unknown to man.

Micah and I followed Jarred who walked through the paths with sure steps. The pendant glowed brightly at his breast as he followed the directions of whatever force led him. Looking at the branches and trails that threaded in our way, I'm sure I would have been lost. Jarred's intense eyes seem to gleam with expectation as we trudged deeper into the forest that never seemed to end.

I don't know when I first saw them. Perhaps they had been there all along, blending into the landscape we passed through. The beasts were still, except for the glowing eyes that watched us with hunger and maybe something else. Fear. I saw the tiny squirming insect type abominations, which slithered and crawled over the greater beasts. The variety of creatures was that of a fevered nightmare. If we were truly in Hell, then these were the appropriate denizens of this domain. But none moved to harm us. In the glow of the blessed necklace that Jarred wore, they shrank as if in fear from the symbol of the mightiest warrior of all. Only their gleaming eyes followed us in the timeless scarlet glow of the great vastness that lay before us.

As we walked, Micah and I spoke of our friends. The warmth of those memories passed the time and seemed to ease the aching of my hip. We chuckled at the good times we had been given, even in the midst of the darkness that had come to our world. We missed our friends and family. A random line of an old BJ Thomas song floated through my mind, *"Friends are like warm clothes. Best when they're old and you miss them the most when they're gone."* Amen, Brother Thomas. I'd drink to that. All the ones we had loved were gone; it was just us now. I hope that I told Micah how much I loved him. It's hard to remember after everything else happened after that. But, I think he knew. We don't know how precious those simple moments are of communion with a close friend or a loved one. I wanted these things more now than ever. They were worth more than all of the worldly treasures you could imagine. Jarred walked on in silence. If he held communion, it was not with us.

My old mind felt as if the fog had been lifted from it. I remembered the faces and words of those I held dear through my long life. I had grown up in a much different world where the supernatural and mysteries did not involve our ever day life. My beautiful Rose and I had a good life. When it ended, all I could see was oblivion. I remember the blue-green eyes of the one we all knew as Maggie, as she covered my shivering body and whispered of wondrous things to come in my ears. I know who she was. I believe it with all my heart. I see the intense eyes of Hans, the warrior-priest who told me of my bit part I would play in this tiny corner of our universe. I remember Sam Cochran who climbed from the pit of insanity as he, Hans and the others spilt their precious lifeblood that day to protect our promised one. I saw the birth of Christina, who would carry the love for this used up world through all of her days. Her compassion would lead us out of the darkness. I saw all of these simple decent people who had made the choices for us when we cowered in fear and despair. Their choice had been hope. The hope that people like Joshua and Rachel Beck would not have died in vain. The hope that the voice of Peter Beck as he spoke of freedom at the brink of his death, would not be silenced. The hope of thousands who had given their life, their deeds written in the books of the fallen in the Hall of Valor, that from their blood would spring life for the children who followed. I am honored to have known so many and read of many more. Now our hope is with the unusual child who leads us. It is that hope and love that will preserve us in this valley of death.

He stood before the judges in chains. The whip marks dripped red from his shredded back. The bones of his fingers had all been broken as well as his ribs, which pulsed from the fractures inflicted there. Even now, he was bleeding internally. If they had been patient, he would have died soon anyway. But they were not patient, they were afraid. The sentence rang through the great hall. Death for the one whom had brought blasphemy to their world. Peter Beck gazed calmly at his accusers and smiled. Already the words of hope were ringing around the world. In a mighty wave that could not be stopped, it would engulf all before it.

The last remnants of the path lay just before us. It ended in the entrance to a massive grotto from which a bloody, foul smelling mist poured forth. We had heard the screams before we saw the entrance. The screams of agony that should not have been made by human voices. The screams of the eternally damned. Jarred waited for us and as I placed my shaking hand in his young one, we walked forth into the lair of the Beast.

In the great cavern, human beings burned while alive, as the smell of their cooked skin and melting organs was everywhere. Demons and beasts ripped them open alive and feasted even as they still screamed. Before us were billions of tortured souls as they begged for the end to their misery. Women held their murdered children as maggots ate into their maternal flesh. The rapist and child molesters were castrated by terrible she-demons with the slice of their curved daggers. Over and over again as did the murderers who suffered the fate of their victims only to return yet again and repeat it over again and again. Flesh was ripped and shredded by the black shaggy beasts that wandered among them. My horror was complete when I realized the beasts still had shreds of clothing hanging from their horrible bodies, which were covered with sores that oozed vile pus and excrement. Somehow I knew that these beasts had once been humans. This was the true nature of their souls, which they had given to the Beast and marked with his number. My mind shut down; it could take no more. I grabbed at Micah's hand and looked into his face. I screamed myself, for his hair had turned solid white. I looked at my beard and screamed again for so had mine. Above my screams I heard the laughter which rolled like dark thunder across the visions before me. Through the smoke and blood, I saw it rise from its throne. And I beheld the Beast. It was known by many names. I called it Satan.

His roar shook the foundations of the abyss. Birds would have fallen from the sky and cattle would have slumped to their knees and died from the hemorrhage of their brains. Thousands of miles away, dogs would have turned on each other in a violent rage and the wolves would have eaten their young. But there were no creatures to hear the fury from the Evil before us. Only a pitiful band of humans that stood in its shadow. How anything could look into that terrible face and live, I do not know. Only that somehow, we did. Jarred's pendant pulsed in a steady beat and perhaps it had protected us all. I cannot adequately describe what stood before us. It was the sum of all nightmares and more. The face did have many horns and the body was like that of a dragon. He towered at least twenty feet above us. The tail was that of a scorpion and the many legs like a spider with each foot the size of a small car. Venom dripped from the curved fangs, sizzling as it touched the blistered red body. Across the great chest was a scar as from the wound of a great blade. The face was the worst. The face of an evil so old that it lit the ebony eyes with flames, the color of burning lava. He laughed as he shook his fist to the heavens, *"Is this the best you can send to me, Hated One? I shall kill them a million times over, just for your enjoyment. They will be honored guests in my home. I have prepared a special place for the pilgrims sent as lambs by their puny god."* With dark glee, he pointed at our "special place" that had been prepared for our arrival. I think I fainted when I saw the three crosses.

A gentle slap brought me awake. I looked into the concerned face of Micah and he sighed with relief as my breathing leveled. I was going to tell him about this terrible dream I had, then the stench hit me and I sadly realized it had not been a dream. I got to my feet as the Evil One glared at me with amusement. Jarred placed his small hand on my shoulder and looked me in the eye and whispered, "You'll be okay. I know what to do." I appreciated the kind words, but unless he could open up one of those portal things and let about a thousand archangels through, I wasn't feeling very confident right now. Jarred started forward toward the Beast and Micah grabbed him. The flickering eyes met Micah's one good one and he said; "It's okay Uncle Micah. You have brought me this far. I could not have asked for any better protector. Now, it is my time to do what I was sent here for. Wait with Theo" We waited and prayed as the tiny boy went to face the Devil alone.

Jarred walked straight and proud right up to the very feet of the Beast. One slap by those talons would shred him to pieces. The Beast stared down at the little boy at his feet. The boys with eyes of blue and crimson flashing across them. *"Why do you come to me boy? Do you think that necklace that hangs from your scrawny neck will protect you? I know who it is from and I hate him even more than I do you humans. He sends a whelp to fight his battles for him. He is a coward."*

Jarred spoke in that soft voice of his. But it was heard throughout the abyss. It reverberated as the pendant pulsed with a powerful blue light. The demons and beasts cowered in fear at the voice of the child. Jarred stepped even closer as the mighty Beast sat down upon his skull-encrusted throne. I did not have to write the words of Jarred Duncan down. I remembered them until the end.

"I am not just a boy. I am the One. In my blood runs that of the First Beloved, your dark dreams and that of the humans. I have come, not to wage battle but to reveal secrets. The secrets from the before and the Time of Sorrow. I know these things as I know Thy secret name." The Beast stood as transfixed by the gaze of the child before him. A great silence reigned in Hell and unknown to us, in Heaven also. Jarred climbed into the great throne and sat on the lap of the Beast. With his soothing voice whispering comfort to the Death before him, he told the story of the beginning and the end. As we listened, Micah and I wept knowing the pain that we had endured had been nothing but a single drop in the vastness of sorrow as it was spoken by the lips of an innocent child. A story that had never been heard in all the time of creation.

In that place called Home, there was silence as the Father sat still by his beloved. His children waited with great wings and weapons of war at rest now. With shimmering blue eyes, the focused all of their hope and will, sending it forth to the tiny voice that whispered in the darkness.

Seth and his fellow guardians sat in the eternal circle formed at the base of the rocks where the Seraphim had written. They held the hands of each other and focused on a tiny circle in their mind's eye. In that small circle beat the heart and fed the love of the child that it encircled.

At the end of the bloody valley, there was silence. Christina listened as the world held its breath. She gathered the young ones to her and they sat holding each other in the darkness praying the simple words that rose as truth from their souls.

Somewhere, millions of miles from the small war torn planet, another hurled through the great silence of space. Rotating around twin suns and lit by the light of three moons. The green and blue lighting had started as the clouds moved toward the hill. A very human man, who had made his choice, walked slowly up the hill. The cross stood waiting, in silence.

The Story of Jarred

"In the very beginning, all was darkness and chaos. Out of the darkness, the One came and was filled with goodness. For what is good, there is evil and He found it waiting for him. The battle went on for an eternity. The battleground was created from all that was. The universes swarmed with dust as the stars were birthed in the midst of the conflict. Dimensions exploded upon one another and in the destruction were the beginning of creation. In all of the things we call time and space, He fought the Dark One for the sake of what would come. In the end, He vanquished the Enemy. Pure evil never dies the final death, but he was banished from the known.

The One sat in his place and dreamed of what could be. He was lonely, so he created another and they were together. Creation was their playground and they loved. As they played among the beauty they had created together, they saw the wonders of beauty as the all was born of their love. Matter took a little from its creator and became beauty and love. They looked upon all they had made and felt sadness. Sad, for they had no one to share it with. With that knowledge and love, they became Father and Mother.

The First Beloved brought the sounds of music and laughter to the place called Home. Beautiful, with their flaming eyes of blue fired by the very energy of Mother and Father. Their snowy white wings were so great; the very molecules of space propelled them. They helped mold the things that man would call time, space and dimensions. They helped chart the myriad of stars and universes and set the motions of the galaxies as they spun through the great vastness. They sowed the seeds of creation on the rocks that rotated around the stars, which bloomed into plants of all the colors of the spectrum and then more. In their artistry, they painted the great oceans and mountains. The hearts and souls of Home rejoiced as the First Beloved grew and multiplied.

They had names of love that they were called by the Mother and Father. The names recorded in the great Book, man would not recognize, but later gave some of these beings the names by which they were known to them. Each of them was precious and brought something individual to the collective of the Home. Michael was the first and as such, was the protector. His loyalty to Home would always be paramount and he stood ever vigilant against the Evil should it surface. Lucifer was the second. He was known as the Prince of Light. His unique ability was that of the fire that would power the stars. He reveled in the freedom as he roamed his Father's domain bringing light upon the darkened infant worlds. Many more brothers and sisters came, each bringing their own personality and unique gifts to that wondrous place of Home. They lived in happiness and peace and thought nothing more could bring any more joy than they already had. Then came the birth of the most special one of them all.

Father looked upon the billions of worlds that floated, lifeless in the infinite places that he had created. He found them beautiful to behold and he loved to share them with his beloved and his children. He found that he wanted more. It was not enough, that this playground be empty except for the visits from Home. In his great mind, he began the design of the animals, great and small. The birds that flew on the currents and the ones that swam in the deep were detailed in perfection with the mechanisms of life and reproduction, so that they could bring life to the barren planets that charted their empty courses through the void. The First went here and there joyfully, placing the designs of the Father into motion and reporting on the development of the dynamics of their experiments. A great Council of the Seraphim was formed to watch over the new forms which now brought life and noise to the before silent planets. The human mind could not conceive of the multitude of the creations that flew, swam and walked upon the worlds. On a tiny speck of a world that would someday be called Earth, life sprang forth in the oceans. Great beasts walked the fields and the winged ones flew high above carried by the currents of the wind. And there was peace among them.

In their Home, Father and Mother looked with satisfaction on what they had created. It was good. They spoke in whispers of how much more could be as they held the small special one to their breast. There was great excitement as well as great awareness of the responsibility that would be. For to give the gift of intelligence and the ability to create, there must be direction. What form would that direction take? Would it be the will of the Creator or must there be more? This was the greatest question of all, as they gazed into the eyes of the little one nestled between them. It was in that gaze and the understanding of his special gift that the answer was found. Believing that to give life would be love, He realized that to give life and allow choice, would be the greatest love of all.

So it was. He breathed forth life and the great experiment began. On a few worlds, beings awoke for the first time to the sounds of the creatures around them and felt the warmth of the suns on their faces. They took their first infant steps to that of becoming. The steps became strides. Societies were formed and civilization rose. Throughout it all, the choices were made and they flourished in their freedom.

Lucifer and Michael went everywhere together and explored as the new life sprang into being. They were inseparable as they spoke of the progress as they played with their baby brother in the gardens of Home and felt the happiness of being with Mother and Father. The angels along with their brothers and sisters kept watch over the new ones that now knew life, as they would tiny children. In the time before, the beings saw the angels and they were not afraid.

The first argument was over nothing. Michael had been by himself that day, Lucifer off lighting another star, no doubt. He had stumbled over a small planet in the corner of a galaxy, which had caught his attention. Something about the blue oceans and the white swirl of clouds brought him closer and he went to inspect it. For the first time since the beginning, the foot of an intelligent being walked on the face of the planet we would call Earth. Michael fell in love with the planet and its lush gardens filled with all sort of wildlife. He swam leisurely in the warm waters of the ocean. Michael felt this would be a special place and told his Father so. The Father's love for Michael was great. He was the first born. Because Michael loved this planet so much, he would give him a special gift. A gift as no other. The Father made man in his image and breathed life into him. And on this planet which Michael loved so much, man was given domain. Michael was ecstatic. He could not wait to tell Lucifer upon his return. Lucifer smiled weakly at the excitement of his brother and hurried away to the garden. In that garden, jealousy was born.

Lucifer spoke before the council trying to humiliate Michael about getting too involved with the children they had been assigned to watch over. Michael was spending way too much time with the beings on that insignificant planet of his and not taking care of other business at home. Lucifer stopped short of openly criticizing the Father for catering to the whims of his eldest. Michael was furious with Lucifer when they arrived at their home. Father was none too happy but he held his tongue at Mother's request.

The man and woman were happy in the garden that had been provided for them. They held communion with the beasts who came to them in peace. Michael came to visit often and enjoyed his time with these special ones. Even, the Father spoke to them, bathing them in his love. They were the center of attention for awhile. Perhaps too long. In time, Lucifer's jealousy turned to anger and then to hate. He would pay a visit to these puny beings that had taken the love of his brother and Father away. Soon.

Soon is a relative term when time and space know no bounds. But, Lucifer did go to the man and woman. They greeted him as they had the others and spoke of their happiness and contentment. Lucifer had to admit this was a beautiful planet and the beings before him beautiful also. Almost as beautiful as the First Ones. They had the potential for greatness. To be as great as he maybe. With that realization, he hated them even more. Like the lesser beings, his Father had created; the First Beloved had been given the gift of choice. It was that freedom that all of their love had been founded on. On this day, as he held darkness in his heart, Lucifer made a choice. He told the first lie. He told the humans that there was more and that is was rightfully theirs.

Lucifer sat in the garden, laden with guilt over what he had done. The young one came to him and asked him what was wrong. He smiled at his youngest brother and the love swelled for him. If anything was right now, it was the love he felt for the special one before him. He did not want to worry that young heart, so he just smiled and ruffled his hair, telling him everything was okay. But it wasn't. He had spoken with some of the others and they felt the same. This experiment called man had gone terribly wrong. It was becoming an obsession for Father and Michael. The ones that spoke in whispers felt threatened and felt something should be done to end this before it went much further. Even if it was harsh and radical. Feelings could be mended later but for now, the man and woman needed to go away. The ripples of rebellion had started.

Lucifer went back to the man and woman many times whispering of secrets that they had not been told. At first, they had shrugged the words off saying they knew nothing but happiness and peace. That was all that they needed. But little by little, the seeds of doubt grew from the poisoned apple wrapped in the lies of the angel before them. Soon, the seeds would blossom into the ugliness of arrogance. Lucifer left and told his followers that soon they would be rid of the pests known as man. Michael had always said that home was never silent. With all the joyfulness, music and the business of the universe there was always noise. On the day that Father spoke to the man and woman, that would change. They spoke to him in harsh words, challenging that they had not received enough. They demanded the knowledge that was their birthright. At that, Father fell silent. For there was no answer to give. There was no more knowledge to give. Father never spoke directly to them again. In the heavens, there was silence as the anger of the Father was seen for the first time ever.

Michael confronted Lucifer in the great hall of their home before their Mother and Father. He charged that Lucifer had sown the seeds of dissent among their brothers and sisters. Lucifer lied again and denied the charges. For the first time, he openly accused the Father of being in error when it came to the matter of man. He had made a mistake in the form he had afforded them and had coddled Michael's selfishness. The bitter words flew between Michael and his brother while the youngest hid behind Mother. Words that could never be taken back. Words that would lead to war.

The young one was afraid for he loved both his brothers so much. He did not understand a lot of the argument but his young mind knew that the terrible charges that flew back and forth would not be left unchallenged. He had seen the agony in his Mother and Father's faces that made him even more afraid.

Lucifer met with the ones who sided with him and told them to prepare. Things were getting out of hand. Michael was enthralled with his new toy, the humans, and Father could not make a decision. Lucifer would make the decision that was right for all of them. Later, the misunderstandings could be sorted out. Lucifer readied to take over Heaven.

Michael spoke with his parents and would not be calmed by them. Lucifer planned to make war against Father and that was unthinkable. He was the first born and the protector. Mother wept but Father said nothing, as Michael girded himself in armor and brought forth the mighty sword that had not been used since the time of chaos when Father had defeated the Evil One. Michael held the sword high and his eyes blazed with fury. War was at hand.

War in Heaven

Father and Mother spoke as they held the young one in the safety of their arms. He was what had been missing but they had not known. In him lay the secrets that would make man and all of the other children of creation one. His power would raise them to the pinnacle of the stars and more. He was what would complete them. That was his special gift. Now, they sat in fear and anger as the sounds of war filled their home.

The battle was enjoined that day as the angels made war. Brother against sister. Clan against clan. Lucifer led his army and was met by the Chief Archangel of the Father, his brother Michael. The blood flowed and the dimensions shuddered as the mighty clashed with sword and will. The battle was fought through the streets of Home and into the very center where Mother and Father watched as their children fought unto their very chambers. Lucifer and Michael faced each other with great swords drawn. The sharp blades had marked both as they danced to the deadly melody. Bodies lay strewn around the once peaceful throne. Loved ones had gone beyond to the Final Death. When the Father saw the carnage, he raised his hands in anger ready to end it all. The soft hand of mother stilled him as she whispered of the choice, which had been freely given and must be freely made. He wept as he stayed his hand because he knew she was right.

In the chaos, no one saw the young one watching as his brothers tried to kill each other. Michael had ducked a mighty swing by Lucifer and parried as the other was off balance. Lucifer fell to the floor and Michael was upon him. The sword held high arched downward in a deathblow. Mother screamed as she saw her son about to kill his brother and with a mother's instinct rushed forward. From the right, the young one screamed and ran toward Michael. He tripped over a small stone corner and crashed into the arm of Michael as it swung downward. Just a tiny push but that was all it took. Both Michael and Lucifer looked in horror as the blood of their Mother spilled onto the floor from where the sword had entered her breast. Somewhere far off they heard the screaming as she slipped to the floor and lay still. They did not realize it was their own screams they heard. Mixed with that of the young one standing there, watching the lifeblood of his mother run in rivulets across his feet. The roar of pain from the giver of life drowned their screams. The Father's eyes blazed with a fury they had never seen and he became the taker of life.

The war ended that very day in the despair and rage of the Father. His punishment was swift. For the angels that had rebelled, he colored their wings the color of their dark hearts and banished them from his presence. Michael, whose wings dripped crimson with the blood of his mother would wear those crimson tips for eternity as would his seed, as a reminder that it was his sword that had plunged into her precious body that he held even now. Man would know the coldness of the world they had abused and be given the knowledge they had sought. To survive, they must struggle. He banished them from the peace of his love and they cowered in the darkness. In his anger, he blamed the one who started this and his wrath was terrible as he killed his son that day. With the sword that had pierced his beloved, he plunged it into the heart of his son and watched as the blue eyes of Lucifer turned dark in his final death. Then he wept at what he had done and for all he had lost. That was not the end though. In their anguish, they had forgotten the small one who had seen all of the horror. The young one that held the promise of heaven in his abilities. In the ancient writings of man, this angel has rarely been mentioned by name. The old ones who had once spoken with angels in the earliest time of man had called him Memuneh, The Appointed One. He was also called by another name. Dispenser of Dreams. Not much was known of him, because he was lost that day. Not in death but in the insanity that incinerated his soul when he saw his mother and brother die.

He went into the dark forest of his insanity and forgot. He forgot his true name and his heritage. And in that forest where he had retreated, he dreamed and his dreams became the nightmare of creation. I know the child and I know his true name: Galen, the Beloved. He is the Dispenser of Dreams."

The Final Seeker

The cross was made of a dull gray metal which reminded Peter of stainless steel. It was not the wooden ones that he had read of as a child. Well over fifteen feet tall it stood, with a cross bar in which was imbedded leather like straps. A rolling ladder type apparatus stood beside it. The night had come and the triple moons rose reflecting off of the adjacent ocean which was the color of a deep burgundy wine. The guards that prodded him with black shock sticks seem to do so more out of fear than anger. A crowd waited on the hillside and watched him with dark eyes. Many, he recognized and he smiled at them in hopes of bringing them comfort. Some shrank in fear. Some hurled stones which struck his already bruised and marked body. At the top of the hill, the Chief Guard removed the shackles. Peter did not resist as he was hoisted onto the pole and his wrists strapped onto the crossbar. He tried not to tremble as he looked down upon the gathered citizens, priests, and politicians. On the ladder stood the Chief Guard. He looked into Peter's eyes with what may have been pity, as he readied the object in his hands.

Peter looked at the spike as it was loaded into the tube and heard the click as it was locked into place. He tried not to focus on it. Instead, he turned to the corners of his memory like sifting through old diaries found in an attic. Peter looked back to the steps that had brought him here. Had he been destined for this from the beginning? His training and work in law enforcement had made him physically tough. His later duties a planetary diplomat had taught him to look beyond his own small world and love beyond the human race. Maggie's unusual eyes and infectious laughter had turned his head. Soon, he had fallen madly in love with a woman who had not been from Earth. His love grew as they had two beautiful children and they were happy together. Until the Beast came. When he returned from Epsilon 7, he knew they were in danger and he had prepared.

They had hidden Joshua and Rachel. Maggie refused to leave his side and Sam, the young brave president, had been a friend until the end. They had killed his precious Maggie. It had been made to look like an accident but no leads were ever developed on the driver wearing sunglasses in the dark sedan that had run her down on the streets of Washington.

Soon after Sam had been assassinated, Peter was arrested on treason charges by Legion's forces. After a quick appearance before a tribunal, he was sentenced to death. The next day, he stood on the platform in front of the Capitol as the executioner prepared the guillotine. He remembered the razor sharp blade glinting in the sun. He had always felt protected even in his young days with the FBI. As he stood in the cold winter breeze, he knew his luck had run its course. As his head was placed in the stainless holder and the camera's zoomed in as the blade fell, Peter thought of what the man had said of choices and destiny. A quick slice of pain and his spirit had soared.

He had gone to the place of transition. He had made his choice. He did not wish to stay, he went on. The wondrous things he saw while in that timeless place took his breath away. Man's knowledge was not a grain of sand in the way of things. He went forward time and time again searching for the final goal. To touch the face of God. He learned from every experience and the mysteries of the all unfolded before him one by one. Before he came to this planet, he had met the one who had marked him for this journey. They talked awhile on the beach of a scarlet sea upon a world that did not yet know life. For Peter Beck, the final mystery was revealed.

Michael told Peter of the war in heaven and man's fall from grace because of the anger of the Father. The guilt felt by the Father was unbearable. He blamed himself for what he had loosed upon mankind. The pleas of his children and beloved had gone unheard in the Father's grief. He could have done no more than he did but that did not bring peace to him. The ones that had sought Dominion before had gone to love the Father and still he wept. The grief of the One, whom had created all, rippled through creation bringing sadness to the ones he had made. Michael had sworn in his mother's blood by his true name that he would make things right. Down through the ages, he and his clan had protected man and had patiently waited for the one who would have the wisdom to know what to do. He could not interfere but wanted Peter to know that his faith rested in him. When the time came, Peter would know what to do. Then Michael was gone. He had in fact sworn two oaths that day. The other was to bring Galen home.

The spike thrust through Peter's right hand. The pain was terrible and the laser immediately cauterized the blood that gushed from the wound. Another spike was reloaded and he heard the thump as the Chief Guard pulled the trigger sending it into Peter's outstretched left hand. These had been small spikes compared to one that was now loaded and shot into his overlapping feet. Peter felt the bite of the barbed point into the metal as the pain fanned along his body like a flame. The great tongs encircled his knees one by one and with a single twist, the snapping of the bones could be heard among the gathered crowd. Peter slumped as he passed out from the pain. As the ones wept in the crowd that had grown to love this man, the skies darkened with red clouds. Green and blue lightning flashed as the rains began washing those below in rain that was the color of the blood that dripped from the lone figure broken upon the towering cross. The clerics and politicians were satisfied. They left before the rain could ruin their fine clothes. Much of the crowd shuffled off. Only the devoted and the guards were left to watch the man die in agony.

The Chief Guard looked into the face of the man before him. The face was so different from his and could not be considered beautiful by any of their standards. There was something though that drew the guard to gaze into that face which even unconscious, rested in something like peace. He looked over his shoulder to make sure the leaders had left. He was just a soldier doing his duty. But he had heard the words of his mother who had spoken of this man. A part of him was horrified by the treasonous ideas that his mother spoke. But some part of it made his heart race as he heard the words of love and peace that the man had said. There was a ring of truth in them that spoke to his soul. The stranger had come from nowhere and had gained nothing from the words he said and the deeds he had done. He did not try to overthrow the government but in his long years of service he knew that did not matter. The man had made them afraid and what they were afraid of, they destroyed. As he gazed into the face of the one before him, he knew he would never be a soldier again. He would take his mother, wife and children this very night and go to a safe place that he had heard of. A place far away where one could be free. His hand touched the dagger that he wore at his side and he waited for the man to wake.

In his dreams, he saw the young boy. Just like any little boy, except this one had the ability to give dreams and the power to make those dreams into reality. He saw a father like any other. Parents were not supposed to have favorites but somehow there was something special about the little one. Peter could sense the agony of the Father of all and did not know how such could be held. It was almost too much to comprehend.

One errant child who had the power to alter reality had looked upon the horror that his young mind could not take. It had crumbled and those dreams had become nightmares. The Father had tried to bring him home from that dark keep but his efforts had failed. Mankind may have been deceived and shouldn't have questioned the gifts they had been given but their punishment had been beyond that of imagination. If man and his beloved Galen could not forgive him, how could he forgive himself?

Peter Beck woke gradually to the searing pain from the mist of his dream. He understood. As he looked into the skies that screamed their anger and sorrow, he cried, "My Father, I know your pain. I am so afraid but I am not alone. I know now why you turn your face. It was not your fault. Not for us, we made our choices. And not for the little one who was lost. Look upon the face of your humble servant. I am man; made from the clay you formed and gave the gift of wonderful life to. I am the best part of you that you could give. I give my life to seal our covenant. The guilt will be washed away and a new beginning will be sealed by the sacrifice I make for you, our Beloved."

The tears rolled down the guard's face as he heard the words spoke with all the heart and passion that the shattered man could summon. The words carried above the rolling thunder as they mounted the currents to heaven itself. Speaking softly to the man, the guard offered and when the pain filled eyes of the man said yes, the guard asked for his forgiveness before he plunged the dagger into the man's heart. Crimson flowed down the blade and dripped from the hilt as the guard fell to his knees while the storm raged and the ground shook.

The Journey Home

I held my breath as the Beast looked into the eyes of Jarred. I saw Micah staring at Jarred in wonder. I knew what we had heard had never before been told to man. I waited for the Beast to burst into a rage so great that he would rend the tiny child before him. I watched those molten evil eyes and they were unreadable. Then I saw the beginning of something in the corner of one of the great orbs. A single blue tear fell down striking the cheek of the Beast and fell to his breast. The façade crumbled. In my fear, I trembled and I heard Micah cry out in wonder.

The forest was gone. We stood in nothingness. The cries of the damned were silenced. They were no more. No beasts growled and crawled through the landscape. The great throne had disappeared. On the ground sat Jarred beside a small boy. A boy who looked about the same age as Jarred. His face was so beautiful as to almost bring tears to your eyes. The dark honey blonde hair hung slightly over the liquid blue eyes. Snow-white wings bound his slight body. The tears fell freely down Galen's face.

The sobs were mixed with the heart wrenching words that flowed as if they could not come fast enough. "I am so sorry. So sorry. I was lost. I couldn't find my way out. I saw my mother die. I saw my brother…I ran. I ran so far and couldn't find my way back. The dreams were horrible. I saw blood and war and the dreams, they never stopped." Jarred stroked the silken hair as he held the boy close to his chest and whispered the simple words over and over, "we love you."

Jarred lifted the young angel gently to his feet and brought him to Micah and me. As the tears dried, Jarred introduced us. Galen stared at us with those beautiful eyes. His voice spoke with awe, "You are the ones my brother spoke of. Michael loved you so much. I can see why. You have beautiful souls." He tentatively touched us as if we would break. I forgot about the ache of my old hip at that soft touch and Micah knelt down and hugged the angel like a long lost son. Galen held on as if he sensed everything that Micah had given to help him come back. Galen turned back to Jarred and asked one question. How? Jarred replied, "It was the love of many who protected me so that I could come to you. I am the only one. I am a part of our Father, a part of your dreams and of man. I would never have made it here if it had not been for those that have protected the hope for so long. Now it is almost complete." Jarred took Galen by the hand and smiled, "There is one other thing. I have a surprise for you."

The light started somewhere to our right. A blue that blazed so brightly in a few seconds, I could only squint. Micah shielded his eyes as well, as the vortex swirled into being. Michael came through with Ashe. Galen's eyes lit up with even more happiness as he ran to his brother. Ashe hugged Jarred and showered him with kisses. Michael swung Galen up and around as Galen's laughter echoed from the cavern. It was hard for my mind to accept this mighty warrior being just another big brother but for the moment that's exactly what he was. As they rested and the mighty figure leaned over to look into the young eyes, it was all said in simple words. "I am so sorry my beloved, I would not have hurt you for anything," Michael said. "I know. I'm just glad to see you again," Galen replied. Then with hope in his quivering voice, he asked, "Where is Father?" The vortex grew brighter and the voice came from it. I could just make out the figure that stood in the circle of flaming light. I could almost see the face and I fell to my knees weeping at the beauty of it. The voice was warm and pierced the very being of my soul. "I am here my son. I have waited so long to hold you again. We have waited." And I saw the other figure, smaller and definitely…female. The voice of Mother was like nothing I can describe. The sweetness of that voice mixed with the scent of fresh honeysuckle just about made my heart stop. "Mother!" Galen screamed with joy and ran to the embrace of his Mother and Father. The love blinded my old eyes. The love of a child's return to his Mother and Father. Michael came to us and spoke his thanks. He looked at Galen, who we could see just inside the vortex. We could hear the words of the joy that his mother had recovered. "Some wounds heal, some will take longer. He will miss his other brother but with our love he will grow." With that, Michael turned, towards the rest of his family. Ashe followed after telling Jarred how much he loved him. The tears stood in Jarred's eyes as his father walked to the vortex.

In the brightness of the blue flame, we could hear the Father as he bespoke his sorrow that he had lost his little one in his rage. My knees buckled and I saw Micah fall. I lay there overwhelmed by the light, which increased in intensity as if governed by the emotions of the celestial beings inside it. I felt the world begin to fade as I heard Galen's words heal all: *"Father,"*

As the last of his lifeblood spilled into the dust of the world he did not know, Peter Beck's words soared to the Father… *"I…"*

"forgive"

"you"

Millions of miles away, a great man gave his love and forgiveness to the Father of us all as a child did the same.

As I sank in that blessed darkness that I knew would be death, I heard the words of the Father:

"What once was will be again."

Epilogue

I woke up lying in the grass on the hillside overlooking Sanctuary. My old journal was still clutched to my chest. My eyes were clear and bright as I looked down the gentle slope and saw the people in the valley laughing and playing. The great waterfall cascaded in the background as the perfect backdrop with sunlight glinting off the mist in the perfect summer evening. The grass was the greenest I had ever seen it and I marvelled at the beauty of the garden like countryside.

As I watched, I understood. I felt it important to write down as much as possible. Lest we ever forget. But I must hurry because the memories already begin to dim. As I look at the happy faces of the ones I've known and loved, the old ways and fears are slipping away like the mist burning off in the morning sun. I will write all I can and place it in the heart of Sanctuary. I doubt it will ever be needed again, but just in case. We protected the children and brought them together again. That is what matters. We did it. The nightmares are no more and it is as it was meant to be.

The beauty holds me in a trance. I must not let myself get side tracked. The great gathering has begun. I see a smiling Peter Beck as he holds his beautiful wife against his chest as they share private jokes. Their children are there. Except this Joshua and Rachel do not bear the scars of war. They spread the blanket for their family, laughing while they prepare the picnic lunch.

Sam Cochran tickles the nose of his wife Jill with a blade of grass while the dark hair of Becky flies in the wind playing with the other children. Saint joins in the chase letting Jarred hang on to his neck. Christina sits with her mother Mary along with Michael and Samantha Duncan. The sight of angels does not amaze anyone. They belong here. Mara stands enfolded in the great wings of Ashe as they watch Jarred tumble with Saint. I see Jack and Shannon wading through the pool at the base of the waterfall hand in hand. In small and large groups, I see the ones that I loved so dearly. I cannot remember much more to write down my friends, they are all here.

Galen plays among the children free from his guilt at last. He chases a young beautiful girl named Jerrie whose laughs carry, as she runs to her father and mother. Micah sweeps his daughter up in those mighty arms while Sarah looks on. This is what I wanted to see and why I struggled to remember until now. Of us all, Micah gave everything and suffered through so much. Without him, we would not have made it.

I doubt I can remember to make a statue of him but I can see him the way he is now. Strong with bright blue eyes filled with love for those with him. Enough love for the whole world.

I can't remember anything else to write. We're going to have supper with Micah and his family. My beautiful Rose is tugging on my sleeve to hurry and so I must. Never keep a lovely lady waiting. I will end my journal now. If I remember more, then maybe. But I think not. It is as it should be. I look around my home and I am filled with it. Do angels weep my friends? Yes they do. In joy and exultation. In celebration of Thy Secret Name.

0-595-30255-6

Printed in the United States
18039LVS00004B/34